Anguish knocks another one out of the park as she perfectly captures the angst in a marriage after the newlywed euphoria wears off. When her fictional couple realizes marriage isn't a fairy tale. That small annoyances can pile up and build a wall hard to scale. That a relationship requires nurturing and tending, sacrifice and compromise, hard work and listening to God. The story sucked me in and I rooted for them as they fought hard for happily-ever-after.

— SHANNON TAYLOR VANNATTER, MULTI-PUBLISHED AUTHOR AND RECIPIENT OF THE INSPIRATIONAL READERS CHOICE AWARD

FOR *Better* OR FOR GRANTED

Amy R. Anguish

Scrivenings
PRESS
Quench your thirst for story.
www.ScriveningsPress.com

Published by Scrivenings Press LLC
15 Lucky Lane
Morrilton, Arkansas 72110
https://ScriveningsPress.com

Printed in the United States of America

Paperback ISBN 978-1-64917-370-6

eBook ISBN 978-1-64917-371-3

Editors: Elena Hill and Linda Fulkerson

Cover by Linda Fulkerson, bookmarketinggraphics.com

All characters are fictional, and any resemblance to real people, either factual or historical, is purely coincidental.

To those who refuse to quit but instead choose to love every day.

What therefore God has joined together, let not man separate.
—Matthew 19:6

1

Finally.

Scott Stewart eased back into his recliner, a tiny bit of the tension in his back letting go. A few flicks of his fingers on the remote, and a basketball game flickered across the TV screen. What a day. This was just what he needed.

"Seriously?" Genevieve's voice warned him a second before a box hit him in the chest.

"What in the world?" He held up the cracker box and frowned. "This is empty."

"Exactly." She pointed at him. "But it was sitting in the pantry."

He set it on the table next to him. "Okay. So, throw it away."

A whistle blew on the television, and his eyes sought out the cause.

Genevieve stepped in front of the screen.

"Gen." Trying to see around her, he straightened some in his chair.

"It's over." Genevieve said the words as if she were greeting a friend in the store. What was she talking about?

Scott waved at the television behind her. "It's only the third quarter. There's still time."

Her hands moved from her hips to the power button with enough force to set the flat screen rocking. "I'm not talking about the stupid game."

"Hey!"

"Scott, it's over. This …" She pointed to him and then back to herself. "Isn't working."

He sat the recliner up so fast he almost fell out. "This? This what?"

"Us." The word hissed between her teeth. "We're not working anymore. I can't keep living like this."

He frowned. "Gen, I don't understand."

She closed her eyes and took a deep breath. "Maybe we need to get a divorce."

Words she wasn't ever supposed to say. Words not allowed in their marriage. But there they were, taking up all the breathing space in their living room. She didn't open her eyes. Surely she was joking. This was all a bad dream, right?

He eased out of the chair and inched across the room, afraid to startle her. "Genevieve."

She jumped. Blinked a few times. Then, shrugged her arms away from his touch.

"I've got to go."

"Go?" He reached out again, but she slid away. "Go where? You can't say something like that and then walk away without at least an explanation."

"Explanation?" She threw her hands up in the air. "Doesn't our life speak for itself? The fact you don't know where I'm going should be your first clue about why I said what I said."

She didn't repeat that awful word again, but it hung there in the air, practically suffocating him.

"What's that supposed to mean?" He folded his arms across his chest, a pose that intimidated quite a few of the students who met him face-to-face in his office, but didn't work on her. No, sir.

"It's Tuesday, Scott." She raised an eyebrow. "What always happens on Tuesdays?"

The light flickered in his mind. "Dinner at your parents'."

"Same thing every week since we got married." She shook her head. "Not that you've gone with me for probably a year now." She glanced at her watch. "I'm already late. I don't expect to see you when I get back."

"What?"

"I'm serious about this. The way our life has been going lately—I can't handle it." She hooked her purse over her shoulder. "This isn't what I signed up for when I agreed to marry you. Please be gone before I get back. We can work out the rest of the details later."

"Gone?" He caught the garage door before she could shut it. "Why should I leave? You're the one who wants out."

She let out a breath but didn't stop. Didn't answer.

"You still haven't told me what I've supposedly done wrong."

"I shouldn't have to tell you." She slid into her car and started the engine before he could stop her again.

She didn't even glance his way as she backed out of the garage and down the driveway. What just happened? Where had all this come from?

Scott sank down at the kitchen table, his head in his hands. Never in his life had he expected his sweet wife to demand a divorce. Their fifth anniversary was still three months away. Hadn't even been able to put all their plans in action.

Plans he'd thought were right on track.

Step one, get married. Check.

Step two, work his way up to principal. Check.

Step three, save enough so Gen could stay home with babies.

"Almost check."

But apparently, Gen had changed her plans. Or something. He still wasn't sure.

Did I forget something important? A glance at the calendar proved Valentine's Day had been the week before. He remembered the balloons in the hallways and all the flowers coming through the office. It had crossed his mind that he needed to pick something up for Gen on the way home, but then he'd gotten caught in a late meeting and completely forgotten by the time he left.

She wouldn't demand a divorce over missing a silly holiday, though. Right?

His stomach grumbled and reminded him he'd been counting on her to figure out dinner tonight. Tuesdays were one of the rare nights he didn't have much else going on. And while he loved his in-laws, he didn't think now was the best time to follow her to their house and join in that standing dinner invitation.

Did they have a clue what their daughter was thinking? Did they support her? Was her dad still going to keep his promise to make Scott regret it if anything ever happened to break Genevieve's heart?

Scott rubbed his chest.

Surely Dan wouldn't stick to that promise if Scott didn't know how Genevieve's heart had gotten hurt in the first place, right?

One thing was for sure. "I'm not leaving. This is my house too. In fact, my name is first on the deed. If she wants to go through with this crazy plan, *she* can leave."

He slapped his hand on the table and pushed up. The fridge showed several leftover containers, but nothing looked appetizing. A sandwich would have to do.

He needed to get some more work done before bed anyway, so it was just as well she'd flown out of here faster than students at the three o'clock bell. Maybe she'd talk to him when she got back. Explain what had provoked such insanity.

With the last few minutes of the ballgame as background noise, he munched his ham and cheese and checked emails. A high school principal's job was never done. But his attention didn't stay on the laptop or TV. It kept wandering several blocks over to where Gen ate dinner with her parents.

DADDY WASN'T GOING to take her side this time. Genevieve released her pent-up breath in a trickle. Her parents would automatically know something had happened. How would she tackle this coming maelstrom?

She steadied her shaking hand and pressed the doorbell.

"Hey, sweetie." Mom's warm hug wrapped Genevieve in a physical embrace as did the floral scent Mom had worn for as long as Genevieve could remember. "We were beginning to wonder if something had happened. You're usually here before now."

"That husband of yours have another ballgame tonight?" Dad leaned against the doorframe, his arms crossed over his chest.

She avoided his gaze. "On TV."

"And that's more important than family dinner?" She didn't have to look to know what expression her father's face displayed. That look of disapproval had made her uncomfortable for years. At least this time, it wasn't directed at her ... yet.

"Dan." Her mother's tone warned to not stir things up.

"What?" He grumbled. "A father can't look out for his daughter's best interest?"

"You know when you put her hand in his on their wedding

day that you were passing that task on to someone else. Now, come on. The pork chops are getting cold."

Genevieve swallowed the lump of disappointment in her throat. Her dad had trusted Scott enough to give him her hand, and what had Scott done with it? She blinked hard. She could do this. Just dinner with the parents, like every week. She sat in the chair between them like she had her whole life. No one mentioned anything else about the empty place setting across from hers.

"This looks delicious, Mom."

They all held hands and bowed their heads while her father rattled off his standard blessing. As soon as the "amen" sounded, he reached out and forked a slab of meat.

"Maybe you should take Scott a plate when you go home." Her mom handed the mashed potatoes her way. "He used to love my pork chops."

Genevieve didn't say anything as she spooned the creamy spuds onto her plate.

"Gen?"

She glanced up. Both her parents stared at her. She pulled her bottom lip between her teeth and passed the bowl to her father. So much for getting through dinner before having this discussion.

"I don't expect him to be there when I get back."

"Some late-night meeting?" Her dad shook his head. "People didn't have business meetings at all hours of the day when I was your age."

"No meeting." Genevieve plopped some green beans next to her pork chop.

Her mom set the meat platter down with a rattle, despite the fact she always chided everyone else to be careful with the family heirloom. "Genevieve Rose? Spill it."

"We might be getting divorced."

What was it about this day that kept making the rooms she

occupied so stifling and airless? She pressed her fork down on her pile of potatoes as if their arrangement were the most important thing in the world. The clock ticked steadily in the front hallway. Somewhere in the back of the house, Mom's cat let out a soft "meow." Genevieve finally looked up to meet the stunned glances of her parents.

"Divorce ..." Her mom's hand reached her way and stopped as if Genevieve's problems might be catching.

"Did he cheat on you?" Her father threw his napkin on the table with such force the saltshaker spilled. "If he did, I'll–"

"Daddy, he didn't cheat on me." Genevieve waved him back into his seat. "Not with another woman anyway."

Her daddy slowly sank back into his chair and set the shaker upright.

"What do you mean?" Her mom shook her head. "What brought this on?"

"Everything." Genevieve shrugged as if the situation weren't tearing her up inside. "Our marriage isn't like yours. We started out okay, but ... but now we're like strangers who happen to live in the same house."

"Gen, that's not a reason for divorce." Her mother straightened her spine. "That's a reason for counseling."

"And our marriage isn't perfect, either." Her father half-grinned.

"Says who?" Her mother chunked the extra napkin at him.

"Mom, you don't understand." Genevieve pushed her pork chop across her plate. "I know this all sounds petty and sudden, but I've been thinking about it for a while now. And I've come to the conclusion, I just can't live this way anymore."

"We raised you better." Her father's voice was gruff, but she could hear the concern lacing the edges of it.

"I know." Genevieve set her napkin aside this time. "Good Christians don't get divorced." She stood up and put her hands on her hips. "Except they do. All the time."

"What?"

"Half my friends are divorced. And some of them didn't make it four years. Obviously, it's not as big of a deal now as it used to be." She waved her hand as if to show her parents proof all around them. "Besides, you don't know how miserable I am."

"So, tell us." Her mom rose and leaned over the table. "Help us understand. You haven't mentioned being miserable until now. How were we supposed to know you two were having problems?"

"Evidently, no one can see it but me." Genevieve shook her head. "Even Scott was shocked when I brought it up."

"What does that tell you?" Her father raised his eyebrows, as if back in college professor mode. "Maybe you're the only one who can see the problem. Maybe if you'd talk to Scott, you two could work it out."

She let out a breathy laugh. "Like Scott has time to talk to me!"

"You promised him for better or for worse." Her mother put a hand on her shoulder. "Obviously, this is a worse time, but that doesn't mean it has to stay that way. How can things improve unless you communicate?"

"You make it sound so easy, but it's not." Genevieve shook her head. "I don't think I'm hungry anymore. Thanks for dinner."

"Stop." Her father's voice carried enough authority to halt her momentum and glue her feet to the floor.

"Daddy, please." She leaned her head back and stared at the ceiling. "This is hard enough as it is. It's not like this was in the plans when I agreed to marry him. I didn't want us to end up this way."

"No one has written 'the end' on your story yet." Her mom's voice was gentle and calm, a perfect contrast to the emotions roiling inside of Genevieve. "There's still time to fix it."

"I'm not sure we can." Genevieve shook her head.

"Divorce isn't the only option in a bad marriage, you know." Her dad turned in his chair. "There are other possibilities."

She continued to shake her head.

Her dad stood and moved to face her directly. "You will always be my little girl, and I will always love you. But until now, I've never been disappointed in you. I don't want that to change. Please, don't give up on this marriage yet. If not for yourself, then for me."

"Daddy." Her shoulders slumped.

He raised her chin, forcing her to look at him. "And for your other Father too."

Her chin trembled. She'd been so sure this was the right decision. For weeks, it had resonated with nothing but truth in her innermost being. Could she be wrong? Or did Dad just want her to be miserable for the rest of her life? Moisture pooled in the corner of her eyes. He didn't understand.

"Have you talked to anyone else about this?" Her mom placed her hand on Genevieve's shoulder.

"No." She took a deep breath. "I only told Scott tonight."

"What if you go talk to Marty?" Her mom tilted her head. "I'm sure he'd be happy to give you guys some counseling."

"But he's known me my whole life." Genevieve widened her eyes as she contemplated baring her soul in front of their associate minister. "Won't that make it weird?"

"Or maybe it will make it easier. After all, you know he loves you almost as much as we do. Wasn't he the one who baptized you at summer camp all those years ago?"

Genevieve's lips turned up at the happy memory. "He was."

"And you know he'd be honest and tell both of you what you need to hear. You just have to be willing to listen." Her dad nudged her.

"And I suppose you don't think I listen well?"

"Never have listened when you didn't want to." He winked.

"But I also know you well enough to know you'll do the right thing."

"Pray about it, if nothing else, Gen. This is a big decision. I know the world takes divorce for granted, but you know that's not the way God intended it to be. And think about talking to Marty."

She nodded. She'd agree for now, if only to get them off her back. They hugged her tightly before she was allowed to leave, a plate of food tucked into her hands in case she decided she was hungry later.

As she neared her house, she searched for signs of life within. Had Scott taken her ultimatum seriously? Was he still here, or had he left for—at least the night? Which one did she want more?

His truck still sat in its spot in the garage. She needed more time before she walked into whatever awaited her inside.

Mary's trash receptacle remained at the edge of her driveway. Genevieve headed to the road and tugged her neighbor's trashcan toward her dark house. Mary must be working a night shift again. As much as Genevieve loved being a nurse, she never envied Mary's crazy emergency room shifts. Working at a high school had been a dream come true for her.

Before she married the man who was now the principal.

She brushed her hands off once Mary's trashcan was in place. If Genevieve had to work such crazy hours, she'd hope someone else would do the same for her.

She spun and faced her own house again. Much as she dreaded going inside, she couldn't stay out here all night. Tomorrow was a workday. Maybe Scott would already be asleep, and she could avoid discussing this.

2

———

The TV was silent, the kitchen and living rooms empty. A lone lamp shone next to the sofa, a habit she and Scott had formed the first weeks of their marriage—leave a light on for the one who wasn't home yet. She hadn't been out that late, but he'd evidently already retired. She put her leftovers in the fridge and turned off the lamp.

He sat in their bed, his back against the headboard, readers perched halfway down his nose as he studied the laptop screen in front of him. She leaned against the doorframe and took her fill. Those glasses always made her heart flutter a bit, reminding her of a stoic professor instead of the basketball coach she married. At only thirty-four, he was one of the youngest upper school principals in the state, and she admitted to being more than a bit proud. Where had they gone wrong?

He glanced up and immediately tensed when he caught sight of her. "Are you going to issue more ultimatums tonight?"

She shook her head.

"Good. Because this is my house, too, and I'm not leaving. If you think it's so bad, you can be the one who leaves."

So much for hoping their marriage might have a chance. She crossed her arms against her chest and tightened her lips.

"Did your parents agree with you and finally find all the bad things your dad's been searching for about me since we met?" He shut his computer.

"Actually, they told me I needed to reconsider." She shifted her jaw. "Mom even sent leftovers."

"I grabbed a sandwich earlier."

"I'm sure that tasted much better than my mom's pork chops."

He tossed a file onto the bedspread. "That's not what I was insinuating. I simply wanted you to know I wasn't hungry."

"I really wasn't worried about you being hungry." She kicked her shoes off in the direction of the closet.

"That much is obvious."

"What?" She spun around from the dresser drawer she'd pulled open.

"It's not like you invited me to the dinner you got so mad about me not attending." He waved his hand in the general direction of her parents' house.

"It's a standing date. We've gone to their house for dinner on Tuesday night for the last four years." She barely kept herself from stamping her foot. "Well, I have anyway. The last almost two years, you've been too busy."

"You knew I'd be busier when I accepted the principal position. But you encouraged me to take it anyway."

"I didn't realize 'busier' meant every waking hour of the day!" She gathered her pajamas and stormed into their bathroom.

How could her parents think things could be fixed? With Scott having an attitude of "I did no wrong," there was no way he'd agree to go talk to Marty. And she definitely wasn't going to go by herself. She stripped her dress off—one that Scott liked in the past but hadn't even noticed the last few times she'd worn it—and took a step toward the hamper to throw it in. A pile of Scott's clothes mocked her from the floor in the doorway of the closet. She kicked his pants closer to where they should've been but refused to put them in the basket. Why should she have to pick up after a grown man?

Comfortable pajamas on, she grabbed her toothbrush and stuck it in her mouth.

And gagged.

Reaching into her mouth to find whatever had poked her, she gagged again when she pulled out a toenail. Someone's habit of propping his feet on the edge of the bathroom counter had obviously continued this evening, with his nails flipping every which way but the sink or trashcan as he clipped them. She gargled an extra two minutes to try and erase the grossness from her memory.

Throwing open the door, she marched back across the bedroom, grabbing her hairbrush so hard that several bobby pins flew across the dresser and dove off the end.

"What now?" Scott's voice carried more than a hint of exasperation.

"Do you know what I found on my toothbrush?" She shook her brush at him. "*After* I stuck it in my mouth?"

"Toothpaste?" He didn't bother to look up.

"A toenail!" She hadn't meant for her voice to be that close to a shriek, but how could she help it when he didn't even care about anything to do with her anymore?

He glanced up with a raised eyebrow.

"Do you pay any attention at all to where those things fly when you're clipping them?" She practically gagged again. "It was in my *mouth*. Your dirty toenail."

"I'm sorry. It's not like I put it there out of malicious intent. It ended up there accidentally."

"If you'd quit clipping them in the sink in the first place, accidents like that wouldn't happen." She faced her mirror again to work on the mess her hair had become through the evening.

"And where would you prefer I clip them? In the kitchen? Off the back porch? Maybe while I'm at school before I come home?" He stashed his papers and laptop into his bag and let it slide down to the floor with a thump. "I told you I was sorry. I'll try to be neater next time."

"That'll happen just like you'll actually put your clothes in the hamper." She muttered it under her breath while working on a particularly snarly tangle. She'd considered cutting her hair, but Scott liked it longer. Maybe it was time.

"And I suppose you think yourself the neatest person in the world?" He fluffed his pillow before slamming his head back onto it.

"Neater than you." She tossed her brush back onto the dresser and faced the bed.

"Ha!"

She froze where she was pulling her covers back. "Ha?"

"Yeah. It's the sound someone makes when he doesn't believe someone else." Scott rolled over on his side, leaving his back to her.

"I was more interested in what part you didn't believe." Oh, how she fought the urge to throw something at him.

"The you being neater."

"I'm neat."

"Except your dresser, your desk, the table beside your favorite chair, and your makeup drawers." He glanced over his shoulder. "Oh, and your shoes."

"At least those aren't things that get in your way." She refused to look at the ankle boots she'd kicked toward her closet earlier. Or acknowledge the bobby pins now somewhere on the floor.

"Not until I trip over said shoes in the middle of the night because they're right in the middle of the pathway." He turned back toward her. "Or when I can't find a stamp because they're buried somewhere on that desk in the living room. Or if you've moved the remote to that black hole which used to be my grandma's side table."

"Heaven forbid you not be able to find the remote control!" She threw her hands in the air. "You might miss a ballgame. There's only forty million on each night."

"You knew when you married me that I liked sports. You even went to games with me once upon a time." He sat up and pointed at her chest. "You get into high school football more than I do."

"Yes. I was aware you liked sports." She shook her head. "I just didn't realize that was *all* you liked."

"It's not all I like." He slammed his hand down on the bed.

She drew deep breaths in through her nose. She would not cry tonight. Not here. Not in front of him. If she could control her tears around her parents earlier, she could do the same now. She grabbed her pillow off her side of the bed.

"You couldn't prove it by me." She started toward the hallway.

"Where are you going?"

"Since you stubbornly refuse to leave, I guess I will instead." She pulled the door closed behind her with slightly less than a slam.

Two steps into the guest room, he grabbed her arm. "This is ridiculous. What is going on with you?"

She tossed her pillow onto the full-size bed. "As if you care."

"You keep saying that, but I don't know what I've done wrong." He clasped her arm. "What started this?"

She jerked away. "Does it matter?"

"It matters to me."

If only she could believe that! The stupid tears were burning her eyes and throat again, begging for escape.

"Gen, we promised each other divorce wasn't an option. That hasn't changed for me. And it won't."

"What?" She glanced over her shoulder.

"Don't you remember?" He started to reach for her, then pulled his hand back again. "Right before our wedding, you got cold feet. You were bawling, going through every worst-case scenario you could think of. 'What if we get a divorce?' you asked."

"And you said we wouldn't because it wasn't an option for us." The words came out softly through her constricted throat.

"We pinky-swore." He chuckled.

She nodded and hung her head.

"So, what changed?"

"We did."

She didn't turn around but sensed him stiffen behind her.

"So, that's it, then? You're willing to throw it all away? Just break your promises and vows? Give up?" He huffed. "That's not the Genevieve I thought I married four years ago."

She chewed on the inside of her cheeks. He wasn't the same Scott she'd married, either.

"If you're so set on sleeping in here, go ahead. I'm going to sleep in our bed down the hall. Feel free to join me if you change your mind."

She flinched as the door slammed behind him.

"*Talk to Scott. It will help.*" She mimicked her mother's thick Southern accent as she pulled back the comforter. "Obviously not, Mom."

Despite having a whole bed to herself, she huddled on the side established as hers from their wedding night. A streetlight shined directly through the lightweight curtains she had hung in here. This was the first time she'd been in here after dark without the lights on. She needed to get thicker curtains if this was to be long-term.

She rolled over and faced away from the window. She

pushed her pillow into a different position under her neck. Shifted her hips to try and avoid an extra-sharp spring only to find another right beside it. Was this bed sinking in the middle? It'd been his bachelor bed before they married, and he obviously hadn't kept to one side all those years.

She shoved some covers into a bunch right next to her legs to try and keep from sliding down into the valley. That only pushed her back onto the uncomfortable coils. She flipped onto her back and flopped an arm over her eyes to block the streetlight. She'd been so tired earlier.

This room was quiet. The slight whiffly sound of Scott's snore bothered her when they first married, but now she found herself listening for it to help her drift off. Of course, it was probably going strong down the hall—in their comfortable bed with the pillowtop mattress that cushioned a person's hips from poky springs. Why was she in here and he in there? Stubborn pride. But she wasn't about to admit whose pride was more stubborn.

She needed to sleep. Why did she have to bring all of this up on a Tuesday night? Because the sight of him sitting there in his recliner doing nothing—again—had fired her up. Sometimes, the only adult thing he did was go to work every day. As soon as he got home, he reverted into a kid again.

A kid who was way too handsome in his reading glasses and striped pajamas. The tears she'd held back all evening came as a flood now. She didn't want to break her pinky promise. But how could she keep it when they couldn't even have a conversation without snapping at each other?

THERE'D BEEN VERY few nights since they married where Scott had slept alone. Maybe a handful—when Gen had gone on ladies' retreats. And he hadn't slept well with her gone.

Had she drifted right off down the hallway with her self-righteous anger? Or was she lying awake too? Tempting as it was to go check, he remained under the covers and squeezed his eyes shut. The next day would be a busy one, and he needed to rest. Why couldn't she have had this mental breakdown over a break? When he had more time and brainpower to figure out what might be causing it.

It was like Genevieve had lost her mind or something. The most dramatic hormonal mood swings he'd ever seen.

Scott sat straight up in bed. "Hormonal."

He glanced toward the door and opened his mouth. Then closed it again. No.

Their original plan had been to start trying to have children around now, but surely she would've talked it over with him before taking that next step. Unless something hadn't worked the way it was supposed to. There was always a chance.

Could she be? Could this simply be raging pregnancy hormones?

"Surely she would've said something." He scrubbed a hand over his chin, the beard making a bristly noise in the still night. "Unless she hasn't realized it, either."

He tried to think back to the last time they'd done anything that might lead to such a possibility. But the more he strained his brain to remember, the more he couldn't. Had it been that long?

Sure, he'd been running crazy with work. And by the time he hit the pillow, he was exhausted. But still.

He flopped backward with a sigh.

So, probably not the reason she'd gone crazy tonight. He made a mental note to check out her waistline tomorrow. See if anything was different.

Because if an expanding family were the reason for the chaos that had invaded his life, at least there was a light at the end of the tunnel. The alternative was much bleaker.

3

The thump of the door woke Genevieve with a start the next morning. It took a moment before her surroundings made any sense. With the speed of a ninety-year-old woman, she rolled from the bed, stretching her achy muscles. If she decided to stay in here too many more nights, she needed to find a more comfortable mattress. She rubbed the small of her back as she padded down the hallway to their room.

The bed was unmade, clothes tossed across the end of it, as if Scott hadn't been able to decide what to wear that morning. In the bathroom, little black hairs littered the sink area, and the toilet seat saluted her from its upright position. She let out a puff of frustration. She hadn't really believed things would magically change overnight, but it would have been nice, nonetheless.

A glance at the clock showed she was running later than usual. She picked up her pace and got ready for work. The note tucked under her coffee mug was almost so small she missed it, but its fluttering movement caught her eye when she picked up her cup to go. She plucked the paper from the counter and recognized Scott's familiar hen-scratch.

I'm still not sure what happened yesterday, but I'd really like to talk things through after work today.

She rolled her eyes. Scott almost never got home early enough on a Wednesday night to do more than scarf a sandwich on the way to mid-week Bible study. She wiped up the ring of coffee he'd spilled earlier, grabbed her own caffeine, and headed out.

The school hallways echoed as her low heels clacked down the linoleum floors. In a few minutes, these corridors would fill with hundreds of voices and locker slams and sneaker squeaks and giggles. The cacophony wasn't something everyone could handle, but Genevieve loved her job as school nurse. Despite the fact she and Scott worked only a few doors away from each other, they almost never crossed paths here anymore. She glanced through the office window where he hunched over his desk, furiously scribbling away in a notepad. Could they find a way to have a conversation without emotions getting in the way this evening?

Opening her door, she flipped on the lights. She pushed the button for her computer to start up, a slow task most mornings, and then wandered down to the teachers' lounge to check her mailbox. As she flipped through several faxes and memos, Valerie Malone came up and swatted her shoulder.

"Still on for lunch today?" Valerie, the art teacher, had planning period right after lunch, so every now and then she snuck off to the local diner with Genevieve for something other than cafeteria food.

"Sounds great." Genevieve straightened her stack. "I've been hankerin' for a Frisco."

"*Mm.* That does sound good." Valerie leaned against the copy machine she'd set humming. "Although I usually order a cheeseburger anyway."

"Always time to change your mind between now and then."

"Your car or mine?" Valerie tossed a stack of papers on the long table in the center of the room and then started her next set.

"Mine sounded funny this morning." Genevieve shrugged. "Better take yours this time."

"No problem. See you around noon."

The bell rang to start the day right as she stepped into the hallway. She picked up her pace to beat most of the stampede. Only a few teenagers had her dodging to avoid their phone-focused meanderings before she made it back to her office. She pulled the bottom half of her Dutch door closed and sat at her desk to enter medical releases into the student database.

Everything was computerized, and it made life easier in some ways, but more difficult in others. Especially when she had to make out the scribbles of a harried doctor who faxed over releases on ancient machines, which often left several lines missing.

"Hey, Nurse Stewart, got a bandage?" A lanky boy with curls hanging over his ears and neck stuck his head through her doorway.

"Sure, Troy. What happened this time?" She opened the drawer with basic first aid supplies and pulled out a box of various-sized bandages.

"So, we might've been playing paper football before class, and might have gotten into it a little too much."

She raised an eyebrow. "You need a bandage for a cut from a paper football?"

"More like a pencil that got thrown after an interception when the kicker got mad." He held up his hand sporting a gash along one finger. "I was the unfortunate goal post."

"What kind of pencil did that?" She gently pressed the wound with an alcohol swap to clean it before handing him the bandage.

"I guess he'd been chewing on his eraser or something, the

metal part was bent, and it stuck out far enough that it caught my skin as it whizzed past."

"What class was this in?" She signed his hall pass.

"Ms. Daughtry's Algebra II." He waved his pass. "Don't worry. She already sent the other guys to your husband, and now it's my turn. I had to get this first. Thanks, Ms. Stewart!"

She shook her head. Scott didn't fool around with kids acting stupid to the point of people getting hurt. Would Troy still be smiling when he headed back to class? The boy wasn't a real troublemaker. Just a handful.

SCOTT REFILLED his coffee cup with a second dose of caffeine as he contemplated the conversation he'd overheard. He knew Valerie and Gen were friends but had no idea they regularly had lunch plans. Not that he could've joined them even if he'd been invited. Not enough time between meetings to get away.

Would Genevieve admit to Valerie what was bothering her?

It didn't matter. Valerie would never break her friend's confidence and tell him what was discussed at their gabfest. And he wouldn't want her to. Mostly.

Back in his office, he found two boys waiting. "Bit early in the day to start your shenanigans, isn't it?"

He motioned them into his office and then listened to their rather crazy explanation of a paper football game gone wrong. Once the third boy joined them, he wrote them all lunch detentions and reminded them to be more careful in the future before sending them back to class. One problem dealt with. How many more to go?

His email held a crazy number of unread messages. A lungful of air leaked through his lips as he waded through them, dealing with what he could. Parents wanting to meet with a teacher regarding their children's grades. A school board member with a question about prom. Several teachers requesting time off or supplies. A reminder for yearbook orders.

He frowned as he noticed several messages all containing similar complaints.

Coach Drake cut the basketball practice short again the last two times. I don't mind my son having more time for homework, but I worry about whether or not the team will be ready for play-offs next month.

Simon said Coach Drake let them go an hour early yesterday. Has something changed in the way school does practices? I just wanted to make sure I was getting the whole story.

We had arranged a ride for Blake after practice yesterday, but we didn't realize the boys would get out early. He had to sit in the cold for forty-five minutes because his ride wasn't supposed to be there yet. Did I miss a memo?

What was going on? Maybe something had come up in Drake's personal life, and he needed to end before the scheduled time. Still, he needed to communicate better with the parents. Scott scribbled a note to himself to talk to the basketball coach who'd replaced him the year before.

Up until now, there hadn't been any problems that he'd heard of, but three messages at once threw up a flag. It was awkward, because he didn't want to come across as knowing better than Drake how to coach the team. But at the same time, it was his job to reprimand the new guy.

He ran a hand through his hair and sighed again.

Wasn't it enough to have problems at home? He had to have more added to his work life?

A rap at his door brought his attention to the secretary standing there.

"What's going on, Marian?"

"Dress code violation, Coach Stewart." She bobbed her grey head to somewhere behind the door. "Tansy Michaels."

"Bring her in."

Marian ushered the teenager in. This was the third time this year, and Scott wondered if something was going on outside school to cause her to act out repeatedly. Tansy crossed her skinny arms and waited. Marian stood right inside the door.

"Tansy, you know why you're here?" Scott made sure to keep his eyes directed at her face and nowhere else.

"Yes."

He paused a moment, debating whether or not to insist on the "sir." Probably not worth it today.

"You know the rules. Ms. Marian will help you call someone to bring you something more appropriate. If no one can come, you're going to have to wear something out of the lost and found bin that meets dress code. And I'll write up another lunch detention slip."

That table would be full today.

Tansy nodded and turned back toward the door without waiting for anything else.

Marian exchanged a look of sympathy with him. Something told him her mind was wondering similar things to his. If anyone could squirrel something out of the recalcitrant teenager, it would be Marian. She was the best secretary he knew.

Maybe he should set Marian on Genevieve.

He shook his head and returned to his emails. Not yet. Hopefully, he could talk to her tonight between work and Bible study.

GENEVIEVE'S MORNING inched along in the normal way. Another bandage. A temperature taken of a girl who only wanted out of her chemistry test. A check for headlice that fortunately turned up clean. A couple doses of ADHD meds distributed. Several other records updated. Still, it was nice when noon rolled around, and she could escape for a bit. She flipped her "out to lunch" sign around and locked her door behind her.

"Hey, girl. Ready?" Valerie leaned against her white Mustang.

"You bet." Genevieve slid down onto the black leather seat and shook her head. When her friend first bought this car, everyone thought she'd gone completely nuts. Now, she couldn't imagine Valerie in anything else. The car suited her free spirit and love of fun.

"What's that look for? Missing your fuddy-duddy sedan?" Valerie revved her engine, making the guys sitting at the picnic tables outside the cafeteria holler and wave.

"I like my fuddy-duddy sedan, thank you very much." She patted the console. "I still can't believe you bought this thing."

"I'd wanted one since I was in high school. When Clara moved out, I figured, why not?" Valerie's only child had been gone for two years now. "Besides, Parker likes it too."

Did Scott have any feelings about Genevieve's car? Would he pay more attention if she traded in for something like this? *Don't be ridiculous.* She gave herself a mental chide. *This car wouldn't be practical if we ever have kids.* And there was another ramification of her ultimatum. Would she ever get to be a mom?

"Earth to Genevieve." Valerie's voice brought her out of her emotional thought process. "You okay?"

"A lot on my mind." To put it mildly.

"Well, come on. Let's go eat." Valerie pointed at the diner they were parked in front of.

How had she missed the whole drive? She followed Valerie through the doors and to their favorite booth. Sometimes it was nice to have your best friend's brother own the local eatery. When Val let him know they were coming in that day, Jimmy always saved their spot.

"The usual, I suppose?" He scooted in next to Valerie with his memo pad in hand.

"You know me so well." Valerie lightly punched his arm.

"Only since you were born." He rolled his eyes. "Cheeseburger all the way except onions. Extra fries. Diet soda." His gaze shot over to Genevieve. "Whatcha in the mood for today, Genny?"

"I'm thinking your Frisco sandwich. And iced tea."

"Sweet, right?"

"With extra lemon."

He nodded and jumped back up to fill their orders.

"So, what constitutes 'a lot on your mind.'" Valerie brought them right back to where they'd left off—exactly what Genevieve had hoped to avoid.

She fiddled with the piece of paper holding her silverware in a bundle. "I don't know, Val. It's like everything is ... wrong."

"Wrong? Like, your job? Your house? Your health? What?"

Genevieve waited until after their drinks had been delivered before answering. No need for this to get out any further than necessary yet. "Like between Scott and me."

Valerie choked on the sip of soft drink.

Genevieve passed her some napkins to mop up the splatters.

"Sorry." Valerie waved a hand in front of her face as if the slight stir of air would dry the tears in her eyes from the coughing fit. "I thought you said things were wrong between you and Scott."

"I did."

"Genevieve Stewart, you can't be serious." Valerie leaned back and crossed her arms. "You and Scott were perfect together from the moment you realized you wanted to be more than coworkers. Really, before that. You just wouldn't admit it for a while."

"I thought so too." Genevieve rearranged the salt and pepper shakers in the middle of the table. "But it's like everything has changed."

"Everything, meaning what?"

"I don't know. Sometimes, it seems like there's nothing he does that doesn't annoy me—the way he leaves the toilet seat up, misses the hamper, spills things and doesn't clean them up. And that's only in the few minutes he's home. I can't honestly remember the last time we had a date. Or even dinner together. His job takes up every moment except the few he's sitting in his recliner watching sports."

Valerie leaned forward, but then straightened again as their meals arrived. Once the waitress left, she reached for Genevieve's hands and gave them a reassuring squeeze. "The honeymoon stage is over now. You've hit a rough patch. That doesn't mean you can't get through it. Those all sound like things pretty much every married couple goes through."

Genevieve wanted to believe it with all her heart. But she remembered too vividly the fight from the night before.

"What's that look?" Valerie asked before biting into a fry.

"I'm not sure we *can* get through it." Genevieve wiped some sauce from the side of her sandwich before taking a bite.

"Well, not with an attitude like that."

Genevieve wrinkled her nose. "It's hard to explain. I've thought about this over and over and over again, but I keep coming to the same conclusion. This isn't going to work."

"You can't be serious. You've only been married for what? Four years? You're still getting to know each other. Good grief!

Parker and I are still getting to know each other, and we've been married twenty-five this June."

"Valerie, I'm not kidding. That list I gave a minute ago is the tip of the iceberg. There are always little hairs in the sink. A toenail was on my toothbrush last night. In my *mouth*, Val! And he didn't even act fazed by it when I told him."

No reply from across the table.

Genevieve glanced up from her food and widened her eyes. "Are you laughing at me?"

"I'm sorry." Valerie wiped her lips. "The way you said it or something. It caught me off-guard." She took a sip of soda. "Okay, keep digging. I really don't think this iceberg is as deep as you think it is."

"From the first week of our marriage, we've been having dinner with my parents on Tuesday nights. But ever since he moved from being a coach and algebra teacher to the principal, I think he's only made it to three. That's almost two years. Last night, when I headed out, he actually asked where I was going. As if it wasn't something we'd done over and over on the same night. It's like all he can think about is his job. Half the time, I'm sort of surprised he makes it to worship services."

"Genevieve, have you talked to him about this?" Valerie wiped up the last of her ketchup with three fries.

"That's what my parents asked last night." Genevieve set aside the last fourth of her sandwich. "Every time we try to talk, we end up fighting. I moved into the guest bedroom last night."

"That's not going to help solve things." Valerie shook her head. "Maybe you need a go-between to help you guys talk it out without the arguments. Marty does counseling, you know?"

"My parents pointed that out too. But I don't know." She tucked her payment under the edge of the plate. "I don't even know if Scott would want to do something like that."

"You'll never know until you try." Valerie gave her a side-hug as they walked back outside. "And marriage is definitely worth trying for."

"I'll think about it. But I make no promises."

"I'm glad you'll at least give it some thought." Valerie paused a moment before starting the car. "Honey, we've been friends a long time despite our age difference. I watched you two fall in love. You can make this work if you want to."

"What if Scott doesn't?"

"Has he said that?"

"No." Genevieve shook her head. "In fact, he reminded me of a pinky promise we made before we got married that we wouldn't bring up divorce."

"There ya go."

Genevieve thought for a moment. As soon as she started talking about this yesterday, everyone had pointed her in the opposite direction of where she thought she was headed. Were they right? How could she be sure?

"Tell you what. You're the second person to suggest counseling with Marty." Genevieve pointed to the sky. "If God sends me one more sign that it's what we need to do, I'll try to work up the nerve to bare my soul to someone who's known me even longer than you have."

"I'll be praying He sends that sign soon."

4

The garage door opened before Genevieve could push the button that evening. She froze with her hand in mid-air. Scott's truck pulled in to his usual spot, and he hopped out with the engine still idling.

"Sorry, I didn't get here sooner. Parents wanted a meeting after school about their son's grades. Right as I was giving up on them showing, almost an hour later than they said they'd be there, they waltzed into my office and plopped themselves down as if there were all the time in the world. You should have seen Kimberly's face. It was her class they were most concerned with. She looked about ready to spit. Of course, there was no way their baby had done any wrong to deserve such a grade, despite the fact he hadn't turned in any of his homework this quarter." Scott shook his head. "Anyway, all that to say, I really did mean to be here in time for dinner."

"Leftovers are in the fridge, but I've got to go. It's almost time for Bible study." She slung her purse farther up on her shoulder and stepped as if to pass him.

"I can wait to eat until later. I just wanted you to know what kept me so long." He opened the passenger side door of his truck and studied her.

She paused, uncertain. She had planned to take her own car.

"No reason for us to take two vehicles when we're headed to the same place." He pointed his head toward his leather seats. "Besides, riding together will keep tongues from wagging too much around town."

She couldn't deny his statement. It didn't take much to set the gossips ablaze in this little town. She gave a quick nod and slid in. Would he feel like he won? Like her acceding to this meant things were good again? No. He simply closed the door behind her.

The ride was quiet for the ten blocks to the church building. She stared out the window on her side, fiddling with her purse handle. Her mind remained fixed more on her conversation with Valerie than on anything else. Valerie was so confident, sure all would come to a happy ending. Could she be right? It was almost scary the way she promised to pray for a sign.

Their silence continued as they walked side-by-side, almost but not quite touching, into the church's classroom building and down the hallway to the room where the young marrieds met for study each week. Genevieve lowered herself onto a cold folding chair. She smiled at the others as if nothing out of the ordinary were happening in her life. As if the man sitting next to her weren't becoming a stranger more and more each passing day.

Parker stood a few minutes later and called everyone's attention. "You all know we've been talking about various ways we can stand out and be different from this world. Tonight, I want to talk about an alarming trend."

Quiet rustles filled the air as people shifted and settled their Bibles in their laps or opened Bible apps on their phones.

"I'm seeing a rise in the number of couples I know who are getting divorced. Some only a few years after they tie the knot."

Genevieve shot a dirty look at Valerie across the room. Had she put her husband up to this? Was she trying to force the sign she'd promised to pray for? Valerie widened her eyes and gave a little shrug as if to look completely innocent.

"This is the young marrieds class, so I want to know, besides Valerie and me, how long have people in here been married?"

"Three years."

"Six!"

"Two months." The recent newlyweds held up their hands amidst the hoots of those married longer.

"Four years, nine months, and three days." Scott's voice was quiet but sure.

He knew down to the day? Even she didn't keep track that closely.

"Wow, Scott." Parker gave him a thumbs up. "That's either really impressive or a little frightening. Do you know the hours too?"

A general chuckle went around the room.

"Sounds like most of you have been married less than ten years. Right?" Parker scanned everyone and nodded.

"Personally, I know ten couples who have gotten divorced in the last five years. Of those, only one had been married longer than ten years."

Silence reigned. Genevieve didn't need statistics to know it was true. She could probably say the same.

"God designed our families in a particular way for a reason. Adam needed a helpmeet perfect for him, so He designed Eve. He knew that combination would be ideal for raising children and making sure life went as well as could be expected in a fallen world. But our culture is taking away the base God gave us and saying, 'No. We want to do life however we feel like it, even if it's not the best way.'" Parker shook his head. "When we destroy the family as God designed it, everything else falls apart. Let me show you something."

He held up two pieces of construction paper, one red and one blue. With a quick squiggle, he squirted glue on one side and pressed the two pieces together, mashing all the way to the edges.

"When a man and woman get married, they become one flesh, right?" He held up the papers to show they were basically one piece now. Everyone nodded, including Genevieve. "There are still two individuals. You can still see the separate parts, but for the most part, they're one."

Where was he going with this?

Parker placed the papers he had glued together into his lectern and pulled out a set that resembled the first. "Let's say this couple has been married a few years and decides to get a divorce. It's simple enough, right? He takes his things, she takes hers, and the stuff they bought together, like the house and couch, can either be sold or divided equally. No big deal."

Parker glanced up as if to make sure everyone was watching. Genevieve held her breath as he gripped a corner of each piece of paper and started to pull. At first, the red and blue came apart easily enough, but then there were some ripping sounds, and Genevieve winced as it got harder and harder to separate the different colors from each other. When he held up each piece, no longer glued together, several chunks of red remained on the blue, with a big gaping hole in the middle. The blue didn't look much better, still gripping a few snippets of the red.

"You see, when you've become one unit, it's not as easy as you think to go different directions. You've changed each other. You've grown together. And you're never going to be the same person you were before you married. God glued you together. And His glue is better than this stuff."

Were she and Scott like that? Had their glue dried enough

that when they went in opposite directions, she'd be missing pieces and torn almost in half? It must be true because she already felt ripped in places from the turmoil of the last few days. Would she be able to function at all if they continued down this road?

The destroyed papers seared themselves in her brain as Parker continued talking about how they all needed to guard their marriages from the devil, to protect this God-given gift and their own hearts. Was it too late? Valerie said it wasn't. So did her parents.

Was this really the sign she had requested from God, or was she supposed to be looking for something else? Did she really need another sign or should she give in and talk to Marty?

The thought still made her inwardly cringe. Marty had known her since the day she was born. He was great friends with her family. What would he think of her needing marriage counseling? Especially after he had done their pre-marriage counseling? What did that say?

And yet, going to a complete stranger didn't seem right, either. Would Scott want to go to anyone? He still acted as though nothing was wrong. He was counting each day of their marriage. Was he counting them because they were limited or because they really mattered to him?

Talk to him. It's what everyone had counseled her. But how badly had that gone last night? She didn't want this day to also end in a huge argument.

A gentle nudge from her right brought her back to her surroundings. People milled about, laughing and catching up. She must've missed the closing prayer while lost in her thoughts.

"Hey." Valerie stood above her.

"Hey." Genevieve's voice was full of caution. "I don't think that really counts, does it?"

"What?"

"Coaxing your husband into teaching a class isn't the same thing as praying for a sign." Genevieve leaned back and crossed her arms. "And you know it."

"He already planned to teach this lesson tonight." She glanced over her shoulder at Parker and Scott talking near the front of the room. "But when I found out this was the topic, I hoped you would take it for that third nudge."

Genevieve ran a hand through her hair. "I don't know."

"What's holding you back?" Valerie perched next to her. "You don't really want to get a divorce, do you?"

"You know I don't." Genevieve shook her head. "You know how it is when you go on a hike and there's this beautiful vista, so you step out a little farther on the cliff, and a little farther and a little farther until you're as close to the edge as possible? And you know you're seriously going to fall off if you don't take a step back, but you're also afraid if you move at all, you might fall off anyway? That's sort of where I am right now. On the edge of a cliff."

"There's a big difference, though." Valerie squeezed her in a side hug. "You have people who want to pull you back, if you'll let them. You don't have to take that step alone."

Genevieve glanced again at the man who kept track of how many days they'd been married. "I'll talk to him tonight."

"Praying for you." Valerie gave another quick embrace.

"So, what's your secret to keeping track of how long you've been married?" Parker slapped a hand on Scott's back after class.

"I really don't know, man. I've always had a knack for numbers." Scott cut a glance across the room to where Valerie talked with Gen. "Not that it's doing me any good."

Parker frowned and pulled Scott away from the crowd a bit more. "What's wrong?"

"I was hoping maybe you'd know more than I did." Scott scuffed the toe of his shoe on the floor. "Genevieve and Valerie talk a lot, and I thought maybe Valerie had said something …"

Parker shook his head. "Valerie is sometimes way too good at keeping confidences."

Scott let out a breath and glanced around before lowering his voice. "Gen brought up divorce last night."

"What?" Parker leaned closer. "Why?"

"I don't know." Scott ran his hands through his hair. "I thought we were doing great. Right on track for the plan we'd set out when we first got married. When she said it, it was like I'd been fouled by a point guard at full speed. I never saw it coming."

"Did you ask her why?"

"Yes. And she never gives a real answer. She was complaining about laundry and toenails, but those aren't enough to warrant ending things, right?"

"I wouldn't think so, no." Parker laid his hand on Scott's shoulder again. "Keep trying. Don't give up. And if I can get anything out of Val, I'll pass it on. We'll be praying hard, brother. I never like to see a couple break up, but especially not one I've watched from the beginning and know can go great places."

"Thanks." Scott choked the word out between his lips. He needed all the prayers he could get. "Great lesson tonight. I'm hoping it paved the way for us to finally have a real discussion tonight when we get home."

Parker nodded his head. "I'd love to be a vessel used by God in that way."

Maryann burst through the door, almost too breathless to understand. "Anyone in here a medical professional?"

"I'm a nurse." Genevieve jumped up, more alive than he'd seen her all evening.

"Eloise collapsed in the other room."

"Let's go." Gen followed Maryann with purpose. Her compassion and care were the first attributes that attracted her to Scott. When she was nursing, she was part saint.

He followed in case there was anything he could do. Genevieve was already kneeling beside the octogenarian when he stepped inside. She checked her pulse, and listened for breathing, all the while murmuring comforting words. The older woman stirred a bit, but not much. Gen squeezed the fragile hand between her own and coaxed her to lie still.

Scott's own heart squeezed as the love and gentleness in his wife poured out on Ms. Eloise. She used to be that sweet with him too. Along with flirty and sassy and fun. What had happened to them? When was the last time she'd held his hand? Was it his fault?

Sirens alerted everyone of the ambulance arriving. Scott moved out of the way, watching as his wife gave the EMTs Eloise's stats and a history of what she had already checked for. Confident and poised, she worked well under pressure. Another thing that had drawn them together—both of them having to maintain their heads in stressful situations and being able to commiserate later.

Scott moved to Genevieve's side after the EMTs had rolled Ms. Eloise out.

"Ready?" He offered his hand to help her up.

After a short pause, she accepted his assistance. "Sure."

Genevieve was quiet as he drove home. Did she think about Eloise? Or was the lesson spinning in her head? Would she be willing to talk to him now without yelling and slamming doors?

His cell phone rang with the tune he'd set for the school board members. He stifled a groan and answered as professionally as possible.

"Sorry to bother you during home hours, Coach Stewart, but I figured you wouldn't answer if you were busy, and I'd just leave a message. Had to call while I had it on my mind so I wouldn't forget." Tim Miles rambled through the line.

"How can I help you?"

Genevieve stiffened in the passenger seat, but there was nothing he could do to change things now. Too late to let it go to voicemail like Mr. Miles had suggested.

"Well, we were all looking over your proposal for closing school early for those ballgames coming up in Jonesboro. We think it's a great idea. Go ahead and set things up for that to work. We'll see how this tournament goes, and then we may need to talk. A few parents have reported some things about Coach Drake that aren't sounding so rosy."

"Yes, I've heard a few of those complaints as well. All right. I'll make sure everything is squared away, and we can set up a meeting after spring break."

"Okay. A few of us might swing by one day later this week to talk numbers. I don't think our budget will stretch as far next year with the cuts the state is making again."

Scott smothered a sigh. "Don't start canceling programs yet. Let's lay everything out and see if we can pinch a few pennies here and there to keep things going a little longer the way they are."

"Yes, sir. We'll see what we can do. I'm no good at numbers, but some of the rest of you are."

"I figured that's why you hired a math teacher for a principal, right?" Scott let out what he hoped sounded like a happy chuckle instead of a grim one.

"Ha. Wasn't a bad idea."

"Right. We'll talk soon and see what we can do."

"Sounds good, sir. You have a good night."

"You too."

He had some work ahead of him. But maybe he could talk to his wife first.

She was out of the truck and in the house before he could get to her side, though. So much for Parker's words breaking down any of the walls she'd erected. Scott let out another sigh and grabbed his laptop. Might as well get a few things taken care of while they were fresh on his mind. No use starting another fight before bed.

5

"Seriously?" Gen kicked a pair of pants and several socks out of the way so she could get to her clothes hanging in the closet. A second night on the uncomfortable mattress hadn't helped her mood this morning, and fighting through her husband's slobishness only exacerbated the problem. Especially after he never found the time to have that promised conversation the night before. Discovering the toothpaste squeezed from the middle instead of the end so it took an extra minute to get the tube how it should be—well, that was yet another straw on her achy back.

With more force than necessary, she wiped up the ring on the kitchen counter where he had sloshed his coffee. She pulled his dishes from the sink and opened the dishwasher to stuff them in. It wasn't even a foot farther down the counter. She double-checked. Yes. The magnet was still turned to say "dirty." This shouldn't be this hard. She slammed the door of the appliance.

With moments to spare, she grabbed some leftovers from the fridge, set the alarm, and headed out into the chilly garage. Late February acted like spring half the time, but it was frigid at night in northeast Arkansas. Her car took a few extra cranks before the engine turned over and set to its normal irregular hum. She patted the dashboard in sympathy. It had been hard for her to get started this morning too.

A quick glance through the office window at school showed Scott already meeting with several people. The school board? From what she had overheard last night, something was going on financially. What would get cut this time? No sports, of course. Not in this part of the world. She sent up a quick prayer that Val's position would be spared. Art classes were often the most vulnerable.

Gen rifled through a stack of faxes and unlocked her door. As her morning progressed, her mood grew worse. Her computer took three restarts and a call to the IT guy before she could get it working well enough to do anything. She had two irate calls from parents wanting to know what she was doing about the lice outbreak they'd heard was running rampant through the school. As if she had any control over it, other than sending students home when the bugs invaded their hair. Somehow, she made it through those calls without saying something she might regret.

As she reached across her desk to grab another pen when she ran out of ink, her elbow collided with her mug, sending it crashing to the floor. Porcelain pieces mixed with the remains of her morning coffee spread quickly over the tile floor. She spun her chair back as the mess crept toward her favorite flats. Only a loud snap gave her a warning before she found herself on her backside, the chair collapsed. A broken wheel skidded across the floor.

She allowed herself one moment of pity party, letting her head fall into her hands, resting on her knees. This had to be the most Monday-ish Thursday she'd ever lived. A rhythmic knock sounded on her doorframe. She jerked forward to see who caught her in such a state.

Coach Harmon Drake leaned against the opening, arms across his chest, one eyebrow raised. "You okay?"

"Just three or four mishaps all at once." She started to push herself to her feet, but he quickly held out a hand to help her before she could move. "Thanks. Let me grab some towels so this mess doesn't spread any farther."

"Sure." He squatted at the corner of her desk and picked up broken pieces of mug, letting them clank into the trash can. She paused for a moment at the sight. A man helping clean up. Now there was a happy thought in this miserable day.

After a quick survey of the back room of her office where she usually kept quarantined students and private files, she had three towels in hand and was back to mop up the cold, creamy liquid. She dropped to her knees on the other side of the puddle and watched the white cloth turn tan. His hand on hers jerked her gaze up to his.

"How did you end up on the floor in the first place?" He thumbed over his shoulder at where she'd been sitting when he first arrived.

"My chair broke." She pointed to the miscreant wheel under the far corner of her desk.

"*Ah.*" He grabbed the culprit and tipped the chair over to slide it back in place. "If you're careful, this will hold the rest of the day. I'll get Pete over here to make it more secure as soon as I can. His boy's on my team, so I see him around practice now and then."

"Thanks." She piled the wet towels into a plastic bag to take home and add to her laundry pile. "Did you need something? In the craziness, I didn't think to ask."

"Carter Phillips. Have you heard anything from his doctor?" He helped her stand again, his hand lingering around her fingers an extra second longer than necessary.

She glanced down and then up at his face again, unsure if

she'd dreamed it or not. Considering how the rest of her day had gone, it was probably in her head.

With a motion at the stack of faxes she'd input that morning, she shook her head. "Unless something has come in since first thing this morning, I haven't seen a release for him."

He snapped and barely covered up the swear word she could see forming on his lips.

"Did he tell you to expect something? I can check my mailbox again, but there's not usually anything more this time of day."

"No need. I may glance in there and see if there's anything new." He lightly hit the doorframe. "He swore he was going to have his appointment yesterday so he could play this weekend. I can't let him play without the release."

"Sorry." She lowered herself into her seat as gently as possible, testing to see if it would dump her again.

"I don't suppose you could look at his leg?" His face was so hopeful, she hated to be the one to crush his expectations.

"Sorry. School nurses aren't certified to give a medical release after surgery. With a torn muscle, the doctor will have to sign off." She reached over and grabbed the new pen that started this fiasco.

"Figured it wouldn't hurt to ask." The muscles in his jaw clenched and unclenched as he stood there a moment longer. "I'll go check your box. I need to run by the office anyway."

"Wait!" But she was talking to no one because he'd already gone. "Coaches."

Halfway through clearing out the three voicemails left while she was cleaning up the rest of her mess, Coach Drake slid into view again as if he'd sprinted down the hallway and had barely been able to stop. She held up a finger as she jotted down the phone number of the parent asking when her child needed to be vaccinated. She pushed the three to erase the recording and set the handset down.

"Is this it?" Coach Drake thrust several papers into her face before she could look up. "I glanced through it but couldn't make out exactly what it was."

"You read my confidential fax?" She shot him a glare. "Don't you know about HIPAA laws?"

"I don't care about hippos. I need to know if this will let Carter play in the game or not." He pushed his finger down on the desk and used his best do-it-or-do-pushups voice.

"Look, Coach." She stood up, still only the height of his chin. Better than him towering over her. "In case you haven't noticed, my day isn't exactly going as smooth as silk. I don't need some antsy basketball bully standing here telling me what to do. I get it. It's playoff season. But that doesn't mean you get to push people around. Give me a minute, please."

She sat down and picked up the papers. "And don't ever look at a private fax again."

All was silent. She glanced up to see him staring at her with raised eyebrows. Half a smile crept up his cheeks and he let out a quick chuckle.

"You're laughing at me?" She leaned back in her chair before remembering the broken wheel. Arms flailing, her world tilted again, but this time strong hands kept her bottom from banging against the still-damp tiles.

"I'm sorry." He gently set her back on her feet and squeezed her arms. "I'm sorry you're having a bad day and that I was being a bully. You didn't deserve that. It's partly my fault for not making sure he brought it straight in this morning instead of having it faxed."

She gave a quick nod.

"Ms. Stewart, can you please look through these papers and let me know if my star player will be joining us for the games this weekend?" He gave her what must be his puppy-dog face, eyes sad and mouth pouty.

"Stop, stop. Yes. Let's see." After flipping through the sheets on her desk, she shook her head. "I have bad news."

This time he didn't try to stop the curse from slipping through his lips. "He can't play?"

"His leg didn't heal properly. The doctor is recommending a second surgery." She pulled up his information in the school database and entered the notes necessary for teachers and coaches. "Sorry, Coach. The team is going to have to pull it off without him."

He swore again.

"Hey!" She gave her sternest frown. "I get that you're upset, but I don't appreciate that kind of language. Quit making my day worse."

He held up his hands. "I know. I know. But now I've got to figure out who can take his place as my point man." He tapped her desk. "Anything I can do to make your day better? Besides telling Pete about that chair."

She shook her head. "You've done more than enough. It would have taken me much longer to clean up without your help. So, thanks for that. Wish I could repay you with better news."

"Not your fault." He pursed his lips. "I warned him if he didn't stay off that leg and let it heal, this might happen. I hate that he may lose a scholarship because of it."

"That's rough."

"Almost as rough as your day?" He shot her a grin.

"Touché." She slid the wheel back into place in the base of her chair and tried it one more time. "My day hasn't been quite that bad. Just a lot of little things."

"Like mad coaches?"

"And spilled coffee. A favorite mug broken. Laundry in the floor. And a car that probably needs something fixed. Dirty dishes in the sink." If she kept talking, she might end up in tears. Over a bunch of miniscule things. "No good-bye kiss."

Had she really said that last one out loud? She clamped her hand over her mouth. Her eyes squeezed closed in humiliation. The last person she needed to share something like that with was the man who'd stepped in to fill the head basketball position when Scott vacated it for the principalship.

"Scott neglecting you?" Drake leaned forward and rested his hands on the edge of her desk.

"Just a bad day."

"Because if you were my girl, I'd make sure you got a goodbye kiss every morning." His eyes darkened a bit. "Probably more than one."

She swallowed around the lump in her throat and leaned back a little. When was the last time a guy studied her like that? She blinked and reminded herself this was the wrong guy.

"Like I said, it's just a bad day." The words came out whispered, and less sure than she meant for them to.

"Let me know if you need anything else." He touched the back of her hand and then straightened and sauntered out of her office.

What was that? Surely, he wasn't hitting on her. No. He was simply one of those guys who actually paid attention to a woman needing help. Unlike Scott lately. Scott wouldn't have noticed the spilled coffee had it been him who came to the door. Not that he ever came to her office during the day anymore.

"It's just a bad day." She flopped her head down on her desk, only to feel the momentum set her chair to wobbling again. "*Uh-uh.* Not this time."

She switched her normal chair for one of the molded plastic ones that lined her wall. Not as comfortable, but at least she wouldn't end up on the floor again. Then, she'd have to call Coach Drake back. And she wasn't sure that was the safest idea, even if he did make her feel more attractive than she had in a long time.

"GOT A SECOND, COACH?" Pete Ransom, the janitor and all-around maintenance guy leaned against Scott's door.

"Of course. What can I help you with?"

Scott set his readers aside.

Pete held out a piece of black plastic. "I don't think I can fix this."

"What is it?" Scott fingered the crack across the top part, and it broke off.

"The wheel from Nurse Stewart's chair."

Scott's head jerked up. "When did this happen?"

"Apparently, earlier today. Sent her to the floor. Coach Drake was able to rig it to hold a little longer, but I guess it broke again because she'd swapped it out for another chair before I could get to her."

The mention of Drake helping his wife sent a shiver through Scott. Why? Jealousy that he hadn't been there to assist her? And why had Drake been there in the first place?

"But unless we have another wheel around here somewhere, I don't know what else I can do." Pete shrugged.

"You know what, Pete? I'll take care of it. I'm sure you have other things to do."

"You sure, Coach?" Pete shuffled. "Basketball practice should be over soon and I'd love to be able to give Seth a ride."

"Absolutely." Scott waved him on. "Go spend time with your boy. I've got this."

Scott glanced at his watch as he gathered his wallet and keys. Still a little earlier than practice used to end, but not as much as at the beginning of the week. Maybe he wouldn't have as many irate emails tomorrow.

Ten minutes up the road was an office supply store he hoped would have something better than the piece of junk in his wife's office. And he had half an hour before they were supposed to close. He rushed in with fifteen minutes to spare. The employees might not be glad to see him, but he didn't care. Because straight ahead was exactly what he'd come in for.

Back at school, he unboxed the pieces and screwed everything together. The building was quiet this time of day, with only a few teachers still around finishing up grades or prepping for the next day. And the play practice across campus in the auditorium. Another thing he needed to do.

6

———

After another morning much too similar to the last few bad ones, Genevieve stopped right inside her office door. Her old rolling chair was missing, and in its place, a brand new one almost preened. Its ergonomic back and seat were a deep maroon color, the armrests were pristine with no marks to show it had been shoved under a desk multiple times, and best of all, every wheel was attached.

She set her bag down and spun the chair in a circle, testing it out. There were no squeaks or hitches. It was a well-oiled machine. She caressed the armrests as she leaned back against a cushion that had to have been made with her in mind.

Coach Drake had definitely come through. He'd said he would send Pete to fix her old one, but this was above and beyond. Surely the school didn't keep such things around. Not that she'd seen in the last six years of working here, anyway. Where had it come from?

This almost made up for the fact that the leftovers she'd been planning to bring for lunch today had been missing from the refrigerator. Almost. She closed her eyes to soak up the luxury for another moment. Then, she'd start her day.

A quick knock startled her out of her reverie. The coach she half-expected to be standing there again, possibly to check up on the chair situation, was not the man staring at her now. Instead, the former coach filled her doorway.

Scott raised an eyebrow. "New chair?"

"My other one broke yesterday." She sat a little straighter.

"Pete told me." He looked like he was going to say something else, but then didn't.

She leaned forward and grabbed her things off the floor where she'd left them to examine her gift. "Did you need something?"

"Playoffs are tonight. I don't know when I'll get home."

She pinched her lips together. This was news, how? Sounded like the same-old, same-old, except that he was informing her he'd be gone instead of just doing it.

"The spring play is this weekend." His words jerked her out of her stewing. "Thought you might like to go see it tomorrow evening."

She loved theater. And for a school as small as theirs, the drama department was top-notch. The performance was sure to be fabulous. Was he asking her out on a date? When was the last time that had happened?

"Or not ..." His eyebrows narrowed as he started to turn.

"Yes. I'd love to." She half-stood behind her desk.

He leaned back in with a relieved grin. "Okay. We'll do it then. Have a great day."

A date with her husband. Did she know how to do that anymore? Granted, it wouldn't be a private thing. They'd be sitting beside each other in the dark auditorium with half the school surrounding them. But still, they'd be together.

Would he hold her hand like he used to?

Did she want him to?

Something told her it would take major self-control to focus on work today. Options for what to wear already raced through her mind. Would he notice if she put on something nice? Only one way to find out.

This day might've started badly with more laundry in the floor and more spills in the kitchen, not to mention the overflowing trashcan by the back door, but it definitely got better when she arrived here. A brand-new chair. She flopped into it, admiring the way it bounced a bit to catch her weight. And an invitation to the play. Any more attention, and it might start going to her head.

SCOTT NORMALLY ENJOYED BASKETBALL GAMES. Especially since half the boys on the team were ones who'd started with him a few years before. But his attention was all over the place tonight.

Part of it kept wandering back to the look on Genevieve's face that morning when he'd invited her to the play. As if she thought she hadn't heard right. Sure, she was happy enough about her new chair, but he'd hesitated to take credit for it at the time. Now doubts niggled the back of his mind as to why. Maybe that would've helped convince her he still loved her.

Now, with his bottom on the hard bench in the gym, he found he missed her. Why hadn't he invited her to come tonight too? She used to come to games with him. Would that have been too much, considering all they'd been through this week?

A whistle on the court pulled him back to the present. Coach Drake yelled and hollered on the sidelines, but the referee ignored him and stuck with his foul. Scott narrowed his eyes at the slightly younger coach.

"Think he's mad enough?" The dad of one of the team

members sitting beside Scott grumbled and motioned toward Drake. "Pretty obvious that was a good call."

Scott made a non-committal *hmm*. He wouldn't talk badly about his replacement, but he tended to agree with the father. What was going on with Drake?

For the rest of the half, he paid more attention to Harmon Drake than to what was happening on the court. But no other blowups occurred. And the boys were doing well. Up thirty to ten at the buzzer.

"We might actually have a shot at state this year, *huh*?" Another set of parents came over to shake Scott's hand while he waited for his order of nachos at the concession stand.

"Looks like it." He grinned and participated in small talk for a few minutes before heading back into the hot gymnasium.

He focused on his cheesy chips instead of the girls doing some dance routine on the floor. It wasn't that he didn't support the cheerleaders, but he wished they'd wear slightly longer skirts. With this being only his second year as principal, and him being a man, he picked his battles carefully when it came to dress codes.

Drake came back out as the boys returned to the floor. He paced the edge of the court, his lips in a flat line. What was going through his head?

When Scott had coached, he'd watched for signs of fatigue or injury at this point. It helped him know who to play more in the second half. But Drake wasn't paying much attention to his players around him. He turned and shot his glare directly at Scott for a second before looking to either side of him. With a smirk, he returned his focus to the game about to restart.

What had that been about?

Scott divided his attention between the boys and the coach through the rest of the game. They pulled it off, but barely, allowing the other team to get within two points before the final buzzer. Scott shook several hands and waved at a few more people before making his way out to his truck. Good thing he'd already put the plans into action for letting kids leave early for the games at the end of the week.

Back home, signs of his wife were all through the house, but she was already shut behind the closed guest room door. He rested his hand on the wood for a minute, debating on checking on her. But he hesitated once again.

"Good night," he whispered before walking down the hall to their room.

In bed alone once more, he sighed. Despite this being the fourth night without her beside him, he still struggled to sleep. And his stomach churned as he thought about tomorrow night. Would she consider it a date? Let him put his arm around her?

When was the last time they'd had a date, anyway?

***

GENEVIEVE SMOOTHED down her skirt once more and touched her hair to make sure the bobby pins were secure. The way the butterflies were grooving in her tummy, one would think she'd never been on a date with this man. And she'd been married to him for over four years. Good enough.

She pulled open the door and gasped. He was leaning against the wall right outside of the guest room. He straightened inch by inch, his eyes taking in her careful outfit of full-length skirt, creamy three-fourths sleeved sweater, twisty hairdo, and the brooch his grandma had given her.

She hadn't realized she was holding her breath until the smile crinkling his eyes caused her to release it. "I look okay to be the school principal's date?"

"More than okay." He offered his elbow. "People are going to figure out I married up."

She only paused a second before slipping her hand through and letting him walk her out of the house to his truck. He put his hands on her waist and easily lifted her up to the high seat so she wouldn't have to climb in dressed as fancily as she was—something he started years ago before they were married. He gently tucked a wisp of hair behind her ear, letting his finger trail down her cheek.

What were those butterflies doing? She placed a hand to her middle to calm them down as he walked around to his side. She hadn't had this reaction to him in months, and it frightened her a little.

At the school, he steered her toward seats not quite in the middle of the room. For some reason, she'd expected him to want to sit farther up, like all the kings did in the old movies. She mentally shook her head. He wasn't stuck up. He simply took his job too seriously.

Several parents greeted them as they settled nearby, many with bouquets for their actor or actress. Valerie waved ecstatically from a few rows over. She probably thought this was her prayers being answered right before her eyes. Genevieve stole a glance at the man beside her.

Maybe it was.

He casually draped an arm across the back of her chair as the lights dimmed and the music started. The school had chosen an obscure play this year, finances being stretched already in the art department. Without a huge donation, they couldn't afford the rights to a better-known production. Still, the thespians acted their hearts out, delivering punchlines with perfect timing, playing up the drama, and wearing the costumes as if they were everyday clothes to them.

Intermission came too quickly. Genevieve thoroughly enjoyed the performance—and the feel of her husband's arm about her shoulders. She took a deep breath before standing to stretch.

"Want some hot chocolate? They're selling it in the lobby." Scott pointed toward the door.

"That sounds nice."

"I'll bring you some. Sit tight." He inched his way past the few people remaining in their row.

"You look to be having fun." Valerie leaned over the chair in front of her.

"I am."

"So, how did this happen?" Valerie pointed between Genevieve and Scott. "You two randomly show up at the same place?"

"Actually, he swung by my office yesterday and asked me to join him." Genevieve's cheeks burned as if the spotlight had suddenly been turned in her direction.

"I'm glad." Valerie squeezed her hand. "This is exactly what you needed."

"I think what I really need is a restroom break before I sit through the other half of this play." She hooked a thumb over her shoulder and left before her friend could gush any more.

The line in the women's bathroom was three deep when she pushed through the door. She waited her turn and gratefully shut herself into a stall before the teenagers she could hear giggling emptied theirs. Their words at the sinks made her pause as she adjusted her skirt and tights.

"Did you see Principal Stewart and Nurse Stewart?" A high-pitched giggle followed the question.

"She looked so elegant tonight." A voice Genevieve recognized as Riley Mitchell, one of the senior girls, sighed. "I want to be like them when I get old."

Genevieve rolled her eyes. Thirty was hardly old.

"I don't know." The other girl's voice was muffled, like maybe she had bent over to fluff her hair. "I don't think I'd like to work with my husband."

"But just think how sweet it would be to have him pop in your office for a quick 'I love you.'" Riley sighed again. "They're totally romantic."

It would be romantic—if it ever happened anymore. Genevieve started to open the door despite the embarrassment it would bring the girls, but Riley's next words stopped her short.

"They're such a good example to us. Even when they were dating—back when we were in eighth grade—we all wanted what they had." Her voice sounded like it was next to the exit now. "I only want to be married if I can be married like Coach and Nurse are."

Genevieve swallowed the lump in her throat and swiped at moisture trying to slip from her eyes. She wasn't that good an example. The way she and Scott had been living lately—no one would really want that. Had they ever been the ideal couple the students spoke of? Maybe at first. But not anymore.

The bell rang to let people know intermission neared an end. One more swipe to her cheeks and a quick check to make sure her mascara hadn't run was all she had time for before slipping back out and into the seat next to Scott. He was finishing a conversation with someone to his right, so she merely accepted the warm drink from him and focused on the change in scenery instead of her heart.

"You okay?" His whisper right in her ear made her jump, some of the chocolate sloshing onto her dark green skirt. "I'm so sorry."

She accepted the napkin he had been holding around his cup and dabbed at the spill.

"Hey." She glanced over at him as the lights dimmed for the play to start once more. "You okay?"

"No." Her whisper was loud in her ears, although no one around them seemed to notice it.

He wrapped his arm around her shoulders again. "As much as I'm enjoying this play, I wish it were over."

She nodded, afraid if she said anything else she would lose it right then and there.

Forty-five minutes later, she and Scott stood and applauded the actors and actresses as they took a third bow up on stage. The play had been great, but the last half had only held a third of her attention. Scott gently wrapped her coat around her shoulders and hooked an arm around her waist as they merged with the mass exodus.

"Coach Stewart, what did you think of that game last night?" One of the dads caught him right before they reached the door.

"They pulled it out, but they'll have to play harder as they go." He shook the man's hand. "Even with the star player on the bench, it's a good team. If they focus and work together, they might have a shot of going all the way. We'll have to wait and see."

"Don't you wish you were still coaching this year?" The man laughed like it was the funniest thing he had ever said.

"I think I'm right where God can use me best. But I'm happy to be rooting for the team with everyone else." Scott steered her around the man and out the doors before anyone else could stop him.

He didn't move away right after lifting her into the truck, his arms staying on either side of her. "What's going on, Gen?"

"I wish I knew." She ducked her head.

"Hey, Coach Stewart!" Several cat calls came from across the parking lot.

"Hang on." He tucked her in and closed her door before hurrying around to his side. "No privacy here."

Words swam in her head on the ride home, but she couldn't quite catch the best ones to be able to express herself. How did she say that the ultimatum she'd given at the beginning of the week was no longer what she wanted at the end? Things still weren't perfect, but this night had shown what could be possible, and she wanted that with all her heart.

Those girls in the bathroom. If Wednesday night Bible

study hadn't been the third sign she was looking for, then the teenagers talking about her being an example must be. Wouldn't Valerie be glad?

"Would you be willing—" She stopped, unsure how this would sound.

"What, Gen?" He cut the engine in their garage and waited for her.

"Several people—" Why was this so hard?

"Several people ..." He prompted her, giving her hand a squeeze.

"Valerie. And my parents—they suggested maybe we should go talk to Marty." Genevieve quickly averted her eyes. Did that make it sound like she'd been talking about their problems to everyone?

"Okay."

Her gaze jerked back toward him. "Okay?"

"If it will help us get past this ... whatever this is." He waved his hand in a circle to incorporate everything around them. "Whatever it takes. I told you Tuesday night, and I'll tell you again. I meant it when I made that pinky promise. And those wedding vows."

"How did we get here?" Tears slid down her cheeks. "Everyone said we were perfect for each other, but it hasn't been very perfect lately."

"Hopefully, Marty can help us figure it out." He came around and helped her down.

She paused in the hallway outside the guest room door.

"That's up to you." He pointed at the lumpy bed. "If you're more comfortable in there for now, I won't stop you." He kissed her forehead. "But I also won't stop you if you come back to our room, either."

She wavered. She hated that bed, and she missed his stupid snore. But she couldn't. Not yet. "Maybe after we talk to Marty."

"Let's catch him tomorrow." He kissed her head once more and then walked away.

What was she doing? She didn't want a divorce. But she didn't want the marriage they had, either. Tonight had been so nice—like the early days. But would they be able to keep it up, or was it all an act they put on for the people at school?

7

─────

The look Scott's father-in-law shot him Sunday morning was one he couldn't read. Somewhere between "don't hurt my baby" and "fix this." He wanted to repair whatever had caused the damage to his marriage. But that was hard to convey from the opposite end of the pew.

Genevieve sat beside him, less relaxed than she'd been during the first half of the play the night before. The way she'd leaned into him, allowing his arm to be around her shoulders, had given him more hope than anything else this last week. It proved she still felt something for him, anyway.

And that was worth fighting for.

Her elbow caught him in the ribs, and he jumped. A snicker from the other side alerted him to what his wife had been trying to draw his attention to. Sloan Matthews stood there, offering the metal tray full of communion bread.

Scott pinched his lips and quickly took the tray, breaking off a piece of cracker and passing it on to Gen. He obviously needed to focus on the here-and-now more than what they planned to do after services. It would take swallowing all his

63

pride to be willing to go to Marty with these problems. Especially since Scott still wasn't sure what the problems were.

That part might be more humiliating than bringing in help. How was he supposed to get help when he didn't know what he needed help with?

He made it through the rest of the service, standing and bowing his head and everything when he was supposed to, although he couldn't have answered any questions on the sermon afterward. His brain was too busy for that.

"Amen." He echoed the end of the final prayer and let out a breath. Now, where was Marty? Gen's hand came into view, pointing to the other side of the auditorium. Her fingers shook.

He gave her hand a squeeze, nodded, and then quickly gathered their things so they could catch the associate minister. Fortunately for them, Marty had been caught by Ms. Priscilla and was nodding as the older lady regaled him with one of her stories. He caught sight of them waiting and winked.

"I think you've told me that one before, Ms. Priscilla. Tell you what? Why don't I come by and bring you a treat sometime this week, and you can tell me some more? Would that work?"

"Oh, you don't have to waste your time on an old lady like me." She waved her hand at Marty.

"It's not a waste. I'll call you and set it up."

Marty easily slipped away with that promise and came over to shake Scott's hand. "How are the Stewarts today?"

Scott cleared his throat. As much as he'd agreed to this idea, now the words were stuck. Genevieve straightened beside him.

"Marty, do you think we could talk in private for a few minutes?"

Marty raised an eyebrow but nodded. "Of course. Why don't you two come to my office?"

Scott followed the minister, the sense of being a teenager in trouble with the principal settling over his shoulders. It was a switch he wasn't comfortable with at all.

This will be worth it. He repeated the phrase in his head. *My marriage is worth it.*

"Now, what can I help you with today?" Marty closed the door and settled behind his desk.

"Our marriage." Scott finally convinced the words to leave his mouth. "We're having some problems. We need help."

MARTY SCRUTINIZED ONE OF THEM, then the other, and back again. How awkward could this get? It was bad enough that they admitted they needed someone to help negotiate their fights. Did he have to look at them with such shock? Or was that love and determination? Was Gen simply seeing what she expected?

"Well, that wasn't what I thought would come out of your mouths when you asked to talk to me." He rubbed his hands together. "But we can work with this."

What other possible reason could they have wanted to talk to him? She dug through scrambled thoughts as quickly as possible but came up with nothing before he started talking again.

"First, let me congratulate you for seeking help." He leaned forward and placed his palms on his desk. "So many people are afraid to ask for help, too ashamed and struggling to do what the scripture commands."

Genevieve's confusion must have shown on her face because he explained. "Galatians tells us to bear one another's burdens. James tells us to confess our sins to one another and pray for one another. What you're doing today is exactly what God suggested. You're letting someone else pray for you and help bear your burdens."

If that were the case, why did she still feel like she was failing?

"That being said, let me tell you how I normally handle situations like this." He leaned back in his leather seat and tapped his fingers on the armrests. "I like to start by meeting with each half of the couple by himself or herself. After I do that, then I bring you in a week or so later and meet with you together. I find this allows me to get both sides of the story in an unbiased manner and be better able to help you negotiate and understand where the other is coming from."

"So, we can't just start right now?" Scott shifted in his club chair. "Spring semester is pretty busy, and it's hard for me to squeeze much else in."

Of course, his work was going to get in the way. Why had she thought he might be changing? Did he even want to make this work?

Marty glanced between them and then focused more on the man next to her. "Scott, I know it's a busy time, but I need you to think about how important your marriage is. You agreed it was important enough to reach out to me in the first place. Is it important enough to carve out an hour here or there to meet with me again and figure out how to make it better?"

Scott gave a curt nod, his jaw set tight.

"Now, I was going to suggest we actually get started this afternoon." Marty pointed a pencil between the two of them. "I know spring break is coming up, and I want to meet with you at least once more between now and then if possible. I'm free this afternoon, if one of you wants to come back in a couple hours and the other an hour or so after that."

"That works for me," Genevieve spoke for the first time since asking him to meet with them. Scott had done the explaining—they were having "some problems" and hoped he could give them a little help. "I can be back in a couple hours."

"Yes." Scott shot a look in her direction before focusing back on the associate minister. "Sorry I assumed you didn't mean to start today. I wasn't sure how all this was going to work."

"Not a problem." Marty pushed up from his desk and offered a hand to shake. "I want you both to be praying about this until you're back in here. I'll be praying for you as well. And, if you don't mind, I'll get Samantha to pray too. My wife is an awesome prayer warrior."

They both nodded.

"See you in a few hours."

The bright sunshine belied the fact that the temperature had dropped into the low thirties the night before. Genevieve pulled her wool coat tighter around her front as the wind whipped around her tights-encased legs. Scott opened the truck door for her and lifted her into the seat. It only took a minute or two for the seat warmers to do their thing, but in a town the size of theirs, that meant maybe five minutes of warm seats before stepping back out into the cold.

"We could pick up some chicken." He pointed to a little gas station at the corner of their neighborhood. After the diner, it had the best fried chicken in town.

"Sure."

He left the truck idling while he ran in to buy their lunch. His self-assurance was obvious. He chatted with the boy working the counter and paid as if money were easily come by. The smell of grease and biscuits filled the cab as soon as he opened his door. The heat of the warm meat soaked into her cold fingertips as she held the bag in her lap the last two streets.

They sat across from each other moments later, crispy chicken and fries loaded onto plates. When they first married, they always held hands and prayed before every meal. Now, more often than not, they ate at different times or in different places. He held out his hand and she tried to not be awkward about sliding her fingers over his.

"Father God, thank you for Marty, who is willing to listen to us and use his knowledge to help us fix whatever has come between us. Please help us use his advice so we can make this marriage stronger and more like what You want it to be. Amen."

It didn't really matter that he'd forgotten to bless the food. Right now, what he prayed for was more important. She pulled off a chunk of crispy crust and popped it into her mouth. Perfect.

"Do you have a list or something you're taking?" Scott's words jerked her out of her enjoyment of the food.

"A list?" She dabbed a napkin at her mouth.

He waved his hand in the air. "All the reasons you think our marriage is doomed to fail. You know, everything you won't tell me."

"Every time I try to tell you things, we end up yelling at each other." She broke an extra-long fry in half. "That's why I suggested talking to Marty."

"I guess I'm trying to figure out why you can talk to him and not to your own husband." Scott worked his mouth, as if trying to figure out how to get the next words out. "Maybe if you'd talked to me before now, we wouldn't have to talk to someone else."

"Well, if you were ever around, I could talk to you." She threw her napkin to the side. "Maybe this is a case where I should be fasting and praying instead of eating." The chair legs screeched across the floor as she pushed her seat back. So much for making progress. Was it going to be better or worse after their separate meetings with the counselor?

"OKAY, GENEVIEVE." Marty leaned back in his chair that afternoon. "Why are we here? You didn't say much earlier, but I have a feeling a lot of this is your idea. What's going on with you two? It's only been a few years since I stood up on that stage out there and pronounced you husband and wife."

Genevieve fiddled with her purse strap in her lap, refusing to look up into the eyes she knew would be full of compassion. "Things are just wrong between us."

"Wrong how?"

"The first couple of years of marriage were fine. We worked and then spent time together at home. Almost every day, he'd swing by my office for a minute or two to say 'hi.' Or sometimes I'd go to ballgames and watch him coach. But despite the coaching, we still had time for each other. Now ..."

Marty didn't say anything, allowing her to try to formulate her thoughts.

"Ever since he was promoted to the position of upper school principal, he's been gone more often than home. I know it takes a lot of work to be a principal. I know that. And I know with him being such a young one, he probably works harder because he wants to prove to everyone he's up for the job. And he's great at it."

"But it takes him away from you."

She finally lifted her eyes. "And the rare evening he is home, all he does is grab something to eat and plop down in his recliner to watch some ballgame. He never offers to help with any of the chores. I work, too, you know. He never eats at the table with me." She gave a short derisive laugh. "When we tried to eat together today, we ended up fighting."

"Okay, so problem number one is you don't spend time together. That is definitely a huge issue. It's hard to have a relationship if you're never with the other person." Marty made some notes. "What else?"

"This is going to sound so petty." She glanced out the window.

"If it's driving a wedge between the two of you, I need to know."

"Not only does he not help with chores, he doesn't make them any easier for me, either." She smoothed a hand across her corduroy pants.

"How so?" Marty scribbled some more.

"Dishes everywhere but in the dishwasher, no matter that I have the magnet turned to show it's ready for dirty dishes. I'm always tripping over shoes he leaves lying around. Clothes on the floor instead of the hamper. He never wipes up things he spills. I don't bother to ask anymore if he'll help fold laundry or cook. He took my leftovers for his lunch the other day—didn't ask if I'd been planning to use them."

She was on a roll, and it was all downhill. "His toenail clippings actually ended up on my toothbrush last week because of his carelessness. And he hasn't made it to a dinner with my parents, something we're supposed to do every Tuesday, in almost two years."

"So, a lot of little things that are all adding up." Marty nodded as he jotted down a few more sentences on his notepad. "Anything else?"

"I can't remember the last time we kissed." She covered her face in embarrassment. What wife wanted to admit something like that? She'd die if he figured out she couldn't remember the last time they'd done more than kiss, either.

"No physical touch," Marty said it aloud as he wrote.

"We went to the school play together Saturday night, but that was the first time we'd had anything even resembling a date in a long time. I ended up moving out of our room last week because all we'd been doing was fighting, and I needed some distance." She shook her head. "I don't know how to get back to the way things were."

Marty scribbled for another moment and then looked up and tapped his pen against the paper. "I'm not sure you can get it back to the way it was before."

The lump in her throat got bigger, something she hadn't considered possible.

"Wait." Marty held up a hand, obviously recognizing her panic. "I don't mean you can't get it back to good. I mean, it probably won't be the same as those first years. Every marriage changes over time. Different jobs, different roles. Children tend to make a big difference. But that doesn't mean changes are bad things. It does mean the couple has to find ways to make it work through their new normal. Scott's job is very time-consuming. You admitted that."

She nodded.

"That doesn't mean he can't find time for you. It sounds like, in some ways, he's taken you for granted. He knows you'll pick up after him, so he probably doesn't realize how much it irritates you. He knows you're there, so he's stopped looking for opportunities to swing by and spend a moment."

"Yes."

"Okay, here's what I need you to be thinking about." Marty ran his pen down the notes as he studied them. "Are you taking him for granted too?"

She could feel the wrinkles deepen between her brows. What? Hadn't she just told him what was wrong? It was all things Scott was doing.

"Listen to what I'm going to say, and then pray and think about it." Marty raised an eyebrow. "It takes two to make a relationship work. You said you're fighting a lot instead of talking with one another. When you bring things up to him, are you doing it with a clear head and a willingness to listen, or are you coming at him with guns blazing and a sense of self-righteous indignation?"

There was that lump again. Had she been looking for the fights they'd had lately?

"One more thing to think and pray about today. We'll work on more after I meet with you both together." Marty speared her with a look that made her fidget. "How many times a day do you drop by *his* office to say 'hi'?"

"What?"

"I realize he's busy, but you mentioned him swinging by your office before. You still work in the same building, right? Why not take a few extra steps and try to have a coffee break with him a couple times a week? Or maybe do a lunch date? He shouldn't have to do all the work. Find at least ten minutes to spend with your husband this week." Marty stood, indicating the conversation was over.

"What if I can never catch him free to have a coffee break or lunch?" Her hackles were up more than they should be. After all, she'd asked for this.

"Then camp outside his office door and wait until you can. I dare you."

8

Genevieve tried not to seethe as she opened the door to Marty's office, but it took more self-control than she had. Scott was the one more at fault. Why should she have to have *homework*? She was the one suffering.

Scott sat on the bench near the secretary's desk outside the minister's offices. He glanced up from his tablet and removed those ridiculously sexy reading glasses. They hadn't spoken since she left the lunch table, but she couldn't get much from his expression to know what he was thinking now. Had she ever actually been able to read him?

"Hey, Scott. Come on in. Let's chat for a little while." Marty waved a hand. "See you soon, Genevieve."

Genevieve reached for her coat on the rack and slid her arms in as slowly as possible. Marty's door hadn't closed all the way, and the words snuck out to keep her from leaving yet. What was Scott going to say about her? Had he asked her about her "list" at lunch because he had one of his own? But she hadn't done anything wrong!

"Scott, I want to be very honest with you." Marty's voice was serious. "How angry do you think your wife is?"

Leather creaked as someone shifted in a chair. Why wasn't Scott answering right away? It took everything in her to not creep closer to the door to hear better.

"I know she's upset." Scott's voice sounded more unsure than she'd ever heard it. "Earlier this week, she was furious. Demanded I move out. Then, as the week went on, things gradually got better. I really thought maybe we were on the right track until she suggested we come talk to you."

Really?

"I'm going to give it to you straight. Your wife is very unhappy with the way your marriage is going right now. If we don't make some major changes, you may not have a wife by the end of the year."

Marty's words pricked her heart. What was she doing? She shouldn't be standing here right now, listening in to a conversation supposed to be private, but her feet were glued to the floor.

"I can't figure out where I went wrong." Scott's voice was muffled, as if he had his head in his hands. "I thought we were doing okay."

The door to the main office opened, and the church secretary swept in. "Oh, hello, Genevieve. Were you waiting to talk to Marty?"

Busted. "No. I just finished and was pulling on my coat. Thanks. See you later."

"... thought this door was closed. Sorry, Scott." Marty's head peeked out, and he shot Genevieve a look that might as well have come from her father. The chastisement written on his face had her almost cowering. "Did you forget something?"

"Nope. I'm on my way out." She spun on her heel and exited faster than the basketball players ran sprints.

Marty had obviously taken her seriously. When she issued her ultimatum last Tuesday, she'd meant every word. Then, after talking with her parents and Valerie, second guesses gathered and made her rethink things. She didn't want a divorce. She didn't want to end up like those torn pieces of construction paper from the lesson Wednesday night. But she also couldn't keep living like they had been. This was what they needed to be doing.

Although she still wasn't thrilled with Marty's recommendations. How was she going to find ten minutes with a man who couldn't find ten minutes for her most days? Would Scott look at her like she was crazy if she camped outside his office until he let her in? He probably wouldn't be the only one. And who would man her office while she did that?

What were Scott and Marty talking about right now? Was Marty telling Scott to go spend ten minutes with her too? It would be hilarious if they missed each other because they were camped outside the other's office—in a pitiful sort of way.

There were so many complications on top of the ones they started with. How was any of this going to work?

SCOTT'S CHEST felt ripped in two. His marriage was on the brink of divorce. *Divorce.*

And his wife not only took her hour to vent to Marty about him—things she still hadn't told him in person—but also eavesdropped on the conversation supposed to be private between him and Marty. Did she trust him so little? Or was she trying to make sure Marty relayed to him whatever she'd said?

"Okay, Scott. Things aren't over yet." Marty sat beside him instead of across the desk, laying a hand on his shoulder. "The fact that she suggested you guys come to me gives me hope for your marriage. Hold on to that, and let's see what we can do."

Scott swallowed a lump of emotion and nodded. "Okay."

"First of all, can you tell me what you think might be wrong?"

Shaking his head, he huffed. "I wish I knew. I've asked her several times to tell me what's going on, what needs to be changed. Instead of answering, she yells at me and acts like I should know."

"Setting that aside for a minute, can you think of anything personally bothering you in your marriage?"

"Besides the fact my wife moved down the hallway to sleep every night?"

Marty smirked. "Yes. Besides that."

Scott sat back and stared at the ceiling, not that there were any answers there.

"She never wants to spend time with me."

Marty lifted a brow. "Explain."

"She used to come to ballgames. Or at least sit in the room with me while I watched something on TV. Now, she just storms off and mumbles under her breath. And I go to the games alone. I was honestly surprised she joined me at the play last night."

"Have you asked her to go with you?"

Scott blinked. He had, hadn't he? Had he assumed she'd let him know if she wanted to join him?

"Your expression answers the question for me." Marty gave a short nod. "Okay. Anything else."

Scott shrugged, leaned forward with his elbows on his knees. Was there anything else? Before her edict Tuesday evening, he'd thought their marriage was rather perfect.

"I guess maybe it would be nice if she acknowledged the things I am doing for our family. I mean, she's good at pointing out the places I seem to be lacking, but—well, for instance, I got her a new chair for her office at work this week. And she didn't even thank me for it."

"Did she know you were the one who got it?"

Scott opened his mouth but then closed it again. Did she not know? If she didn't realize it came from him, who did she think had put it there? After all, he'd hinted about it when he stopped by to ask her to go to the play. Hadn't he?

"Okay. I gave Genevieve some homework. Now, it's your turn."

"Homework?" Even as a principal, that word had him cringing.

"It's nothing hard." Marty tapped his knuckles against the arm of the chair. "But it's something you need to be intentional about."

Scott nodded. If things were as serious as Marty said—and his gut said they were—he should be willing to do some work to fix it. "Lay it on me."

"You said she didn't want to spend time with you—although I have it on good authority that's not true. I want you to ask her to join you."

What? Marty's words spun in his head. She *did* want to spend time with him? Then, why wasn't she?

"Ask her." Marty play-punched his shoulder. "For the big things like the plays and ballgames *and* for something as simple as snuggling on the couch."

"Okay. That shouldn't be hard, right?"

"Right."

Scott started to get up, but Marty snapped and pointed back at the chair.

"I'm not quite done yet."

Scott slank back down onto the leather.

"Pray your heart out. Constantly. And if you want praise from her, maybe try offering some first."

"Do you really think we have a chance of saving our relationship, Marty?" Scott's voice was more of a whisper than anything, but it was all he could muster.

"Until both of you give up, there's always a chance. Samantha and I will be praying too."

Scott didn't plan on giving up. Not even if Genevieve had. That had to count for something.

MONDAY. What was it about the first workday of each week that made it so awful? Her car coughed and spluttered for almost five minutes before the engine hummed. She really did need to get it checked out, but Scott normally took care of their vehicles, and he probably didn't know there was a problem.

That right there gave her a reason to swing by his office today. Could she do it? She was more nervous than the first time they'd gone on a date over five years earlier. *Get a grip, Gen.* But her pep talk didn't calm the typhoon raging in her belly.

A quick glance through the main office on her way down the hall showed his door open, but he wasn't in her range of sight. Should she try to catch him now? She couldn't remember the last time they'd seen each other in the morning. He always came to work before her and returned after. Despite working only three doors apart, she never saw him for more than a moment before he returned home in the evenings.

She took a step to enter the office, but then he appeared, flipping through notes and talking with three teachers, probably wrapping up an early morning meeting. He wouldn't have time for her now. Maybe later.

And she talked herself out of entering his domain every other opportunity that day. Four times. She would wander by, glance in to see him busy, and keep going, as if she'd walked that way on purpose. No one had to know she took the long way back to her office so she wouldn't have to walk past the same doors and look ridiculous.

She gathered her things ten minutes after the last bell, pulled her door tight, and started down the corridor she'd traversed more times that day than she should have. A glance toward his office showed his door closed. She expelled a lungful of air and kept going. Maybe tomorrow.

"So, we noticed you talking to Marty after worship Sunday. Was he able to help you?" Her father leaned over his plate and took a big bite of roast beef at their Tuesday evening dinner.

"Dad, honestly." Genevieve pushed a bite of carrot through her gravy. "It's not like almost two years of problems can be fixed in one meeting."

"Well, I'm glad you're at least trying to fix it." Her mom, ever the Southern gentlewoman, held her elbows back as she cut a potato into bites. "It shows gumption."

"Not to mention good sense." Her dad's words were mumbled, but she could still hear him.

"Can we talk about something else?" Scott's empty seat across the table mocked their conversation. There was obviously much more work to be done.

"Of course." Her mother waved a hand in Genevieve's direction. "How's it going as the school nurse? Are the students still trying to get out of tests by faking fevers?"

"Always." Genevieve speared a green bean. "Although there is a real stomach bug going around this week. I've had to send four students home in the last two days."

"Are you using hand sanitizer? Disinfectant?" Her mom leaned forward. "I stocked up the other day if you need some extra."

Genevieve started to reassure her mother all precautions were being taken, but the sound of the front door stopped her cold. Were they expecting someone else?

"Knock, knock!" Scott's voice came from the front hallway. "Sorry, I'm late. The softball game went to extra innings." He pulled his seat out and sat as if it were the most normal thing in the world. Could everyone hear her heart? It reverberated in her ears.

"Well, we're glad you made it." Her mom passed him the platter of meat. "Did the girls win after all?"

"Pulled it out with a two-run homer right at the end." He forked some beef. "This looks great."

"How about those basketball boys?" Her dad banged on the table. "They're doing well this year too."

"If they win the two playoff games they have this week, it's on to regionals." Scott poured gravy over the top of his meal. "It's the closest they've been in about five years. A hard thing for me to admit, since I was coaching three of those."

Would no one address the elephant who snuck into the room with her husband? They all acted like her parents hadn't been grilling her five minutes before about the troubles in their marriage. Instead, her parents picked up with Scott as if he'd been coming to dinner every week for the last two years.

He finally met her gaze and gave her a look that seemed to say, "I'm sorry." Is that what that expression meant? She'd fully admitted to herself Sunday afternoon that she was terrible at reading his body language. She forced the corners of her lips up into what she hoped resembled a smile and then focused back on her dinner.

If he could find a way to make it to Tuesday dinner, then surely she could find ten minutes to spend with him at work tomorrow. Marty said it took two. Time to step up her game.

9

Scott's Wednesday morning was already off to a rough start. Two more emails from upset basketball parents. With playoffs tomorrow, everyone should be in full excitement mode. Instead, there were complaints about another shortened practice, certain boys not getting enough play time, and a seeming lack of attention from Coach Drake.

This was a conundrum Scott hadn't foreseen. Last year had been a smooth transition to the new coach, and he'd expected things to go better the second year in. What had changed? What could be distracting Harmon Drake so close to regionals?

A knock at the door pulled his attention from the computer screen.

"Sorry to interrupt, Scott, but can I come in for a minute?" Marian rung her hands and had a frown on her normally sunny face.

"Of course. What's going on?" He'd never seen the older lady look so upset.

"I had run to the restroom, and normally I use the faculty one, but it was occupied. Anyway, so I jaunted down to the junior hall one. You know, near Misty Smith's room?"

He pinched his lips together to keep from urging her to get to the point. Instead, he gave a nod to encourage her to continue.

"Well, there were a few girls in there already, but I guess they didn't hear me come in, because they just kept going with their conversation." Marian threw a glance over her shoulder through the crack in the doorway then turned and quickly whispered the next part, "Talking about Coach Drake. And how touchy-feely he is sometimes when greeting students or as they leave his room."

Scott's brows drew down. "Did it sound like he was doing anything inappropriate? Could you tell if the girls were feeling harassed?"

Marian shook her head. "I couldn't even tell you for sure who it was. And only one expressed feeling uncomfortable. But it sounded like mostly hugs or him tugging their hair or running a hand up their arms. Still ..."

"Yes. Thanks for bringing it to my attention." He let out a slow breath. This was much worse than the parent emails already on his plate.

"I know it's not how you wanted to start the day."

A chuckle burst from his lips. "Or any day."

"Let me know how I can help."

"Thanks, Marian. I'll send him a message that I need to see him." He pulled up the chat window on his computer as the secretary slipped back out to her own desk.

As soon as he'd sent the memo, another knock interrupted him.

Riley poked her head in. "You ready for us, Coach Stewart?"

Right. Student council meeting. "Come on in, guys."

At least this meeting wasn't stressful. And from the graphs and charts in their hands, it might even be entertaining.

"Okay, tell me your plan."

"Hello, dear." Marian glanced up from the front desk in the main office. "Here to see your sweet husband?"

"If he's free." Genevieve rocked back on her heels.

She'd forgotten there would probably be an audience if she visited Scott at work. She twisted the new coffee mug in her hands. When she'd seen it in the coffee shop this morning, it called out to her, and she made the impulse buy if only to force herself to have a reason to come down here. Now, the coffee inside the shiny metal cup might be cooler than ideal if she had to wait.

"He shouldn't be long." Marian waved at his closed door. "The student council is trying to convince him to put a vending machine in the cafeteria."

Every year at least one student ran for student council on the grounds they would be able to convince the administration they needed more access to candy bars and sodas. And every year, they were shot down, their promises unkept. It wouldn't be any different this year. Those machines were expensive, and the upkeep ridiculous. Not to mention the students didn't really need access to more sugar.

Genevieve leaned against the wall right inside the door. The clock behind the secretary's desk ticked loudly, there to proclaim boldly how late a student was or the exact moment he signed out early. She followed the progress of the second hand with her eyes.

"I'm going to run these numbers down to the cafeteria. Back in a jiffy." Marian scooted out the door, a stack of papers fluttering in her hands. She'd been the school secretary for as long as Genevieve could recall. Possibly all the way back to when Genevieve's mom attended school here.

A musky cologne came in on a breeze as Coach Drake dashed into the office. He stopped suddenly before he reached the closed door of Scott's office. A quick pound of his fist on the counter said he was more upset about Scott being tied up than she was. He spun on his heel only to throw on the brakes again.

"Well, hello."

"Hi." She released her fingers from the warm mug only enough to give a stiff wave.

"Waiting on him?"

She nodded.

"Did Pete get your chair fixed?"

Didn't he know? "Got me a brand new one."

"Hey, hey. Maybe I need to break mine." He leaned against the doorframe right next to her.

She inched over a step. Strange he didn't know about her new chair. If he hadn't been behind getting it, who had? She traced the vinyl design on the side of the mug. The school mascot's wings were bumpy under her fingers.

"Has he kept you long?" Drake thumbed over his shoulder at the closed door.

"Not too long. I was talking to Marian, but she had to run down to the cafeteria." Was she rambling?

His finger traced her shoulder. "It's a shame he doesn't have more time for you."

A shiver ran down her arm, her heart rate accelerating. "It's okay. He's meeting with the student council for a few minutes."

"Still, I think if it were me, I'd schedule time for you to come see me every day." His voice was low and barely above a whisper, shooting chills down her back.

She blinked and took another step away, unsure how to respond. It was exactly what she wanted, wasn't it? Except the wrong man was saying it. Still, it reminded her she must be a desirable woman. Otherwise, he wouldn't say things like that.

"Back again." Marian breezed through the doorway. "Are they still in there? They must be more convincing this year."

She stapled something together. "They did go in with graphs and charts."

"Ms. Marian, can you tell Mr. Stewart I came by at his request but he was tied up, and I couldn't wait? I'll try to catch him later." Coach Drake gave a dewy-eyed look to the older woman.

"I can definitely tell him, but I know he really did need that answer sooner rather than later." She tutted. "Don't you have a few more minutes to wait?"

"Nope." He nodded toward Genevieve. "Especially since she was here first. I don't want to jump in line."

"Maybe you could write out a message." Marian handed him a notepad and pen.

"*Nah.* I'm more of a face-to-face kind of guy. Thanks, though." He spun on his heel and shot a wink in Genevieve's direction. "Catch ya around."

His musky cologne lingered behind him. Marian shook her head and tutted again. Excited voices filled the space as the door to Scott's office opened.

Riley led the pack of four students, each clutching their visual aids. "You're sure there's nothing else that could speed this along, Coach Stewart?" The students continuing to refer to him as "coach" sounded much more respectful than when Coach Drake had thrown his *Mr.* around earlier.

"Sorry, Riley. My hands are tied." Scott blinked as he caught sight of Genevieve waiting and seemed to work to refocus on the task at hand. "You guys keep working on a game plan and see what you can do on your end. If you hold up your end of the bargain, I'll take it all to the higher-ups and see what we can get done."

"Sadly, that's the most hopeful thing anyone's said to us so far." She crushed her notebook to her chest. "Thanks again."

Once the teenagers were clear, Scott walked over to Genevieve. "You okay?"

"I'm fine." How sad was it he thought the only reason she'd be down here was if something were wrong? Maybe Marty had been right. "I got you this."

He barely caught the mug as she thrust it his direction. If not for the lid, coffee would have splashed onto his sleeves. He turned it around in his hands, checking out the school emblem.

"It's great. Thanks."

"It's supposed to be one of those that keeps the coffee hot for a long time. I guess we'll find out how true that is because it's been almost an hour since I bought it." Rambling again. What was wrong with her today?

He took a sip and smacked his lips. "Perfect temperature. Thank you."

"You're welcome."

They stood awkwardly next to each other, the discomfiture growing with each passing tick of Marian's clock. She chewed her bottom lip. He took another sip of coffee. Maybe she should have asked Marty what to do after camping outside her husband's office.

"Scott, Coach Drake came by." Marian's voice broke through their self-imposed silence. "Said he didn't have time to wait and would catch you later."

Scott ran his hand through his hair, leaving several strands sticking up in all directions. He shot an apologetic look at Genevieve before turning to face the secretary. "Thanks, Marian. I'll try to head his way in a little bit."

"Sorry. It was so quiet, I thought Genevieve had left." Marian's face reddened as she noticed her still standing there.

"It's okay, Marian. I only came down for a minute— to give him the coffee." She gave a half-hearted smile. "I should probably go and get some more work done. In a few weeks, we'll be entering the vaccination records for next year's freshmen. Better make sure everything else is squared away before then. Not to mention be available if another student comes in throwing up. At this rate, we may need to quarantine the sophomore class."

"If only we could." Marian pointed to a bottle on her desk. "I think I've used more hand sanitizer in the last week than I have in the whole school year."

"You're using hand sanitizer and stuff, too, right?" Scott turned back to Genevieve.

"And disinfecting spray. I'm about to fog myself out, but at least there won't be any germs."

"Can't have the nurse getting sick." He squeezed her arm, but the squeeze to her soul hurt more. Was that really all she was to him? The school nurse?

She gave a curt nod and started toward the door.

"Hey." He pulled her into a quick hug. "Thanks for the coffee. Really. This mug is great."

The bell for the end of first period reverberated in the previously quiet building. Doors slammed open, locker doors crashed into each other, and squeaky sneakers echoed off the tile and bricks. One hot shot hollered as he passed the office, "You go, Coach Stewart!"

Genevieve hadn't realized Scott's arm was still around her. She started to pull back, but he tugged her close again.

"You might as well stay a few more minutes until that mayhem clears out. You're liable to get run over out there."

"I can cut through the workroom." She pointed at the hallway that ran past his office. "I need to check my mailbox again anyway."

"See you tonight?" He held her hand a moment longer in front of his door.

"Will you be home for dinner?" She ducked her head, afraid of the answer.

"That's the plan."

That was always the plan. How well he actually pulled it off was another issue. She accepted one more press to her fingers and then slipped away.

———

It was the end of the day before Scott finally caught up with Drake. Good thing he hadn't waited until five because everyone from practice was filing out a little after four. Great. There'd probably be more irate emails in the morning.

Drake turned from loading balls back onto the cart in the corner of the gym. "Mr. Stewart. Sorry I couldn't wait around. I only had a minute, and someone *more important* was waiting for you."

Genevieve. Her timidity when she handed him the mug had stirred up several emotions—hope, frustration at her shyness, a wish for more time, maybe even a moment to steal a kiss like he used to. But the way Drake insinuated things with his "more important" set Scott's teeth on edge.

"I noticed you didn't try again."

"In case you forgot, we've got playoff games tomorrow. I'm a little busy."

Scott tightened his jaw, praying for the right words. He'd struggled all day with how to put this. "I need to talk to you today. I take it practice is over?"

"Yeah. I let them go early so they'll be fresh for the games."

Sounded legitimate enough, if Scott hadn't already received all those emails. "So, you're free now."

"I really need to get home—"

"Not yet." Scott pointed to Drake's office. "We can do this here, or we can do it in my office, but you're not leaving until we talk."

Drake raised a brow, yet still didn't look concerned. "At your pleasure."

Drake leaned against a filing cabinet, arms crossed over his chest. A look of boredom on his face made Scott want to punch him, but he reined the feeling in. He had no real reason.

"Something has been brought to my attention of a serious nature."

"Oh?"

Scott narrowed his eyes. "You know our policy on hugging and touching students, right?"

Drake straightened and scowled. "Of course, I do. What are you insinuating?"

"It's been reported about how touchy-feely you are when greeting students. I wanted to confirm there was a misunderstanding. Because in this day and age, unfortunately we can't hug students. There are too many ways things can be misconstrued."

"Who on earth told you this pack of lies?" Drake slashed a hand through the air. "As if I have time to do anything besides teach and coach? You know from personal experience this is the busiest time of year for a basketball coach."

"It doesn't take long to hug or touch someone as they walk into class, Drake. But I wanted to let you know the rumor is out there. And I will be watching you."

"Watch all you want." Drake's face was red. "But you won't find me stepping out of line."

FRIED PORK CHOPS grew cold in the middle of their table. The mashed potatoes crusted on the top, and the gravy was a congealed mess. She rested her head in her the crook of her elbow on the wooden surface.

I'd schedule time for you. Coach Drake's words echoed through her head.

Her trip to Scott's office hadn't gone how she'd planned. She'd expected him to ask her in for a minute, maybe see how her day was going, share a funny anecdote or possibly a kiss. He'd acted happy enough with his mug, but other than that, it all went wrong. Being out in the public area hadn't really allowed for anything more than the hug, and even that had received a catcall.

His plan to be home for dinner had obviously fallen through. She waited half an hour after the food was ready before giving up and eating hers. He'd have to live without. It was Wednesday night, which meant Bible study in a half hour. She pushed her chair back and rose. Might as well stick this in the fridge and go get ready.

The back door burst open and he rushed in. "I'm so sorry!"

She pinched her lips closed.

"Honestly, Gen. I meant to be here." He pointed at the table.

"I'm tired of you being sorry." She slammed her chair into the table. "Enjoy your cold dinner. I'm going to go get ready for Bible study."

"I couldn't help it. I tried all day to have that meeting earlier and couldn't catch him until the end." He followed her down the hallway, loosening his tie.

She spun to face him, her breath catching a moment when her nose struck his chest. She took a step back. "You could have at least texted. I sat here for over an hour waiting for you. I could have gone to meet someone and eaten with them. Instead, I was alone ... again."

"This isn't what I wanted. I really did want to be here with you." He reached out and cupped her shoulders.

She shrugged away from him. "Then maybe you need to quit accepting such late meetings."

"Gen!"

She slammed the door in his face. So much for the hope that a mug of coffee could fix their problems. Gallons and gallons of coffee wouldn't be able to cover the gulf between them. And even if it did, would either of them be willing to build a boat or bridge to reach the other? He'd be too busy. She slammed her fist into the pillow on the guest bed. He was always too busy.

She ran a brush through her hair with a bit more veracity than her scalp was used to. Several extra strands came away in the bristles. Giving up, she grabbed a ponytail holder and pulled the whole mess into a knot on top. It would have to do. If her parents didn't see her before or after Bible class, they would worry. She wasn't in the mood, but she grabbed a heavy sweater and headed out.

The kitchen table was empty of the dishes that had filled its surface only a few moments before. Scott straightened from putting a dish in the refrigerator. She paused in her path across the room.

"Ready?" He grabbed his keys off the hook.

Her hesitation must have been evident because he stopped and studied her a full minute. "We're going the same place. We might as well take the same car. No point in both of us using gas."

He opened the passenger door of his truck and turned to lift her in like he had for years.

"I can do it." She swatted his hand away and started to climb up.

"If you want to give me full view of that perfect backside, by all means. Climb on up by yourself." His voice was teasing, as if he could break through the wall that had grown higher only moments before with a little joke.

"Don't." She glanced at him over her shoulder. "You don't get to do that right now."

"Do what?" He crossed his arms.

"Get to joke about my backside. Get to flirt."

"If I don't get to flirt with my wife, then who does?"

Coach Drake's face flitted through her mind. There was a man who flirted to make her feel wanted and not only to make nice after a fight. She squeezed her eyes closed for a second and then shook her head.

"Just don't, please."

He shut the door with extra force behind her. She should've taken her own car. Maybe should've skipped going entirely except she didn't want to answer the questions her parents were sure to ask—not after they accepted him back so readily the night before. How was she going to act like everything was okay in front of her church family for the next hour when the wrongness of it all echoed through her body with each breath?

"Hey, guys." Marty caught them outside the classroom. "How are things going?"

They exchanged a look, and she knew exactly what Scott was thinking for the first time in years.

"Looks like we need to set up our next appointment." Marty's voice held caution.

"Ask him. He's the one with the crazy schedule." Genevieve walked into the room and left the men to talk. She wasn't exactly thrilled with Marty, considering how the coffee idea failed. Why would any of his other advice work?

Scott slid into the seat next to hers as if nothing were wrong. Valerie shot her a concerned glance from across the room. Genevieve hunkered down to survive the class and planned to dash home again as fast as she could.

Their front of a perfect marriage wouldn't hold much longer.

10

"Hey, girl." Valerie leaned against Genevieve's door the next morning.

Genevieve held up a finger. "Sick student in my back room right now."

Sounds of the stomach bug prevailing once again made both women grimace. The virus had claimed another victim with vengeance. Genevieve ran a hand over the back of her neck and tried to stretch the ache out of her back.

"*Um.*" Valerie opened the bottom half of the door and laid a hand against Genevieve's forehead. "How are you feeling? You're burning up."

"Am I?" Genevieve leaned back and touched her cheeks. They were warmer than normal.

"I think you're catching it, honey. Why don't you go get Scott to take you home?"

Genevieve stood and then placed her hands on her desk to catch her balance. "I can't. I have a sick student here whose parents are still at least thirty minutes away."

"I'll sit here. You go get Scott." Valerie picked up the can of disinfectant and sprayed the chair while pushing Genevieve toward the doorway. "Go."

The moment Genevieve stepped out of her office, the bell rang. Timing was everything. She walked half in a trance toward the teacher's lounge. It would be faster to cut through there and down the hallway than to weave between students wrapped up in their phones or significant others.

A peek inside his office showed no Scott. "Marian, have you seen Coach Stewart?"

The secretary glanced around with a concerned frown. "You okay?"

"Pretty sure the stomach bug has caught me." Genevieve put a hand to her tummy.

"Last I saw him, he was headed toward the gym." Marian pointed to the left. "Something about setting up for a pep rally."

Genevieve waved as she left the quiet office and entered the chaos of the hallways once more. Only four students jostled her before she reached the heavy doors that opened into the gymnasium. She squeezed the handle and pulled with what little strength she had left. It was fading fast.

Angry voices came at her from both sides as she took a step into the half-lit gym. "That's not what he said!"

"Yeah, well, why should you believe him now? You never have before."

Of all the things she didn't need right now. Two seniors stood toe to toe, yelling into each other's red faces, several of their friends milling about. No other adults in sight. If she threw up on their shoes, it would serve them right.

"Maybe I believe him now because he's telling the truth." The taller boy scooted closer, a feat she hadn't thought possible. "Several others saw you with her too."

"Guys." She held up her hands as she neared the fracas. "That's enough."

"She has a choice of who she's with, ya know."

"Not if it's with someone like you."

"Hey!" She was right next to them now, but they didn't seem to hear her. Fists were pulling back, and it didn't look like they would stop now. She had to try, though. Right as she got to the danger zone, what felt like a freight train barreled into her and took the blow that would have turned her face black and blue.

Scott's cheek throbbed from the punch he'd taken, but he didn't care. When he'd walked in and seen Genevieve about to be hit, his heart had skipped several beats. It was one thing for kids to be stupid to each other. Another thing completely to take their idiocy out on his wife.

"Coach Stewart!" The smaller boy backed off, hands raised, but the one who'd punched his principal glowered with an expression that said, "Whatcha gonna do about it?"

Scott knelt down and helped Genevieve back to her feet. "You okay?"

She barely got a nod out before he faced the teens. "You. You. My office. Now. Everyone else, clear out!"

If he were taller, he might have thought someone kicked an ant bed the way the students scattered. Scott wrapped an arm around Gen's shoulders and pulled her to his side as they followed the culprits back down the hallway. Most students were in class again now, so there was minimal risk of them being run over. Still, she leaned into his strength more than normal.

"Were you looking for me?" He paused outside the main office, resting a hand on her shoulder.

"I need to go home." She frowned. A look of confusion crossed her face as if she'd forgotten what she was going to say.

"Hey." He lifted her chin so he could see her face. "You okay?"

She shook her head. "Sick."

"Give me a minute to get Anne started handling these hooligans, and I'll give you a ride." He gently pushed her into one of the plastic chairs in front of Marian's counter.

"You don't have to." She gripped the edge of the seat. "You're busy."

He knelt down in front of her and smoothed her hair back from her face. "The school can live without me for half an hour."

Could she hear his sincerity? He wanted her to know she was his top priority. She gave a short nod and leaned back against the window. She must not have the energy to argue.

"Hey." His hand on her forehead woke her up ten minutes later. "Let's get you home."

He led her down the hallway to her office, where Valerie was camped out making sure all was well until the student got picked up. Since most of Val's students were on a field trip, she waved them on. Genevieve grabbed her purse and thanked her friend.

"Do you need to go to urgent care or anything?" Scott zipped through a light as it turned red.

"No." She rested her head against the glass of her window. "If it's like all the others, it will run its course in about forty-eight hours."

By the time she got the door open, he'd come around the truck and lifted her out, but he didn't set her on her feet. Instead, he carried her through the house and into their room. Her little squeak of protest didn't stop him. He laid her on the bed and ran to fetch her pillow from the guest room. Within moments he had her tucked in.

"You going to be okay? Anything you need before I go?"

She opened her mouth, but then clamped her hand over it, eyes wide. Throwing off the covers, she dashed to the bathroom and lost her breakfast. He hovered beside her, holding her hair out of the way, rubbing her back. She blinked a few times as if confused or maybe concerned he might catch the bug. But she couldn't protest because her stomach rebelled again.

When she finally leaned back, he handed her a wet washcloth and a cup of water. "I could call Marian and tell her I'm out until tomorrow."

Genevieve waved her hand. "No point in us both being here. I'm probably going to sleep for the next while anyway. You might as well be where you're needed most."

"I want to make sure you're okay." He scooped her up and carried her back to bed. "Can't have the school nurse gone for too long, you know."

She stiffened in his arms, but he had no idea why. Had he said something wrong? Nothing sounded bad when he replayed the words in his head.

She curled up on her side with her back to him, a clear sign she didn't want to talk anymore.

"I'll be home as quick as I can." His hand rested on her shoulder for another minute. "Call me if you need anything at all."

When was the last time she had called him for anything? He couldn't remember. Before he was three steps away, her breathing indicated she was asleep.

Maybe he could find a way to convince her he still cared, and she could rely on him.

HER EYES DIDN'T WANT to open. She parted her lids to the width of a tiny sliver, enough to see light coming in the window. With a bit more effort, her range of vision widened to include the fact she was in her own bed for the first time in over a week, and her husband was in her cushy reading chair in the corner of the room. She tilted her head to see the clock.

"What are you doing home?" Her voice cracked, and she winced at the memory of earlier that day.

"I told you I'd be back as soon as I could."

"It's three-thirty."

"And school is out at three." He rested his elbows on his knees.

"I guess I didn't realize you could get off that early." She rolled onto her back and licked her dry lips.

"Do you need anything? Are you hungry? I swung by the store on the way back and grabbed ginger ale."

"Ginger ale sounds good." She ran her tongue over her teeth and grimaced.

He was back quickly with a glass full of the sparkling soda. The cup even had a straw hanging over the side. He ran a hand over her forehead as he helped her sit up a little more.

"Do you want anything? You still feel a bit warm."

She studied him—really studied him—for the first time in weeks. His hair stood on end as if he'd been dashing his fingers through it. His tie was gone, and his shirt unbuttoned at the top. A deep purple spread over his cheek.

She reached out and feathered her fingers over the bruise. "Was he suspended?"

"I didn't really have a choice." He pulled her chair over close to the bed. "When I walked through that door and saw you heading right into the path of his fist, I was afraid I wouldn't make it on time. What if he'd hit you?"

"Then I guess I'd have a bruise on top of my virus." She lifted a shoulder. "The fight needed to be broken up, and there weren't any other adults in the vicinity. I didn't really see an option. And they weren't listening to me, so the next step was to try and separate them physically. I didn't see you until you'd jumped between me and that punch."

"Scared me half to death." He laid a hand ever so softly on

her leg. "And then when you almost passed out walking back to the office ... I really was worried."

"You held my hair earlier." She frowned.

"I didn't want it to get in the way." He leaned forward and brushed a strand back.

"Most people can't be around when someone else is throwing up. It kicks their gag reflex into high gear, and they end up joining in." She took a sip of the soda and could almost imagine it dripping into her empty stomach and fizzling away.

"I guess this is the first time you've really been sick in the last four years." He leaned back. "Amazing, considering how often you're around sick people."

"Usually, the disinfectants and hand sanitizer keep me healthy." She shook her head. "It seems to have failed this time. Don't tell Valerie."

"Valerie?"

"When I left earlier, she was spraying things down to keep herself from catching it." She rubbed her forehead. "I'll feel worse if she gets sick."

"She knew the risks when she sat in your chair." He squeezed her arm. "Feel up to sitting on the couch? I ordered a movie I thought you might like."

Her mouth fell open.

"What?" He paused where he'd been moving her chair back.

"Who are you?" That probably sounded wrong, but it was all she could come up with.

"Stick around." He pulled her covers back and helped her stand. "Maybe you'll find out."

Friday evening found Scott once again home early.

"But the playoff games!" Genevieve pointed as if she had a clue which direction they were being held in.

"The team knows I'm cheering for them from here. I didn't want to be two hours away from you when you're so sick." He handed her a bowl of chicken soup. "What if you needed me?"

Confusion muddled her already mushy brain. Was this the same man who hadn't made it to her parents for dinner on a Tuesday in years? The same man she never saw despite the fact they lived in the same house and worked right down the hall from each other? Where had this man come from?

"Eat your soup before it gets cold." He pointed at the bowl in her hands. "It's better than the canned stuff. Marian sent it."

She blew on the spoonful before taking a taste. This would be the first thing heavier than saltine crackers she'd tried since breakfast the morning before. The broth felt good on her throat, and the chicken and noodles didn't seem to bother her. She gratefully took another bite.

"I don't know how you've been sleeping on that awful mattress for a week now." He sank into his recliner. "That thing sleeps worse now than it did before we got married. Why did we ever keep it?"

She barely kept herself from spewing the mouthful of soup across the couch as she snorted. "I was planning to go pick up one of those eggshell toppers to see if it would help, but I hadn't gotten around to it yet."

"Why don't we replace the mattress before we have anyone stay with us? I can move out here to my chair until you're better."

Was he expecting her to move back to their room for good now? Should she? She'd indicated she might after they talked with Marty, but things had remained rough until now. She'd have to wait and see what happened after she got well.

He rented another movie for them to watch together, and he snuggled her into his side the whole time. They hadn't sat like this since she couldn't remember when. She'd forgotten how her head fit so perfectly in the little curve between his shoulder and collarbone. His arm tucked around her waist, and his laugh reverberated through them both. If she'd known he'd react this way, she might've tried getting sick before now.

She gave herself a mental shake at that thought. Her good health wasn't something to make light of. But she wished they could find a middle ground where they could be like this more and less like they were when she was well.

SATURDAY AFTERNOON, while Genevieve napped, Scott drove to the church building for the meeting scheduled with Marty. It had originally been for both of them, but now he was almost glad it was only him going. He needed to hash some things out.

"Hey, Scott. No Genevieve today?" Marty shook his hand and offered a cup of coffee.

"She caught the stomach bug going around on Thursday. I didn't think you'd appreciate it if she shared."

"No, no. She can keep that one to herself." Marty chuckled. "But she's okay?"

"On the mend. But still weak."

Marty nodded. "The fact that you're here instead of canceling until you could both come tells me you've got something on your mind."

Scott ran a hand over the back of his neck. "I keep thinking about what you said. About her wanting to spend time with me. I missed it before somehow."

"What's happened to make you believe me?"

"When she got sick Thursday, I brought her home, took care of her, tucked her in. I even rented a chick flick."

"Above and beyond." Marty winked. "And?"

"She stared at me like she had no idea who I was. When I

told her to call me if she needed anything, it hit me I couldn't remember the last time she had. Is she so independent, or have I given her the impression that I'm too busy for her?"

"*Ah!*" Marty waggled a finger at him. "Now we're cooking with peanut oil!"

Scott had never understood that saying, but he got the gist. "So how do I fix it? How do I get it back to where she doesn't think I've lost my mind when I do something little for her, like bring a ginger ale?"

"Don't stop."

"What?"

"Don't stop doing the little things. Don't stop finding ways to spend time with her, including watching a chick flick every now and then. Invite her to go with you to things. Bring her a drink she loves. Because by thinking of her throughout the day and making sure she's thinking of you—in a good way—it's going to make it that much better when you get to spend time together in the evenings."

Scott nodded. Little things. Surely he could do little things.

11

"Good morning!" Valerie turned from the coffee pot in the teacher's lounge as Genevieve entered on Monday. "How's the patient?"

"Much better, thank you." Genevieve grabbed an extra-large stack of faxes and memos. "How about you? Still feeling okay?"

"Right as rain." Valerie stirred some creamer into her mug. "Want to do lunch?"

"Maybe." Genevieve lifted her pile. "Looks like I have quite a bit of catchup to do this morning."

"I bet it'll go fast." Valerie waved before heading the other direction. "Just send me a text. I'm flexible."

By the time Genevieve tackled her multiple voicemails and caught up on entering medical notes and excusing absences, as well as the normal morning students, the thought of lunch with her friend sounded delightful. She quickly tapped out a text message and smiled when the reply came almost instantaneously. Valerie must've been expecting it.

Across from each other in Jimmy's Diner, Genevieve took a long sip from her iced tea. Valerie watched her. Genevieve ran a finger around her lips, wondering if she had crumbs or something—a feat in and of itself, considering they hadn't eaten yet.

"What?" She finally gave up trying to figure out what Val was looking at.

"I was trying to decide if it would be safe to ask how things were going." Valerie folded her straw paper. "I wanted to ask the other day, but there were too many germs around to have a conversation. And I can never really get a good read on you in Bible study."

"Well, if I'd had time to tell you Thursday, the answer probably would've been different anyway." Genevieve scooted the saltshaker over. "But we had a good weekend. That sounds funny, doesn't it? Since I was sick and all."

"You can still have a good weekend even when you're sick." Valerie waved her hand in the air, showing off red paint under her fingernails. Must be time for her class to paint poppies.

"You know he took a punch for me?"

"I noticed the results on Sunday." Valerie shook her head. "What happened?"

"I was looking for him to tell him I was sick and came upon the fight. Except the boys weren't listening to anything— probably not even each other, honestly. So, I headed in to physically pull them apart. The next thing I knew, Scott was whisking me out of the way. I heard the impact of that kid's hand. I don't know how he kept from hitting him back."

They paused while their food was delivered, and Valerie led them in a short prayer.

"Well, I'm glad he was there to intervene, for sure. How on earth did you think you were going to pull those two guys apart?" Valerie picked onion slices off her hamburger.

"I have no idea. I really wasn't thinking straight by that time." Genevieve popped a tomato into her mouth and chewed while she thought. "Then, he insisted on driving me home. And carried me into the house and straight back to bed.

Tucked me in. Held my hair while I ..." Genevieve shot a glance at their food and grimaced. "Well, you know. Lost my breakfast. He came home early, waited on me hand and foot, rented movies he thought I might enjoy, and sat on the couch with me. I can't remember the last time we've spent so much time together."

"That does sound nice." Valerie rested her chin on her fist. "If only you'd been healthy enough to enjoy some kissing too. I know if my man took a punch for me, I'd be kissing all over him."

"Valerie!" Genevieve wasn't about to admit how tempted she'd been to kiss her husband over the weekend.

"If I remember correctly, you and Parker kiss all over each other no matter what." Jimmy's teasing voice interrupted their private conversation.

"This is the problem with supporting your sibling's business." Valerie swatted his arm. "It lets him get all up in yours."

"Everything taste okay today?" He laid their bills on the end of the table.

"It's great, Jimmy. Just like always." Genevieve shot him a grateful glance to show how she appreciated his intervention.

"Holler if you need anything. I'm around." He gave his sister an affectionate squeeze before heading off to chat with someone else.

"He's always been a menace." Valerie popped in the last bite of her burger.

Genevieve shook her head. "You love him to pieces, and you know it."

"That doesn't make him less of a menace." Valerie winked. "But back to you. I'm so glad to hear you saying all these nice things about Scott."

Genevieve frowned. "What do you mean?"

Valerie leaned back and pursed her lips as if thinking for a minute. "For the last almost year, it seems like all I ever heard from you was the bad stuff."

"What?" Was that true? Really? Surely, she'd said at least one good thing in all those months. Hadn't she?

"I almost cautioned you about it several times, but I could tell from the mood you were in you wouldn't take it well." Valerie gave a little shrug. "Maybe I should have anyway."

"What do you mean?" Genevieve pushed aside the last few bites of her salad.

"You were so focused on the negative. I get you needed to vent some, so you hopefully wouldn't explode at Scott." Valerie held up a hand. "Trust me. I get it. Every now and then, I use you for the same thing with Parker. But that's *all* I was getting from you."

"That's all there was to get for a while." Genevieve ran a finger around the top of her tea glass. "Only bad."

Valerie leaned forward and touched Genevieve's hand. "That can't possibly be true."

Now Valerie didn't believe her? This discussion had gone well up until a few minutes ago. How did this turn from a gush-fest to a reprimand?

"You heard all the things I was complaining about. That's all there was. There wasn't anything else." Genevieve grabbed her check and started to stand.

"Wait." Valerie held her back with a gentle touch. "Will you listen for another minute?"

Genevieve eased down into the booth.

"I've known Scott since he first moved here six years ago. I've known you your whole life. When you started dating, I could see it was going to work." She held up a finger to keep Genevieve from interrupting. "A lot of the stuff you were complaining about—dirty dishes and laundry, spills, shoes everywhere—those are normal things every couple has to find a method of working through. But I know that man. He's a good guy. And if you look hard enough, you'll see the good too. You're simply letting the bad keep you from seeing all the way through."

Genevieve sat, frozen in place. Was that true? Was she keeping herself from seeing the good?

"Think back to when you first fell in love with Scott. What was it about him that drew your attention and caused your heartrate to speed up?" Valerie tapped the table with a red-painted nail. "Those things are still there. You've just forgotten them because you're around him all the time. Try to remember what attracted you to him back then and look for it. From now on, for every bad thing you tell me about him, I'm going to expect to hear one good one as well."

"Am I really as bad as all that?" Genevieve asked when they were back in Valerie's convertible.

"Honey, you're not bad, either. Like I told you last time, you're going through a rough patch, but you can get through it." Valerie gave her arm a squeeze. "You two are perfect for each other. You've just forgotten it."

12

Monday evening was the first chance for Genevieve to practice Valerie's most recent advice. Scott made it home only a little late for dinner. But then he camped out in front of the televised baseball game, and she was left to find something else to do. She worked a sudoku puzzle, curled into the corner of the couch, hoping against hope he might start a conversation or even just share a thought or two on whatever he was busy with. Instead, they remained two people in the same house but nothing else.

When she tripped over his dirty clothes on the closet floor again, she took a deep breath before she approached him. "You'd think a basketball coach would have better aim." She dangled a sock in the air with a smile meant to add a little lightness to her words.

"Sorry." He glanced up from his laptop only for a moment. "I'll get it later. Gotta get these last few messages sent before I call it a night."

Think of something good. Think of something good. It became a mantra, playing over and over on a loop in her head. *He was home tonight. He did help with the dishes earlier. He promised to get it later.*

She replaced the dirty sock in the pile on the floor and finished getting ready for bed. In the ten minutes it took her, he had already shut off his light and closed his eyes. A little snore escaped his lips as she crept to her side of the bed. So much for a good-night kiss. Should she sleep here tonight? It was the first night he'd come back to their bed. The bed they hadn't shared in two weeks. Fatigue won over pride, and she slid between the covers.

Were things better? Worse? The same? She honestly wasn't sure.

"Oh!" Genevieve rolled her chair backward as fast as possible.

The beast stared at her from under her desk, one leg raising a tiny bit as if he prepared to charge after her.

"What's wrong?" Coach Drake filled her doorway.

"Sorry." She pointed toward the culprit. "Spider startled me."

"I'm on it." In one fluid motion, he was through the door, around her desk, and crushing the arachnid under his black sneakers. She had to admit the crunching sound was satisfying, though it did send a shiver down her spine. He quickly wrapped the corpse in a tissue and disposed of it in the trashcan.

"Thanks. I don't usually shriek like that, but this one snuck up on me."

"Not a problem." He bowed at the waist. "Always happy to rescue a damsel in distress."

"Well, thank you again." She started to scoot back toward her desk, but he didn't move from where he leaned against the edge of it. "Did you need something, Coach?"

"Thought I'd stay and chat a minute." He nonchalantly crossed his arms over his chest. "I'm going to be on the road quite a bit over the next few weeks. We made regionals, you know."

"I do know. Congratulations to your team."

"Noticed you and the principal weren't there Friday night."

"I was sick, and he stayed home to take care of me." She crossed her legs and leaned back a little farther.

"I'm so sorry. I didn't realize you were sick." He reached for her hands, but she tucked them under her legs. "You're better now?"

"I'm fine, thanks." She pointed at her computer. "But I should probably get back to work."

"Right." He straightened and moved to the side of her desk but didn't leave yet. "Maybe you can make it to one of the regional games. The first ones are close—in Jonesboro."

"Maybe." She used to go to the basketball games all the time. But that was when she'd been dating and married to the head coach. When was the last time she'd gone to support school athletics? "I'll see what Scott has planned."

"I'm sure he'll be there." He paused in the doorway. "Although I hardly ever see you two together. You're okay?"

"We're fine." The lie slipped easily through her lips. She wasn't about to admit the problems they'd been having. Especially not to him, even if he had come to her rescue several times lately. "Maybe you'll see us there together this time."

He studied her for a moment more before giving a short nod. "I'll be checking the stands for you."

Genevieve let out a slow breath. His musky cologne lingered in her small office, making her wish for a break. Maybe this was a good time to wander down and try the coffee thing again. She still needed to tell Scott about the troubles with getting her car to start anyway.

Marian held up a finger as Genevieve entered the office.

The secretary finished up the phone call she was on, scribbled some quick notes, and then cast a beaming smile at Genevieve. "He's just stepped out. I think he was headed to the lounge for coffee. You might try to catch him there."

"Thanks." Genevieve wandered down the hallway and nearly collided with Scott as he returned. "Looks like we had the same idea."

"Oh." He glanced down at his mug—the one she'd given him—and then to her empty hands. "*Um.*"

"I was coming to see if you wanted to get coffee together. Guess I should've grabbed my mug." She shrugged. Things shouldn't be this awkward between a husband and wife. Why was she always stumbling over herself lately?

"I'm actually about to have to jump on a conference call." He glanced at his watch. "Can I take a rain check?"

"Oh." Disappointment coursed through her. "Of course. I'll see you this evening, I guess."

"Right." He pressed a quick kiss to her forehead and then continued on his way.

Evidently, it was time to practice Valerie's advice again. What good could she find? That he promised to have coffee with her another time? It wasn't like he'd known she'd want coffee at this time. He couldn't help it he had a phone call to make. And at least they'd seen each other for a few moments. More than they had time for most days at work.

What else had Valerie suggested? To remember why she fell in love with him in the first place? Bittersweet memories washed over her as she sat back at her desk.

When Coach Stewart poked his head into her office with more and more regularity five years ago, it was thrilling. After all, how often did a school nurse get regular attention from her coworkers? Usually, they only remembered her presence when something was needed, like to quickly evict a vomiting student or a case of head lice. In most coaches' cases, she was needed more for the receipt of release forms from their players' doctors, stating the kids could return to play.

That might've been what started his visits, but it soon became evident they continued for another reason entirely. He would show up between classes with the coffee pot, smuggled from the teachers' lounge, to see if she wanted a refill. He'd come to give her personal invitations to attend the ballgames, apologizing he couldn't sit next to her and keep her company. That led to them going out for ice cream or coffee afterward. And that led to dates on nights when there weren't games. And sitting next to each other in church services. And marriage.

Where had things changed? It wasn't the wedding that had lessened their time together. For the first few years, he still swung by her office almost every day for one reason or another —usually to steal a kiss. She touched her lips. When *was* the last time he'd kissed her? Christmas? Under the mistletoe? This was the first of March. That made it over two months since she'd had a proper smooch.

The clock showed four hours until time to go home. As if she were a student, she groaned and laid her head on the desk for a moment. This day was taking forever!

ON TUESDAY, Scott's chair sat empty again. Every car passing on the street, every leaf that blew across the sidewalk, every shout from a neighbor had her fighting to stay focused on her parents and forcing one more bite into her mouth. He had come in late last week. It could happen again. But it didn't.

Genevieve's parents didn't ask this time. And she wasn't going to make excuses for him. If he could be adult enough to be a principal, then he could be adult enough to keep standing engagements. She gave her Mom a quick hug and accepted her jacket from her Dad.

"You okay?" He helped her zip up the front like he had when she was a little girl.

"I'll be fine, Dad." She kissed his cheek. "Thanks for dinner, Mom. See you guys tomorrow."

Two weeks. It had been exactly two weeks since she announced they were having problems. Since then, things only pretended to change. But they remained enough the same that she knew nothing really had. She swung into the store and picked up a mattress pad that promised to hide the lumps and bumps of an old mattress.

"WHAT'S THAT?" Scott straightened his recliner when Gen came in with a large bag.

"Something to hopefully help me sleep better." She dropped her keys in the middle of the table and wandered down the hall to their room. Then, back to the guest room.

"What are you doing?" He stood in the doorway, arms crossed across his chest.

"Accepting reality." She pulled back the covers and tugged at the fitted sheet.

"And what reality is that?" His voice dripped with sarcasm, but he couldn't hold it back.

"That nothing is getting better." She unrolled the bumpy foam rectangle on top of the bed and started putting the sheets back on. "Nothing except hopefully this mattress."

"I told you I'd get a new one." He stilled her hand where she was tucking the blankets under the end. "Why did you waste your money on that thing?"

She jerked away from him and stepped back. "Because I don't want to be uncomfortable every night until you get around to buying a new bed."

"What does it matter when I buy a new bed? We have a

perfectly good one down the hall." His voice rose in volume with every sentence, but the thought of her moving back out of their bed tore him in two.

"Well, you enjoy it. I'm going to sleep in here."

"No." He stepped in front of the drawer she was trying to pull open. "You're not. This is ridiculous."

"You're right. It *is* ridiculous." She tugged the drawer harder and a glimmer of a smile crept across her face when it banged into his hip. "But here we are. And if you're sleeping in the bed down the hall, then I'm sleeping in here."

"Is this about the coffee earlier?" He braced himself right in front of her so she couldn't get around him. "I couldn't help it that I had that call. It had been scheduled for two weeks."

"No." She pushed at him, though it did no good. Her five-foot-five frame would never move his six-foot-two body. "This is not about the stupid coffee. I don't know why I bothered to take Marty's advice about that coffee anyway. In fact, I'm very tempted to not answer his text message about when we can meet next. Nothing has changed."

"Will you please tell me what needs to change?" He caught her arms in his hands so she couldn't beat against him anymore. "What's so wrong that you can't even share a bed with your husband?"

Her breaths came fast, and she squeezed her eyes shut.

If only she'd talk to him. Tell him what he needed to do to get them back to good. Because he thought they'd been doing pretty well the last few days.

"Gen, please." His voice was softer now. He rested his forehead against hers. "Tell me how to fix it."

Could it be fixed? Her parents thought so. Valerie did too. And Marty said they had a chance. So, why couldn't she believe it?

"When's the last time we kissed?"

He jerked back and studied her. That was the last thing he'd expected to come out of her mouth. "What? You're making us go talk to Marty and sleeping in this bed because of a kiss?"

"No." She rubbed at a spot on the side of her head. "But it's an example of everything that's wrong with us."

"I don't understand." He shook his head.

A small growl of exasperation escaped her. "When's the last time we kissed?"

He shook his head. "I kissed you earlier today."

"You pressed your lips to my forehead. That's not what I'm talking about, and you know it." She wiggled out of his loosened hold and took a step back. "I was trying to remember earlier, and I'm pretty sure it was at Christmas. And I'm pretty sure it only happened because there was mistletoe at your brother's house."

He blinked. "Really?"

She nodded.

It had been more than two months since he'd kissed his wife? How was that possible? It definitely put a stop to any hope of his original theory being true. If they hadn't kissed in that long, there was no way she was pregnant.

What should he do? He stepped her way. "We could change that, you know."

"Scott." She extended her hand to stop him. "No. I don't want to kiss simply to say we've done it recently. I want it to mean something. I ... I want to *want* to kiss you."

"You don't want to kiss me?"

"How can I want to kiss a complete stranger?" She sat on the edge of the bed.

He waited another moment, gave a nod, and then turned and walked away. A complete stranger. That's how she pictured him.

What had happened to them? Last week, she snuggled into his side, and it was as if nothing had ever happened between them. Last night, they'd gotten along, and she'd even teased him about his laundry instead of yelling. But today, she threw a fit out of nowhere over them not kissing? If it had been that long, why hadn't she said something earlier?

And why hadn't he realized it? Used to, he hadn't gone more than a few hours between stopping by her office to sneak a peck on her lips. Now, she didn't want him to kiss her goodnight.

A stranger.

How did he get from there to here? And how could he get back again?

13

"Come on. Come on." Genevieve pressed the gas pedal down while turning the key this time, but still nothing. Not even a click or whirr or buzz or clunk. Her head thunked against the steering wheel, and she let out a groan.

Scott was already gone. She'd checked his office on her way out. It was one of those rare occasions where she left work after him, but the higher-ups had wanted an update on how the new system was working, so she'd had to stay late.

And now her car had given its last. Why hadn't she mentioned it to Scott one of those times they'd actually been together last week? She'd had opportunity. Had even meant to several times. Although, when he'd have had time to do anything about it, she had no idea. He barely had time to eat and sleep, from what she could tell. So, here she sat, in a useless hunk of metal that would get her nowhere.

The parking lot was mostly empty. She already knew the school building was too. Stranded. It wasn't that big of a town, but she didn't relish the thought of walking the one-and-a-half miles to their house in her high-heeled boots with a fine mist falling from the sky. Time to bite the bullet and call her husband.

A tap on her window startled her as she dug for her phone.

"You okay?" Coach Drake shouted through the glass of her window. She would roll it down, but her battery wasn't strong enough for that.

"My car died." She yelled and then reprimanded herself. She cracked the door and used a normal voice. "My car died."

"Want to try jumping it? I've got cables." He hooked a thumb at his Jeep sitting several spots over.

"It's raining. You don't need to stand out there in this weather."

He shrugged as if he did this kind of thing all the time. "It's not coming down hard. Pop your hood."

She did as he said and watched through the spotty windshield as he pulled his vehicle closer and hooked the two engines together with the red and black cables. He gave her a thumbs-up, and she turned the key again. Still nothing. She shook her head.

"Not working?" He peeked in her still-cracked door.

"Not even a click." She turned the key again to show him.

"Okay. Get your stuff, and I'll give you a ride."

She started to protest again, but he was already gone, unhooking the two vehicles and slamming hoods. She pulled her key out, grabbed her purse and slid out into the wet. He held his passenger door open for her.

"Thanks, but I can call Scott. It's no big deal." She hesitated to get in his Jeep, though not sure why.

"Your house is on the way to mine. You'd have to wait for him to come all the way back up here before you could leave, and it's not safe for you to sit in a parking lot by yourself." He motioned with his head for her to climb in. "If you accept my offer, you'll be home in a few minutes."

She nodded and scooted into his SUV.

"Was your car acting up before?" He easily steered them to the exit of the parking lot.

"Off and on for a couple weeks now." She held her hands closer to the vents to let the warm air thaw out her fingers. "This is the first time it didn't start after a minute or two."

"Why did you wait so long to get it fixed?" His words set her on edge.

"Scott usually handles the car stuff. I just hadn't had a chance to tell him." She gave a shrug like it was no big deal. "He's been pretty busy lately."

"I've noticed." Coach Drake narrowed his eyes. "Does he ever spend time with you? I always see him with … other people. I almost never see him with you."

Other people? What's that supposed to mean? She straightened her back. "I told you. We spent the whole weekend together."

"While you were sick …"

"Yes. While I was sick." She tried to think of when else they'd been together recently. "And he was home all evening on Monday. And we bumped into each other several times at work this week."

"Bumped into each other on purpose or on accident because you happened to be in the same place at the same time?" He hit his blinker to turn onto her street.

"I don't know what you're getting at." She crossed her arms.

"Look, Genevieve. You put on a good front, but I can tell something's going on between the two of you. I've heard talk he neglects you." Drake shot her a look dripping with concern. "And that's not right in my book."

"Heard talk from who?" Her heart pinched. Could people tell she and Scott were having problems? People other than those closest. If it was that obvious to everyone else, why wasn't it obvious to him?

"So, it's true then?" He parked in her driveway and let the engine idle.

"We're in a bit of a rough patch, but it's going to be okay." She studied her hands which were clasped in her lap. Once again, she spouted off what others kept telling her, even though she hadn't completely convinced herself it was true.

"The house looks dark."

She glanced at the windows but couldn't tell if a light was on inside or not, since the sun hadn't set yet. "Scott may have had a meeting."

"You don't know?"

Her gaze swung to him. "I don't know every single meeting on his schedule. I keep up with mine, and he keeps up with his. Especially since his fluctuates quite a bit as things come up."

"Sorry." Coach Drake held his hands in the air. "I didn't mean to insinuate you were doing something wrong. I'm worried about you."

He was worried about her? Was anyone else? Her parents were concerned about her marriage, but they hadn't expressed anything like that for just her. And Valerie checked on her regularly, but more because she wanted to make sure things were working out with Scott. Had anyone asked how she as an individual person was doing lately? Not that she could recall.

"Well, you've rescued me several times lately." She choked out a short laugh. "Spiders and stalled cars have nothing on you."

"Any time you need to be rescued, you let me know." His hand covered hers. Her breath caught and her eyes lifted to his. What was he doing? He leaned closer to her. "I'll be there as quick as I can be."

She cleared her throat. "Thanks. I'll keep that in mind."

"I mean it, Gen."

She tugged her hands gently from his. "I better get inside before these clouds decide to do more than drizzle."

He paused and then nodded. "Hang on, and I'll come get your door."

She took several deep breaths the moment he was out of the vehicle. Her brain was a scrambled mess. Maybe she needed to go eat something. Had she had lunch today? She couldn't remember. Her door opening pulled her from her worries.

She pushed the button on her seatbelt, but the strap didn't release. She tried again, this time wiggling it a bit. Still nothing.

"Oh. That sticks a bit. I keep meaning to have it checked out, but I rarely have anyone up here." He leaned across her. "Hang on."

His hands right next to her hip was a bit disconcerting, but if she tried to scoot away, she'd only end up closer to the rest of him. She sat frozen while he finagled the buckle into releasing. The strap flipped back with a vengeance once freed, and the metal part caught his chin. He hissed and grabbed at the skin.

"Oh!" Her hands automatically reached out to check the damage. Too much nurse instinct to keep her from at least making sure there was no blood. "Are you okay?"

"It just startled me." But he let her fingers probe the spot that was turning an angry red. "What do you think, Nurse? Will I make it?"

Her lips turned up. "Not even a scratch."

His hand covered hers where she was still examining his jawline. Her eyes moved up the contours of his face, suddenly aware of how close they were with him on the running board leaning over her like this. And then they were closer still as he pressed his lips against hers. She couldn't breathe for a moment, so stunned was she.

It took her another second to get her brain back in gear enough to push him away. "What are you doing?"

"Got caught up in the moment." His voice was husky, his eyes dark as they studied her. "It's not every day the one who usually does the rescuing has a pretty lady to check his wounds."

Her phone chimed before she could formulate an answer. "That's probably Scott."

"Right." Inch by inch, he unfolded himself and got out of the way so she could exit the car.

She dug in her purse to find her keys.

"I'm not sorry it happened." Drake's whisper in her ear sent shivers down her spine.

She should tell him it shouldn't have happened. Maybe slap him. Where were the words she needed to do the right thing?

"I better go in now." She pointed up to the sky as the rain grew heavier. "Thanks for the ride."

She hurried up the steps and slid the key into the doorknob before he could say anything else. Safely inside, she leaned against the solid wood that separated her from outside and let her head fall back against it with a bump. Had that really just happened?

Her phone chimed again before she could contemplate it anymore.

Where are you?

Scott's message flashed across the screen.

Just got home.

Your car is still at school, but no one is here except Pete.

It died. I got a ride.

Her fingers hovered over the letters as if wanting to give more details. Instead, her thumb hit the arrow to send the message back to him.

Three little dots jumped up and down to indicate he was typing a message, then disappeared. A moment later, they started again. She waited until the message arrived.

I'm on my way.

She dashed down the hallway and stared in the mirror. Her cheeks were flushed, but that could be from the cold weather. She touched her lips. No visible sign that anything crazy happened less than five minutes ago. Why did she expect there to be? She didn't look any different when Scott kissed her. Right? But he was the one who was supposed to be promising to rescue her and kissing her and helping her when her car died.

Pressing a hand to her forehead, she closed her eyes. Everything that had already been wrong was now a thousand times worse. How had any of this happened? She should've stayed in her car and called Scott like she said she was going to. But Coach Drake made it all sound so reasonable.

Had he given her a ride with the hopes he would be able to kiss her? He *had* been giving her more attention lately than normal. Or had she only noticed how much attention he'd given her because of the lack of attention from Scott?

"I don't know!" Her whiny voice broke through the silence and startled her. Scott would be home any minute. She had to get herself together.

"Genevieve!" Speak of the devil. Did his voice sound suspicious?

"In here." She stepped out of the room and right into him. "*Oof!*"

<hr>

His heart still raced from all the scenarios that had run through his head earlier. He didn't dare admit how fast he'd driven to get here as quickly as he had. And having her step basically into his arms wasn't about to make him complain.

"Sorry." He held her back and studied her. "You okay? I was scared sick when I saw your car and couldn't find you."

"I was going to call but then got offered a ride and figured since your truck wasn't there that I'd just tell you when I got home." Her voice sort of faded at the end. Was that doubt threaded through her statement?

"I met up with Marty for coffee."

She blinked, her face growing paler. What was that supposed to mean? Was she worried he'd been bashing her to their associate minister?

"I hoped maybe talking to him would help me figure some things out." Scott ran fingers through his hair. "I guess your words the other night pulled me out of the cloud I'd been living in. I couldn't believe it was that long since we kissed."

Her lips pinched together as if holding back emotion.

"I'll get a tow truck there for your car first thing in the morning." He gave her a quick squeeze. "How long was your car acting up before this? Normally, you tell me before it gets to this point."

"There never seemed to be time." She shrugged.

"I'm sorry." He pressed his forehead to hers. "I'm so sorry you felt like I didn't have time to deal with something like that. And grateful you were able to find a ride home."

A look crossed her face so quickly he didn't quite grasp its meaning. Was it guilt? What for? Not telling him before it got so bad? The way things had been at their house, there was no reason for her to feel guilty over that.

"What say we go grab a quick bite and head to Bible study?" He stepped back, loosening his tie. Maybe she was just still shaken up over having to find a ride home.

BIBLE STUDY! How could she face everyone at Bible study? Valerie would know the moment she spotted her that something had happened. She might as well have a red *A* written across her chest. Her fingers ran over the front of her shirt to confirm there wasn't one.

"Hey." He stuck his head out the bedroom door again. "You okay? You're pale." It only took a few steps for him to be back in front of her, turning her head this way and that. "You're not having a relapse of that bug or anything, are you?"

The temptation was strong to claim a headache bad enough to get her out of going. But adding a lie to everything else wouldn't help matters. She shook her head.

"I'll be okay. Probably just hungry."

"Let's go, then." He slid her jacket back over her shoulders and tugged her hand as he led the way out to his truck. "How did your meeting go?"

"How did you know about my meeting?"

He paused with his hands still at her waist after lifting her up into her seat. The similarity to the situation earlier was not lost on her. Earlier when she told Coach Drake that she and Scott didn't keep up with each other's schedules.

"I ran into Boyd as he came in. I was headed out, and he mentioned he was on his way to see my wife." He ran a finger under her chin. "I told him he was much luckier than I was."

If the knife went in any further, she was sure it would start sticking out her back.

"What sounds good to eat?" He started the vehicle.

"Whatever you're in the mood for." She leaned her head against the cool window. She had barely over an hour to get her thoughts and emotions under control before she had to face her church family. If Coach Drake had been right about people noticing her and Scott's problems before, how would she pull off a performance that convinced them otherwise now?

"Are you sure you're okay?" Scott frowned.

Genevieve's favorite coconut shrimp remained mostly untouched on her plate, along with the majority of her salad. While he normally ate faster than she did, there shouldn't be that much of a difference between his completely empty plate and hers. Especially since he'd ordered twice as much food.

"*Hmm*?" Gen nibbled a shrimp as if to hide the evidence she'd not eaten more than three before now.

"Genevieve, please." He reached over and clasped her hands. "Are you mad at me because I wasn't around to help when your car died?"

"No." She jerked away, but a blush rose in her cheeks.

Strange.

"And you're sure you feel okay? Not having symptoms like last week?"

"I'm not sick, Scott. I promise." She finally met his eyes and didn't appear to be lying. Maybe he was being paranoid because of everything else going on lately.

"Okay, then. You'll need to finish up soon, or we'll be late to Bible study."

"I don't know if I want much more." She pushed her plate away. "Not very hungry tonight."

"Want to get a box to take it with us?"

"It would get yucky sitting in the car while we're at the church building. Sorry I wasted money on this."

"Don't worry about it." Money was the last concern he had right now.

The two private meetings he'd had with Marty in the last week niggled at him as he helped her into the truck. He was supposed to be doing little things, and he'd let a big one slip through the cracks, leaving her stranded with a broken vehicle. When they first married, that would've never happened.

He was also supposed to be inviting her to do things together, but he hadn't found a chance to ask her to go to the ballgames with him over the next few days. The way she was acting, would she be amenable to the idea?

God, I'm more lost now than I was before. What do I do?

14

Marty caught them before they could enter the classroom. "Hey, guys. I wanted to follow up and see when you wanted to meet together." He glanced between the two of them. "I know I've met with Scott several times now, but thought it might do us some good to get you to hash a few things out instead of just continuing to act like those issues aren't there."

Several times? Genevieve hadn't known Scott met with Marty more than the first time and today. When had he squeezed it in?

"Our boys have regional games starting tomorrow. The way they've been playing, it could last all weekend. We're having early dismissal so as many can go over to Jonesboro as want to." Scott lifted a shoulder. "But next week is spring break, and I should have a bit more flexibility."

"That work for you?" Marty asked Genevieve.

"Yeah." She glanced over at her husband. "I mean, I thought I might go to some of the basketball games too." If she could get over the dread of facing Harmon Drake again, that is. Scott's face lit up, at least proving it was a good idea on some level.

"Sounds like you're on a good track for the weekend, then. How about early next week?" Marty pointed between them. "Maybe take an afternoon one day to sit and talk things out?"

"I'm free Monday afternoon, as far as I know." Scott scrolled through the calendar on his phone.

"I'm free next week." Genevieve nodded.

"Okay. I'll see you after lunch on Monday, then." Marty rubbed his hands together. "Anything specific you want me praying for between now and then?"

Were her cheeks as hot as they felt? She pushed her hands further into her pockets to keep from reaching up to rub them. Would she have to admit on Monday what had happened this afternoon? Or even before?

She lifted her head and realized both men were looking at her expectantly. "Sorry. What?" She hadn't said any of those thoughts out loud, had she?

"Marty asked to pray with us before class starts." Scott raised an eyebrow.

"Sure." She bowed her head, grateful for the excuse to hide her face once more.

"Lord, we ask you to be with this couple. They're struggling with some things right now, but we know You are the One who gave us marriage and designed it to be a good thing. Help me have the right advice for them. And help them to be willing to keep fighting for this marriage, to remember why they decided to be married in the first place, and to once again light that fire so they can choose to love each other and stay together. We thank You for loving us first. In Jesus' name, Amen."

They slid into seats as Parker tapped on the lectern to get everyone's attention.

"You're sure you're okay?" Scott's whisper in her ear sent shivers down her back, and not just because of the tendrils of hair his breath stirred into tickle mode.

"*Mm.*" She hoped it sounded enough like an "*mm-hmm*"

that he would accept it as more than the noncommittal grunt it really was. She didn't want to risk lying in a church building.

He draped his arm across the back of her chair and opened his Bible app to follow along with Parker as he read. She flipped her Bible open, too, although she hadn't heard a word that had been said. A quick glance upward was a mistake. Valerie's stare from across the room told her immediately that she wasn't going to leave tonight without being grilled. Everyone else seemed to be focused on the lesson, but Valerie remained zeroed in on Genevieve the whole time. And Genevieve knew because she met her eyes every single time she glanced up.

If there had been an ejection seat in Valerie's chair, she wouldn't have made it across the room after the final "amen" any faster. "What's wrong?"

"You said you were okay." Scott looked between the two women. "What's she talking about?"

"It's nice to see you, too, Valerie." Genevieve made a big production of stuffing old bulletins back into various spots in her Bible. "Are you free to do lunch tomorrow?"

Valerie narrowed her eyes and pursed her lips as if trying to decide to play along or pounce. "Why don't you walk me to my car? I cleaned out my closet and thought I'd see if you wanted anything."

Scott arched an eyebrow at his wife's friend. That was a ploy if ever he'd seen one. Valerie was trying to get his wife alone so she'd be more willing to talk. Genevieve took her time zipping her Bible cover and pulling her purse over her shoulder. She stretched as she stood, making the motion last as long as possible. Valerie appeared ready to spit.

What was going on?

"Okay with you if I go see what she's got?" Genevieve shot him what was probably supposed to be an apologetic look but didn't quite work. "I won't take long."

"Doesn't look like I have much of a choice." Scott crossed his arms.

"What's up with those two?" Parker thumbed at their retreating wives.

"I have no idea, but something tells me Genevieve will tell Valerie whatever it is bothering her tonight, and I'll still be in the dark."

Parker cringed. "Still rough going at your house, *huh*?"

"That's putting it mildly. Her car died this afternoon, and I didn't even realize it had been having problems. She had to get a ride with someone else because I wasn't there for her. And then all evening, she's been acting stranger than she has the last few weeks."

"Man." Parker patted Scott's shoulder. "Sounds like we need to be praying harder than we were."

"At this point, we may need the whole congregation praying twenty-four-seven to survive the disaster our relationship has become."

"Surely you've had some good moments in the last few weeks."

Scott gave a reluctant nod. "Some. I guess the bad ones are just overshadowing the good."

"They can do that if you let them. Don't let them, brother. That's the devil at work." Parker clasped his bicep. "Focus on the good. Focus on what's gone right. And don't give up, no matter what."

Easier said than done.

"I better go and see if she's ready to go yet." And maybe catch a snippet or two of whatever she wouldn't tell him to his face. Had he sunk that low? Eavesdropping on his own wife?

"Don't forget to trust her." Parker's parting words churned

in Scott's stomach, mixing with his fish dinner from earlier. Not a good combination.

He did trust Genevieve, didn't he? So why was he so uneasy?

VALERIE GRABBED Genevieve's elbow and practically speed-walked out to the parking lot. Once they were out of earshot of everyone, she froze, causing Genevieve to almost tumble into the car. Valerie poked her arm. "Okay, spill. What has you looking like you know the end of the world is coming at any minute?"

"I completely messed up." Genevieve leaned against the side of Valerie's car. "I mean, big time."

"What could possibly be that bad?" Valerie popped her little trunk and handed a garbage bag her way. "Here. In case he comes out, I really did have clothes for you."

"Thanks." Genevieve set the sack by her feet. "Coach Drake ... I ... I'm a horrible person. I kissed him."

"What?" Valerie clapped a hand over her mouth after screeching the word so loud. She glanced around the parking lot and leaned closer, her voice much more like a hiss. "Please tell me you did *not* just say what I thought you just said."

Genevieve cut her eyes sideways and then back down to the ground again. "I said it. And it's true. But I didn't mean for it to happen." She covered her face with her hands.

"How? When?" Valerie pulled her hands back down.

Genevieve quickly recounted the whole series of disasters, ending with, "And he kissed me." She sucked in a huge breath to replenish all the air she'd used, saying it without a pause. "And I didn't even try to stop him."

"So, he kissed you. He instigated it." Valerie frowned. "Had he been acting like he wanted to kiss you? That seems sort of sudden."

"He's shown up randomly several times lately. He came in right after my chair broke the other day. And he killed a spider for me. He ran into me in the office one time when I'd gone in to see Scott for a minute. And then, today, he gave me the ride. We joked about how he'd been rescuing me a lot." She rubbed her temple. "I don't know. I mean, I thought he was just being friendly because I was so down or something. And it was nice to have the attention."

"Oh, honey." Valerie pulled her into a hug. "No. You don't need his kind of attention."

"And to make it worse, I found out Scott had been meeting with Marty. That's why he wasn't at school when I got stuck." She sniffled into her friend's shoulder. "He was trying to make things better for us ... and I made them worse."

"You know you have to tell him." Valerie pushed her back to look into her face.

"No." It came out a forceful whisper. "I can't."

"If he finds out another way, it's only going to be worse. At least if it comes from you, you can make sure he knows your side."

Genevieve let her head fall back and stared up at the moon peeking out from behind a cloud. "I don't want him to find out."

"If I had an eraser big enough, I'd let you remove all traces of what happened this afternoon. But God doesn't put erasers on the pencils He gives us to write our life stories." Valerie squeezed her arms. "Ask for His strength and guidance and the right words to say. Scott isn't going to be happy, but at least if you tell him at home, he won't be able to walk down the hallway and punch his employee."

Genevieve hid her face in her hands again. "*Ugh.*"

"Gen, you about ready?" Scott's voice came from several feet away.

She peeled her fingers away from her eyes and peeked around her friend. "One minute."

"This isn't ideal, but you guys can make it through." Valerie picked the sack back up. "It sounds like you didn't really do anything wrong. Remember that. You were caught in a bad situation. Now, own up to it and move on. Because from what I can tell, Scott really wants to make things work. That should help."

"He hasn't heard what happened yet." Genevieve let out one more groan.

"Better to hear it from you than someone bragging in the locker room. The sooner you get it over with, the sooner you can move past it." Valerie widened her eyes and then gave Genevieve a little push in the right direction. "Go."

Genevieve gratefully released the overloaded trash bag into her husband's hands. "Lots of clothes to go through, evidently. I don't know why she thinks any of these will fit me. She's at least five inches taller."

"I take it you two got whatever talked out that you couldn't discuss in front of me?" The furrow between his brows showed how upset he was more than his voice.

"What do you mean?" She slid her legs around in the seat so he could close the door.

"Don't play stupid with me, Gen." He cranked the engine harder than he needed to. "I know we haven't spent much time together lately, but I can still read you like a book. Something's going on, and obviously you've decided I'm not worth talking to."

She pulled her bottom lip between her teeth. Valerie said she needed to just be out with it. And it wasn't really her fault. Maybe ...

She opened her mouth to try and explain what had happened, but the words wouldn't come out. She caught him glancing at her out of the corner of her eye and quickly shut her mouth again. How did a person go about telling her husband that someone else—a trusted coworker—had kissed his wife? It wasn't exactly something to blurt out. But it had been several hours now. Trying to lead up to it in any way wouldn't work well, either.

He sighed and hit his palm against the steering wheel. "Fine. Don't talk. See if that helps our marriage."

She winced.

"Or do you even want to save it? It was your idea to end it, after all." He turned the engine off and punched the button to close the garage door behind them. "Maybe all this stuff about talking to Marty was simply to appease your parents."

"That's not true!" She slapped the top of her Bible. "I don't want to be divorced. I just can't—"

"Can't, or won't?" He practically growled. "I'm too tired to figure this out tonight." He got out of the truck and went inside without bothering to help her out of her side. She slid down from her high perch, finagled the bag over her shoulder, and followed him in.

The water was running in their bathroom. She sat on the edge of the bed to wait for him. What happened to their agreement to never go to bed angry? They'd broken that promise more often than any other lately.

He paused when he saw her there, but continued on to his side of the room, tugging his shirt off and undoing his belt.

"I'm sorry." It was all she could come up with. It wasn't enough, but it was better than leaving it the way it was.

He turned, leaned against the chest of drawers, and crossed his arms over his bare chest. She dragged her gaze away from a sight she hadn't had in too long and focused on his face again. The bruise on his cheek had started to fade. The mark he gained when he rescued her. A real rescue, not something inane like a spider or a broken chair.

His expression was a cross between expectancy and

disappointment. Disappointment in her. Would she ever be able to fix this?

"I can't give you more right now." She picked at a loose thread in the comforter. "I know that's not what you want to hear. I just ... I guess I need to think about it more before I try to explain further."

He inhaled deeply through his nose, his jaw tight, his broad shoulders tense. "I guess I don't really have a choice."

He turned back to where he'd been getting out his pajamas.

"What time I should I be ready to go in the morning?" She stood stiff as a rail beside the bed that used to be theirs.

"Seven, if you can. It won't kill me to go in a few minutes later, if you need me to." He pulled the drawstring on his pants tight. "I'll call the tow company as soon as they open."

She nodded. So many things hovered in the air between them, as if all they had to do was reach out and grab the unsaid words. Instead, she walked back out and down to the guest room—her personal prison of choice. Sentence unknown.

15

Genevieve twisted her purse strap in her hands. "Were you wanting to leave for the ballgame straight from school?"

Would he still want her to join him? He paused where he'd been about to exit his truck. She stared at the building and not him, afraid of what she'd see written on his face.

His hand covered hers lightly. "We can run back by the house if you need to. Assuming you're still planning to go."

"I am." She glanced his way. "If you don't mind me tagging along."

"I love when you tag along." One corner of his mouth tipped up. "It hasn't really happened in a while."

She nodded.

"Hang on, and I'll come help you out." In a quick moment, he had her door open and his hands on either side of her waist. Unlike the day before, this situation wasn't awkward or wrong. She wrapped her arms around him for a minute before he could let her go once her feet hit the ground.

They broke apart slowly, then he took her hand as they walked up to the school building. She scanned the almost-empty parking lot for a certain Jeep, but it was still missing. Her plan was to check her mail and get settled in her office before Coach Drake could catch her in the hallway.

She might even lock the door today. Not that anyone couldn't reach through the open half and undo the clasp. Still, it would give her an extra minute to find a way out. Hopefully, the tournament would have him so distracted he wouldn't have extra time.

The coffee in her mug was pure black. She wanted the maximum caffeine available, so left out the creamer she normally used. Running on maybe three hours of sleep was going to have her pushing all limits to get done what needed to be accomplished before the pep rally this afternoon.

An hour into her morning, a quick rap at her doorway startled her. She quickly set her mug back upright before more precious liquid leaked onto the floor. At least catching the spill gave her an excuse to not see who was visiting yet.

"Sorry!" Scott's voice slowed her heart rate down. "I didn't mean to scare you."

"It's okay." She plopped some tissues on top of the small puddle.

"What?" Scott jiggled the door handle, but it didn't budge.

"Oh. Hang on." She stepped over and turned the bolt.

"Do you normally do that?" He pointed at the lock.

"Been too many people randomly barging in lately." She avoided his eyes. "Thought that might deter a few."

He set a donut on her desk, frosting flaking off the sides. "These were in the lounge, and I noticed this was the last chocolate one. Didn't want you to miss out."

"Thanks." She shot him a genuine smile. "That looks great."

"The tow company came and got your car. I should hear back from the shop in the next hour or so. Tom promised they weren't too busy this morning." He picked up her mug. "Need a refill?"

"Might go well with this donut."

They walked side-by-side the short distance to the lounge. He topped off her cup with a pot that smelled freshly brewed. She waved him aside when he started to add her favorite creamer.

"Straight black today, huh?" He returned her beverage.

"I didn't sleep much last night." She traced her finger around the edge of the lid.

"Me, either." His voice was low and throaty. "Maybe we can talk some on the way to the game."

She twisted her lips, nibbling on the edge of her bottom one. "Maybe."

"Hey, Stewart!" Coach Drake's voice rang down the hallway where Scott's office was.

She stiffened despite her good intentions of not letting him get to her. "I better get back to work if I'm going to have everything squared away in time to leave."

He frowned in the direction of the interruption, but nodded. "Sure."

"Thanks for the donut."

The corner of his mouth turned up. "You're welcome."

She reached the door before she heard Coach Drake behind her. "Oh. Didn't realize you were busy. Marian said you were getting some coffee."

"I was. Just took advantage of the fact that Gen needed some too." Scott's voice sounded natural, no suspicions or worries in it. As if she and he met in the lounge for coffee around this time every morning. There was a thought. Would Marian be amenable to scheduling a coffee break for him the same time each day? Something told her the older lady would.

She tucked the idea away as she settled back in at her desk. Then, she got up and locked the door again, just in case. And pushed the top part almost all the way closed. Maybe it would keep some distractions at bay. Not that they weren't far from her mind regardless. What was she going to say to her husband on the almost hour drive to Jonesboro this afternoon?

SOMETHING ABOUT HARMON DRAKE made Scott's skin crawl. Especially the way he'd peered at Genevieve when he walked in on the two of them a minute before. And the way she'd jerked when she heard his voice.

But he didn't have time to analyze the alarm bells going off in his head. Because the annoying man wouldn't wait for whatever he needed to talk about.

"We're set to leave early, right? Busses are gassed up and ready?" Drake practically vibrated with energy.

"Yes. I told the drivers to be ready to go right after the pep rally at noon. That will give you plenty of time to get over there and warm up before the game at four-thirty."

"I don't know. They want us there several hours before we play."

"This is the exact same protocol we went through last time our school went to regionals. It will work fine. Keep your head on your shoulders so you can coach our guys to victory."

"When was the last time we went this far? When you were coaching?" Drake raised a brow, something almost wicked in his expression.

"About seven years ago." And Scott wouldn't add any more to it than that. Drake was obviously fishing, though Scott couldn't understand why. Surely it wouldn't do him any good to rile his higher-up.

"Right. Well ..." Drake chuckled.

"I'm sure you have much to do before the rally. I won't keep you any longer." Scott kept his face as neutral as he could.

"Sure. Sure." Drake chuckled again. "Seven years."

He barreled out of the lounge, practically running over Kimmy Watson, a ninth-grade science teacher.

"Oh!" She shuddered as she glanced over her shoulder where Drake had disappeared. "That man!"

"Okay, Kimmy?" Scott frowned at her reaction. Not that he didn't get a similar vibe when Coach Drake was around. But hadn't his wife reacted similarly?

"*Um*, oh. Yes. Well ..." She glanced over her shoulder again and then faced him. "Actually, do you have a minute?"

"Sure. Want to come in my office?"

"Probably for the best."

That set off a new alarm bell. It was never a good indication when a teacher needed privacy for a conversation.

"Would you be comfortable if I had Marian or Anne step in with us? For propriety?" He held his door open for her.

"That would actually be great, thanks." Kimmy perched on the edge of one of his leather chairs and twisted her hands together.

It only took a moment to round up the vice-principal and have her join them.

"Okay, Kimmy. How can we help you today?"

She opened her mouth, closed it again, and then sighed. "Can you tell me—"

Scott waited, fearing what might possibly be so hard to define.

Kimmy cleared her throat and started over. "Can you please tell me what constitutes sexual harassment?"

His stomach lurched. Though he'd half-expected it, it still sickened him. Was it Drake?

God, help me! I'm supposed to be Your servant here, but I may want to punch someone before this is all over and done with.

———

Genevieve was ready when Scott picked her up that afternoon. He sat, tense and distracted, but she was afraid to ask if it was because of something she'd done or work-related. After their sweet moments earlier, she'd hoped maybe the rest of their day could continue the same. Now the earlier concerns settled back in.

She needn't have worried what they would talk about on the drive, though. The discussion ran through all sorts of normal things, from how the boys were back off suspension after the fight last week, to her car needing several large repairs, to whether or not they should do something about the loose piece of siding on the house. Through it all, the unsaid things grew larger in the cab of the truck, taking up more space and using more of the air. She was glad when they pulled into the almost-packed parking lot.

"Want a hot dog or anything?" He pointed to the concessions window where the buttery smell of popcorn wafted out.

"I wouldn't turn one down."

"You go find a seat, and I'll bring it."

She scanned the crowded gymnasium, easily picking out the side their school was on by the multitude of maroon shirts. She wove her way through the students clustered around the outskirts of the floor and headed toward a pocket of space where Valerie waved like mad. She plopped down next to her friend, glad to be away from part of the chaos reigning below.

"I watched your car get towed off." Valerie bumped her arm in a friendly greeting. "How'd you get here?"

"I'm here with him." Genevieve pointed at their school principal, who appeared in the doorway. "He wanted to get hot dogs first."

"See? I told you he'd be okay if you just told him." Valerie grinned widely.

"I haven't told him yet." Genevieve scrunched her face up as she forced the words out.

"You what?" Valerie shot a look between her and Scott and then to where the team warmed up, led by Coach Drake.

"Please don't say anything." Genevieve squeezed her friend's arm. "I promise I will. Soon. I couldn't last night."

"It's not my story to tell." Valerie shook her head. "But you don't need to wait too long."

"Hey, Valerie." Scott handed Genevieve a cardboard tray with a corndog covered in mustard, corn chips, and a lemon soda. Perfect. He settled next to Genevieve with his own tray of food.

"Where's mine?" Valerie's voice was teasing as she spread her hands out to show how empty they were.

"Do you need ..." Scott started to rise.

"Stop, stop." She waved him back down. "Parker's on his way, and I'll eat when he gets here."

"Oh. This was probably his seat." Genevieve quickly swallowed the bite she'd just taken. "We should move."

"We'll all scoot down and make sure he has room. There won't be many seats available anywhere else."

The gym had indeed filled up more since they came in. The buzzer on the far wall sounded, indicating warmups were over, and the game would start in a few minutes. The boys filed off the court, already sweaty in the overcrowded room.

The sense of being watched brought her gaze up from her dinner and down to the floor. Coach Drake stood, clipboard in hand, his stare fixed right on her. A slow smile crept across his lips. She slid a hand under Scott's elbow and leaned into him.

"WHAT'S UP?" Scott squeezed Genevieve's hand tight to his body for a moment.

"Just thinking. Chocolate donut this morning and corndogs this evening." She beamed at him. "You sure do know how to make a girl happy."

"If all it takes to make you happy is donuts and corndogs, I think I'm set." Confusion filled him as memories of the last few weeks contradicted her words. "Why didn't you tell me sooner?"

The buzzer marking the start of the game kept her from replying.

He wouldn't complain about his wife showing affection, for sure. But something seemed off about it. The sense of her hiding something from him the day before still hovered like a thin wall between them, despite the packed bleachers pushing them close. Was she putting on a front for everyone around them?

The first half went quickly, both teams evenly matched. Parker joined them ten minutes into the game, and Genevieve scrunched even closer to Scott. No choice but to sit with her arm tucked under his now. He couldn't complain, though.

Chaos that had been kept semi-reined in during the game was set loose at half-time. Scott stood to stretch and helped her do the same.

She twisted to work the kink out of her back. Teenagers milled around, munching on candy, laughing, taking selfies, and throwing awkward waves every now and then when they passed by her and Scott. She declined his offer to buy her something else to munch on and sat next to Valerie again.

"I take it you two made up last night?" Parker motioned back at their wives as he followed Scott to the concessions.

"Not really?" Scott shook his head. "I still think there's something she's not telling me. But I guess we've both pushed it aside for now."

"I can understand the desire to do that, but it's not necessarily healthy for your relationship."

"I know." Scott sighed before stepping forward and ordering popcorn.

"Sorry, man." Parker joined him a few minutes later with his nachos. "I'm not trying to make things worse. Just concerned."

"Thanks for caring. Keep praying because we definitely need it."

"You got it."

They started back, but Scott's progress was slower than his friend's. Several people stopped to talk to him about things that had been on their mind lately. Most of them, he asked to send him an email or swing by the school one day to have time to talk. But his pace was still slower than he wanted.

When the cheerleaders started their halftime routine, he had the perfect excuse to cut out of a few conversations. Who could hear anything over that music?

<hr>

"You two are acting friendly tonight." Val nudged her and wiggled her eyebrows.

"You know what's sad?" Genevieve wrinkled her nose. "I don't even know if it's real or if it is an act since we're around everyone right now. Gotta put on a good front, after all."

"It doesn't look like a front." Valerie shook her head.

"It is sort of nice. To simply be together." Genevieve followed his progress back with her eyes. He chatted with almost everyone he passed, holding his popcorn up high so that it didn't get bumped, an easy task for someone so tall.

"Hey." He scooted back into his seat.

"Hey, yourself." Her gaze never left his face.

"What?" He rubbed against his cheek, as if checking for mustard.

"In this lighting, that bruise looks greener than it did earlier." She traced the outlines of the remains of his black eye.

"Green is good, right?" He caught her hand before she could lower it away again. "Doesn't that mean it's healing?"

She could only nod. Such a simple thing to have taken her breath away. When was the last time that happened? Something in his eyes told her if they weren't in a crowded gym, he'd close the small space between them and kiss her. And she wanted him to.

If only someone else hadn't kissed her yesterday, leaving her lips feeling so ... contaminated. She had to tell him first. He might not want to kiss her if he knew.

She turned her attention to the cheerleaders in the middle of the court. She wasn't familiar with the song they were doing their routine to, but it didn't sound like anything appropriate for teenagers. Not that their outfits were much better. She cautioned a quick glance at her husband to see if the half-clad girls had his interest, but he faced the other way, talking to one of the players' dads.

The teams came back out and prepared for the second half. As Coach Drake took his place on the sidelines, a pretty brunette and a little girl came over and wrapped him in a hug. He grinned at them and scooped the toddler up in his arms. The woman laid her hand on his bicep and smiled at him, a smile Genevieve could tell was beaming, even from this distance. He was married—and a father. He definitely hadn't been acting like it lately.

"You okay?" Valerie whispered.

She met her friend's look of concern. "I guess I didn't realize."

"Realize what?" Scott's voice had her thoughts scrambling further.

"Didn't realize how many on the team were seniors this year." Valerie leaned around Genevieve and distracted Scott. "Next year is going to be rough, *huh*?"

"It's possible." Scott was always good to talk about

basketball, especially since he'd been the coach only two years before. "There are some good prospects coming up, though. Nate Malone is really great. And Spencer Willis."

"I haven't had either of them in class, so I don't know much about them." Valerie shrugged. "But I know you know your stuff."

"I used to, anyway." He focused back on the floor as the buzzer sounded for play to resume.

The image of Coach Drake with his family stayed in the front of Genevieve's mind. It shouldn't change anything. What had happened was wrong whether he was single or not. But it ate at her more now. Not only had someone kissed her who wasn't her husband, but he'd betrayed his wife in doing it. It wasn't only three people who could get hurt from this. It was five, counting his little girl.

Five people injured because of a bad decision on her part and a worse one on his.

And the way those girls smiled at him, they obviously adored him. That was no act, for sure. No front for the world to think all was right. They had no idea.

And she hoped they never would.

16

With the boys pulling out a win in the last two minutes Thursday night, their school would move on and play again tonight. Another early release day was declared, and Genevieve agreed to accompany Scott to Jonesboro once more. Part of her was elated at the chance to spend more time with her husband. The other part of her dreaded the other person she'd have to see.

At least with Drake being so wrapped up in the basketball games, he didn't have time to drop by her office.

Tonight. Genevieve gave herself a mental pep talk. *Tell him on the way home from the game. Or maybe right after you get home. But definitely before this drags out any longer. Maybe meeting with Marty on Monday will help work out any leftover anger.* She cringed. She didn't want anyone else to know it had happened.

"Knock, knock." Scott's voice interrupted her internal argument. "Ready to go?"

"Sure." She shut down her computer and grabbed her purse. "The kids aren't going to want to go back to regular days after spring break, *huh*? After getting out early these last few."

"The kids don't want normal days even when they haven't

153

been getting out early." He laughed. "How they'll ever survive working a nine-to-five job, who knows."

"Maybe they'll find a school to work at like we did and not have such long hours." She waited while he opened the truck door.

"I don't know. Sometimes I think I work more than a regular nine-to-five job." He lifted her into the seat.

"Sometimes I think you do too."

He paused at her quiet confession. But he didn't say anything, just nodded and walked around to his side. Had she upset him? She'd only repeated what he admitted himself.

The ride this afternoon was quieter than the day before. She almost blurted out her confession if only to find something to break the silence but caught herself before she could. She didn't want Scott to walk into the gym and punch their head coach right before a regional game. It would be bad for more than just the two men. It would look horrible for their school, possibly ruin Scott's career, and might make the team lose. Better to stick with her earlier plan.

The crowd this afternoon was bigger than the previous. She stuck close to Scott's side as he wove through the people milling about and wound his way over to the bleachers. Valerie wouldn't be here today because she and Parker already had plans to go visit their daughter. She and Scott were on their own.

"Hey, Stewart." Coach Drake cut them off before they could start up the stairs. "Or should I say Stewarts?"

"Coach." Scott gave an amicable enough nod, but his arm tensed under her hand. "Think we've got a good chance today of moving on?"

Coach Drake shrugged. "This Newport team is strong. I'm going to keep our guys focused, but they're still pretty tired from last night."

"We'll do our part to keep the morale up." Scott pointed up

into the bleachers where several kids were already brandishing rally towels. "Maybe we can snag one of those rags to wave."

"Harm!" A voice called out from near the door. Genevieve picked out the pretty brunette hailing him, one hand holding tight to the little girl.

"Daddy!" Faster than Genevieve had thought possible in this crowd, the two girls made it through, and the toddler leaped into Coach Drake's arms. "Daddy, guess what?"

"What?" He gently removed the little girl's hand from his mouth.

"We came to watch the ball game." The girl bounced, her curls jumping right along with her.

"Sounds like fun, Buttercup." He set her on the floor and accepted the hug the other lady gave him. "Shanna, this is Scott and Genevieve Stewart. Scott is the principal, and Gen is the school nurse where I work." His eyes focused on her, though she couldn't decide if it was to gauge her reaction or swear her to secrecy. "This is my wife, Shanna, and my daughter, Isabelle."

"Hi." Shanna thrust her hand out so fast, Genevieve almost had to dodge it. "Nice to meet you both. I'm always happy to meet more of Harm's co-workers."

Genevieve gingerly accepted the handshake. How many other staff and faculty had Mrs. Drake had the chance to meet? This was only the second time Gen had seen her, although she hadn't attended many ballgames the last few years. Could she have stopped what happened Wednesday if she'd known about Shanna earlier? No. Her existence didn't change anything.

"We'd better go grab a seat while we can." Scott's hand applied a gentle pressure to Gen's back. "Nice to meet you."

"That little girl is adorable." Genevieve settled onto a bleacher.

"Yeah." Scott thumped down beside her. "Imagine, a guy like him ..."

"*Hmm?*"

"Nothing. Forget I mentioned it." He pointed across the court. "That other team is so tall."

She paused only a moment before accepting his change of subject. Although he wasn't normally the kind of guy to make such judgmental statements. Had he guessed more than she thought? Or was there something else going on? She pulled her gaze away from the apparently happy family and followed the direction of her husband's finger to the giant players on the opposite team.

"Well, I guess height gives a little advantage in this game. But that doesn't mean we can't win."

<hr>

GENEVIEVE SQUIRMED BESIDE HIM. "If we do win tonight, I think I want one of those cushy stadium seats to bring with us, the kind with a back. These bleachers aren't comfortable at all."

"If we win, we'll go pick you up one on our way to tomorrow's games." He chuckled and nudged her arm. "Whatever it takes to keep you coming with me to some games. I really like having you here."

She leaned over and laid her head on his shoulder. "I like it too."

Perfection. If only he could stay like this right here forever —minus the uncomfortable bleachers and enormous crowd— their marriage had a great shot. But he was reminded all too quickly that they weren't alone.

"Hey, Coach Stewart!" Riley and a couple of other girls waved at him.

"I love that they still call you that." She smiled as he lifted his hand in greeting.

"You do?" He focused on her. "Why?"

"It shows how much respect they have for you." Her

shoulder lifted in a half-shrug. "They had you as a teacher for a while and got used to referring to you that way, then, sure, but not all of them still use the 'coach.' Some of them use 'Mr.' now, and you can hear it in their voice they only use it because they have to. But when students like Riley say *Coach Stewart*, you can hear the admiration and respectfulness."

"I guess I never really thought of it that way. Most of the time, I'm just glad they're using something besides my first name." He laughed. "Or one time a kid actually tried to show off by shortening Principal. Unfortunately for him, he didn't think it all the way through, and when it came out 'Prince,' it actually sounded like he wanted to show me more honor than necessary."

She giggled.

The buzzer drew their attention back to the court. The game started out okay, but the further into it they got, the more frustrating it became. Like a few games before, when Scott had noticed Drake not giving his all to the game, tonight was proving similar. Except this time, Drake's focus was obvious— and it was on a person it didn't need to be anywhere near.

With each mistake, and each glance into the bleachers instead of toward the court, Drake raised Scott's blood pressure. If he had some sort of proof, he'd go down there and sock the coach right in the kisser. Scott was actually sitting on his hands by the time the first half ended.

"You can't help yourself, can you?" Genevieve nudged his arm.

He took a deep breath to try and cool his anger before answering his wife. "What do you mean?"

"It's intrinsic. You want to be down there coaching."

Her answer pulled him back to reality and gave proof she hadn't noticed what he had. "I guess that's part of it."

"Part of it?"

"You haven't noticed?" He looked her square in the face.

"Noticed what?" She stood and stretched her achy back.

Scott shook his head. "Coach Drake has been watching you more than the players."

Her gaze darted down to the court, but of course, the team had gone into the locker room. She glanced back at Scott with a frown. "Maybe he's not used to seeing me beside you?"

"I can't imagine that would draw so much attention. I mean, he's seen us together several times at school recently." Scott drummed his fingers on his knees. "I don't know. Seems a little strange."

Her cheeks looked pale, but with her face turned toward the court again, he couldn't tell for sure. He didn't need to be overanalyzing things like that here and now anyway. Maybe something cold would help cool his insides.

"I'm going to go get something to drink. You want anything?" He rose and started down the steps without listening for her reply.

THE TRUTH of everything hung over Genevieve's head like a boulder ready to smush her. When she finally worked up the nerve to tell Scott what happened, would he be mad? Hurt? Or simply enlightened. If only there were a way to make it all go away!

She was so busy watching him walk across the gym that she didn't notice Shanna Drake until she plopped down next to her.

"Hey!"

"Hi." Why had Scott left her now? Or had Shanna been waiting until Scott left to come up here? She didn't seem suspicious or outraged. But maybe she had also noticed where her husband's focus was tonight.

"So, are you guys and Harm pretty close?" Shanna caught Isabelle before she dove headfirst off the bleacher below. "He never really talks about other people from school. I think you're the first ones he's actually introduced me to."

"Oh. *Um* ..." How was she supposed to answer a question like that? "I don't know that we're all that close. Honestly, I don't get to interact with most of my coworkers. I sort of stay holed up in my little office much of the day."

"Wow. That sounds boring. How can you stand it?"

"I have students in and out all day long for one reason or another. And I field phone calls and keep records up to date. On slow afternoons, I get to work sudoku books or listen to audiobooks. It's not so bad." Her heart rate slowed when Scott came back through the doors. "And my husband's right down the hall. We've been having coffee breaks together the last few weeks, which is nice."

"That does sound nice." Shanna let out a sigh. "I'm glad for Harm that his team is doing so well and everything, but it seems like it takes him away from us so much. Sometimes he doesn't get home from practices until after I've tucked Izzy in bed. And game nights are even worse."

"You must put her to bed early, *huh*?" Genevieve reached out to catch the rambunctious two-year-old from tumbling this time.

"By eight." Shanna shook her finger at the little girl. "Isabelle, you're going to fall and bump your head. Please be careful."

Eight? Practices were over by five when Scott was coach. Maybe Coach Drake had been having longer ones lately due to the tournaments. But that couldn't be right, either, because most of the cars were gone when she left the other day around four, the same time he had been leaving.

"I got you a water. Hope that's okay." Scott held out a bottle covered in condensation.

"Perfect." She smiled up at him.

"Guess we'll catch you later. Gotta sit closer to the action, ya know?" Shanna herded her daughter back down the steps.

"What's up?" Scott nodded toward Mrs. Drake's retreating back.

"She said we're probably the only ones of Coach Drake's coworkers she's met. She wanted to know if we were close." Genevieve took a sip of her water. "She's lonely. Said he doesn't get home until after eight a lot of nights."

A piece of her own heart thumped in understanding. Yet, Scott was usually home by seven, even on the late nights. It didn't make sense.

"Wonder what keeps him out so late." Scott's forehead furrowed as he watched the team come back out onto the court.

"She said their practices have been running long."

Scott let out a huff. "Short, more like it. I've had several complaints lately from parents who thought their precious darlings weren't getting enough time from their coach in the afternoons."

"What?" She frowned up at him.

"I'm not sure exactly what's going on, but I don't think I'm going to like where it ends." He took a swig of his soda.

She knew he wasn't going to like at least part of it. The part that included her.

<hr>

THE SECOND HALF of the game went worse than the first. If Scott hadn't received a text message that distracted him from the coach, he might've confronted him tonight. Good thing his mom sent the news they'd been waiting for over a week now.

The final buzzer sent the other school's crowd into a frenzy, while those around him slumped, their faces long. He commiserated with a few parents as everyone filed out. There was no way he needed to stay here any longer this evening, though.

During the awkward meeting with Kimmy the day before, she'd admitted someone on the staff was making her uncomfortable, but she wasn't sure if it was sexual harassment or simply his personality. She wouldn't give his name, though. Normally, Scott didn't jump to conclusions without concrete evidence, but after Marian had come with the story about the teenage girls, he'd immediately been suspicious of one man. And when that man couldn't keep his eyes off Genevieve tonight ...

"You okay?" Genevieve squeezed his hand as they waited their turn for the stairs.

"Disappointed, I guess." He pulled her a bit closer. No need to tell her his dissatisfaction was more in what he was afraid was coming in regard to the coach instead of the lost game.

"It's good that the boys made it this far, though."

"Yes."

As they stepped down onto the court floor, he didn't let his gaze wander toward the coach. Focus on the woman beside him and the text message from earlier. Since today had been the last day before spring break, he had a whole week to figure out what to do about the other problem.

17

"Hey." Scott passed Genevieve his phone once they were settled back in the truck. "Look at that."

"Oh!" A brand-new baby face stared back at her from the screen, all red and squishy and ready for kisses.

"It's our new niece. Lacy had her this afternoon. Mom sent the picture." He started the engine. "Want to go meet her?"

"What? Now?" She laughed.

"Spring break is next week. We could take a day."

"We have that meeting Monday." Her stomach tightened at the thought.

"Since the boys lost tonight, we don't have anything tomorrow. We could drive over in the morning and back after supper. It's not like they live that far away."

"You're really itching to get your hands on that baby, *huh*?" She grinned.

"Gotta make sure little Beth knows who her favorite uncle is right away." He shot her a look full of mischief. "Todd probably won't be able to get away until later next week."

Of Scott's two siblings, Todd was the one who lived the farthest away. The rest of Scott's family lived near Little Rock,

163

but Todd was down in Shreveport. Todd also got the most ribbing about moving to a different state from where they'd all grown up.

"I'm fine with a trip if it's okay with Lacy. You might check to make sure she wants your company before forcing us onto her."

If they went, she'd once again have him as a captive audience for hours in the car. Plenty of time to tell him everything that had happened. But then he'd go into meeting his new niece with the horrible truth hanging over him. She didn't want to mar his memories with something like that. Sunday afternoon. She mentally pointed a finger at herself and commanded her to do it then ...

"I'll send her a text back. By the time we get home, it'll be later than I usually try to call anyone, but she'll more than likely be up some tonight with the baby. That way I'll probably have a response when I get up in the morning." He steered them down the highway toward home.

"Makes sense." She focused her gaze on the world outside. An almost-full moon illuminated the newly furrowed fields, ready for crops of rice and soybeans and cotton and corn. Some people found this part of the world boring, but she saw the beauty in the patterns of the fields, the stretches of land perfect for a sunset, and the slightly rolling hills closer to their town.

It took a lot of work to make those fields produce to their best. Genevieve couldn't imagine being a farmer, though she appreciated their efforts. She couldn't even get her marriage to flourish.

"You okay?" He reached over and gave her hand a squeeze.

"Just tired. It's been a long couple of days. And another tomorrow if we're headed down to see family." She shot a smile his direction. "Not that I'd turn down a chance to hold that sweet baby, either."

"Babies are definitely special." The look he gave her out of the side of his eye sent a thrill through her. But also left her wary. What was he thinking? "Maybe someday we can have one or two of our own."

Oh.

They'd always talked about having babies down the road. Once he was established in his position as principal, and they had a little tucked away so she could stay home while the children were little. They hadn't discussed it in a while, though. One of the many things pushed aside in their recent disputes.

"Might be nice." She dipped her head. They still weren't sleeping in the same bed, and she couldn't even let him kiss her until she confessed what happened earlier in the week. Would he want her to have his baby if he knew all? "May be something to talk about more after we work through some of these problems."

His shoulders visibly slumped. Did he think they were already back to a better place in their relationship? Surely not. If that were the case, they wouldn't need to keep the meeting with Marty on Monday afternoon. And she wouldn't still be sleeping on that uncomfortable mattress. She grimaced.

Scott eased the guest room door open the next morning. Genevieve's breathing was steady where she lay curled on her side, closer to the middle than the edge of the mattress. Though, if he remembered correctly, the bed sank a bit in the center. Much as he hated to disturb her sleep, he couldn't wait much longer to leave and meet his niece.

"She said to come on down." Scott's voice held as much excitement as a kid on Christmas. "Let's go."

She rolled over and groaned when she picked up the clock. Six-thirty ... on a Saturday. "Thirty more minutes."

"Okay, sleepy-head, but then if you don't get up, I'm going to drag you out—or go without you."

She chunked a pillow at him as he dashed out the door. But a little smile remained on her lips. Her eyes drifted back closed, and he sighed. Might as well go make some coffee. Appeared he needed fortifications to drag Gen from slumber.

Right at thirty minutes later, he was back. Her arm was thrown over her eyes, and a slight snore whistled through the air. In years before, he'd have woken her with kisses, but had no idea where he stood on that front right now. Time to break out another method.

"I warned you."

Her eyes popped open a second before he pulled the covers off her feet and set to work. She shrieked and kicked and giggled. He was the only one who knew she was ticklish on the tops of her feet, and he was taking full advantage—especially considering he hadn't heard her laugh in far too long.

She aimed a kick at his arm hard enough to get him to quit. "I'm getting up. Stop!"

He held his hands in the air. "Okay."

She swung her legs over the side of the bed fast enough he couldn't have grabbed them again had he tried. When her toes hit the floor, he backed out of the room.

She shook her head. "Worse than a kid on Christmas."

"A new niece is way better than Christmas." He waggled his eyebrows. "Hurry up. I'll get your travel mug ready."

FORTY-FIVE MINUTES LATER, they were in his truck driving south. It took a little less than an hour and a half to get to the hospital in North Little Rock, where his sister and niece were. It would be the perfect time to talk.

But they didn't. Maybe they were out of practice. Or had spent so much time together over the previous few days that they didn't need to fill the silence.

He drummed his fingers against the steering wheel to the beat of the country song on the radio. She watched out the window as the scenery change from the plains of northeast Arkansas to the rolling hills of central. Not much longer.

"She's in room 402." Scott scrolled through the text messages his sister had sent the night before as they walked across the parking lot. "She said knock before we enter in case she's feeding Beth."

"Oh. That would be awkward. Maybe we should've waited until they got home." Genevieve followed him into the elevator.

"She'd still need to nurse the baby." He pushed the button for the fourth floor. "And I really don't know when we could've made it down here between now and Easter. Spring semester is pretty full."

She couldn't argue with that. They stepped off the elevator and were immediately hailed by his mom. She drew them both into a hug at the same time and kissed their cheeks.

"Lacy was feeding the baby a few minutes ago, so I stepped out for some coffee." Her mother-in-law held up a steaming cup. "Want to go grab one for you too? It'll be a few more minutes before we can go back in unless you want to see more of your sister than you've seen since you quit taking baths together."

Genevieve smirked as Scott reddened and swatted at his mother. "Mom, seriously. No one wants to know about that. Yes. We'll go get a cup of coffee. Anything to keep more mentions of my past from coming up."

"I think it's sort of cute." Genevieve giggled. "Why don't you go get some coffee for me, too, and I'll stay here with your mom."

"Oh, no. I don't even want to think about all she might tell you while I'm gone. You come with me." He grabbed her elbow and helped her back onto the elevator.

His mother shot a wink through the closing steel doors, and Genevieve giggled again.

"How about I ask your mom to tell me some stories next time we're with them?" He sulked beside her, his arms crossed.

"It wasn't that bad, Scott. As far as I know, most siblings took baths together at least once or twice while growing up. I took some with cousins if it makes you feel any better."

"I think it's the way she puts things. It makes it sound so much worse." He pointed to the sign for the café when the doors opened again. "Looks like it's this way."

The line wasn't long, and they procured their drinks quickly. After a short stop to doctor the black brew, they were on their way back. The smell of their caffeine mingled with the antiseptic scent permanent in hospitals. Their shoes squeaked on the linoleum floor as they walked down the hushed hallways.

His mom wasn't out in the waiting area anymore, so they found the room and rapped lightly on the door. A soft "come in" had him looking at her with a grin of expectation that made her smile. If he were this excited about seeing his niece, how wound up would he be when their own children arrived?

Their own ...

The coffee suddenly felt heavier in her stomach. Evidently, the discussion in the car the night before was getting to her because she hadn't thought about having babies of their own in more than a year. She followed him into the room and made sure her smile was in place as she greeted his family members.

Lacy sat in the hospital bed like a queen on a throne. She handed over the wrapped bundle in her arms to her brother as if it were no big deal. But she beamed as he exclaimed over every little feature of the baby within the blankets. And her husband Brian's expression was even brighter.

Genevieve perched on the armrest of a chair out of the way while the family caught up. Scott's mom sat in the other chair and smiled at her children while she held Lacy's two-year-old son Paxton in her lap. Her eyes wandered over to Genevieve, and she raised a brow as if wondering why she wasn't over there fawning over the baby. Why wasn't she? What held her back?

Scott finally glanced up from counting toes and motioned for her to come over. She rose and walked close, peeking past his arm to the tiny human in his hands. Beth yawned and stretched her miniature fists, scrunched up her nose, and then relaxed. Genevieve smiled.

"You want a turn?" Scott placed the bundle in her arms before she had a chance to say *yes* or *no*. Even though she knew humans started out small, she'd forgotten how teeny they really were. The baby's fingers wrapped around one of hers but didn't cover half the length. If she were brave enough, she could probably hold the child in one arm instead of two, but she didn't dare risk dropping her.

A flutter in Genevieve's heart set to beating, drumming up a lump in her throat. If Scott had taken her ultimatum seriously, they'd never have a chance to have a baby of their own. Considering what she was keeping secret from him, they still might not. She blinked a couple times to hold renegade tears at bay. No use borrowing trouble. Instead, she focused on the conversation floating around her.

"WHERE'S DAD?" Scott sat on the end of Lacy's bed and patted her feet. "I would've thought he'd be over here soaking up the new princess."

"You know your father." Mom waved a hand. "If it can be done today, why wait until tomorrow? He's at the office for a few hours but promised to swing by and take me to lunch and get a few kisses from those here."

Genevieve glanced his way, a look flitting across her face he could almost guess the meaning of. Was she comparing his work ethic to that of his father? Had he fallen into the habits he'd so despised when growing up? And if so, how could he undo it?

His wife was stunning holding baby Beth. How amazing would it be if she were to have their own child? Would they be able to find time to be together long enough to have children? After all, it took more than a few dates and a kiss on the cheek to make a baby.

He fought back the cringe wanting to escape as his cheeks heated. *Ugh.* When was the last time he'd blushed? If he'd been embarrassed at what Mom said earlier, how bad would it be if his family found out how little time he'd spent with his wife over the last few months?

Genevieve blinked a few times as if her thoughts had followed a similar path.

"You okay?" Scott pitched his words low, for her ears only, although several others had been paying an awful lot of attention to her as well.

"Just soaking up the sweet goodness of a brand-new person." Her voice sounded mostly normal, but he could hear the strain.

"Isn't it about time you two started making a brand-new person or two yourselves?" Mom pointed between Scott and Genevieve. "After all, your fifth anniversary is coming up this summer. If you don't get started soon, your kids aren't going to be close enough to Lacy's for the cousins to play together."

"Mom." Lacy spoke up before Scott or Genevieve could formulate a reply. "Give them a break. Every couple gets to decide when the right time to start a family is. Scott's been busy becoming the youngest principal in the state. Just be proud of him for that for now, and they'll let you know when they're ready for other things."

Good thing his sister was as outspoken as his mom. He couldn't have said it better. And knowing his temper, it was better to let Lacy handle this one. Beth waved her fists in the air and let out a little mewl of a cry.

All attention was off of the grownups as everyone rushed to make sure the "princess" had all she needed.

But Scott couldn't shake off the small yearning inside him that grew every second he or Gen held the baby. Would that longing ever come to fruition? Or had they messed things up to a point they couldn't be fixed ever again?

18

"Well, now. Let's see." Marty tapped a pencil on one list while he ran down a second with his finger.

Monday snuck in quicker than usual, with their fast trip to see the baby Saturday, potluck after worship services Sunday, and dealing with the rest of her car repairs this morning. She hadn't found a good chance to fill Scott in on what had happened the week before. And now, they sat in front of their associate minister and friend, due for their follow-up counseling session.

"We've really been doing better the last few days." Scott reached over and caught her hand in his. She didn't know if it was to still her nervous tapping or for his own comfort. "Are you sure we need to meet this afternoon?"

"I'm glad to hear you're doing better, but I have a feeling some things still need to be talked out." Marty speared them with a quick grin, probably to reassure them. Instead, it intensified her feeling of sitting in the principal's office—and the irony of that was not lost on her.

Scott shifted forward in his seat, rested his elbows on his knees. "You're the expert."

"I'm no expert." Marty laughed. "Samantha would vouch for that. We've been married over thirty years, and I'm still learning more about her each day."

Over thirty years. She and Scott hadn't made it to five yet. They were a few months off from another anniversary. Were they just that bad at marriage, or had Marty and Samantha had rough times too?

"You said there were things we needed to talk out?" Scott leaned back. Was he uncomfortable being on this side of the desk? Or we he as scared as she was that Marty wanted them to hash out something they weren't ready to touch?

"Have you guys talked about how much you're working?" Marty fixed Scott with a stare.

She took a deep breath. So, they were going to talk about things Scott was doing wrong. Maybe this would be good after all.

"What about unrealistic expectations?" Marty focused on her this time.

What? Did she have those? What could he mean?

"How about the things you were wishing he would help with around the house, like dishes and laundry?"

Scott raised an eyebrow.

"Or about your desire to have a baby?"

Genevieve's gaze darted from her husband to Marty and back again. Scott was ready to have a baby? And he talked to Marty about it instead of her? "A baby?"

Scott shrugged, ducked his head. "We tossed the idea around early in our marriage that we would maybe start trying once I worked my way up to principal. We mentioned it again a couple times right after we found out I got the position, but never actually decided anything. Then, when you started acting all crazy the last little bit ... I was stupid. I sort of thought maybe you had quit taking birth control after that last discussion and might be pregnant."

"You thought I was pregnant?" She frowned. "You do realize how all that works, right?" Her face burned. Was she really having this conversation in front of a man old enough to be her father?

"Yes, I know how all that works. I told you I didn't even realize we hadn't kissed … or anything … for that long until you brought it up the other night. It blew my mind. It wasn't like I meant to quit kissing you."

"You just didn't have the time or energy because you were pouring it all into your new job." She leaned back in her chair and crossed her arms over her chest. If Marty wanted to witness one of their fights, he picked a good way to start one.

"Time out!" Marty held up his hands before Scott could reply. "Everyone, take a breath and slow your heart rates. Let's take this one issue at a time instead of trying to tackle them all at once, shall we?"

Genevieve pulled her bottom lip between her teeth and breathed in through her nostrils. Scott stood and leaned against the wall farthest from her, tucking his hands in his pockets. His jaw remained tight, and she could tell he wasn't controlling his anger easily.

"Okay." Marty moved to lean against the edge of his desk and glanced between the two of them. "Scott, why don't you tell Genevieve what you told me the other day about why you feel the need to work so hard? Calmly." He stressed the last word.

Scott's jaw worked again, and then he gave a sharp nod. "I work so hard because I want to make sure I'm bringing in enough so Genevieve can stay home and take care of any children we might have. It was our plan. This was only my second year as principal, and I'm one of the youngest in the state. I want to make sure I get everything right so I don't lose my position and have to take a pay cut. Then, she wouldn't be able to do what she wanted to do."

She didn't comment on the fact that he had still directed it to Marty. She was too much in shock that he had been working for *her*. Sure, she knew about the youngest principal thing, how he wanted to make sure he could live up to expectations. But she hadn't realized she was the real driving force behind any of it.

"Even if you had to go back to being a teacher and coach, we could still afford to have me stay home with babies. We've saved enough over the last few years to make sure it would be possible." She shook her head. "And you've done an excellent job as principal. I can't imagine anyone finding fault in you relaxing a little bit."

Scott's eyes rose to meet hers from where they'd been staring at a random spot on the floor. "You think I've done an excellent job as principal?"

"Of course, I do!" She hit the armrests of her chair. "Everyone does."

"But have you told him?" Marty leaned forward to catch her attention.

She frowned. Surely, she had. Hadn't she?

"That expression pretty much answers that question." Marty hooked a thumb at Scott. "Do you remember me talking about love languages when we did your marriage counseling? One of Scott's top love languages is affirmation. He needs to hear that you appreciate him. He needs to know you think he's doing a good job."

She swallowed. "I'm sorry. I guess I didn't realize I wasn't doing that."

"Okay, Coach Stewart." Marty focused on him this time. "While we're still on love languages. Guess what one of Genevieve's is."

Scott licked his lips and studied Genevieve. "When I bring her gifts?"

Marty made a buzzer sound. "Wrong. She loves to spend time with you. That's all she wants. Don't get me wrong. Every person enjoys getting a present. But it's not going to get you the brownie points like taking her on a date or staying home and snuggling."

Genevieve nodded. Marty's words rang true. All she'd been wanting lately was to spend time with Scott. That's why she'd been wanting to kiss him more the last few days ... they'd been together almost non-stop.

But if Scott still had to work crazy hours as a principal, there wasn't an easy fix for this one. Not like just telling her how much he appreciated her. Time was a rarer commodity than words.

As if Marty could read her mind, he clapped his hands. "Let's brainstorm some ideas on how to find time for you to spend together that won't make Scott feel like he's not living up to the requirements his job demands."

It was like being called on during class when you hadn't been paying attention. No matter how much she tried to find the answer, she couldn't pull it out of thin air. Scott seemed to be having the same problem.

"How has the coffee break idea been going, Genevieve?" Marty broke through the awkward silence.

Scott frowned. What coffee break idea?

Genevieve shrugged. "We were able to spend a few moments together last week. But he's not always the easiest person to catch during the day."

"You were trying to catch me?"

"Marty suggested I camp out by your office until I could sneak a few minutes to have a cup of coffee with you sometimes." Genevieve studied her own worn spot on the carpet.

"Hence the new mug last week. And the run-in in the

hallway the other day." Scott sank into his chair. "Why didn't you say something?"

"You were busy." She tilted her head. "Meetings and phone calls and such. I considered asking Marian to schedule me in a couple of times a week. Something tells me she might enjoy that."

"She's always after me to slow down." Scott leaned forward and caught her attention. "Maybe you should."

Several emotions raced across her pretty features. From disbelief to relief to joy, as if she'd been worried he wouldn't want to take a coffee break with her. He needed to do better at reminding her he wanted to spend time together. But they needed to block out those breaks and make sure they happened.

"I'll catch her next Monday."

"Okay. That's one idea." Marty's voice reminded Scott he wasn't alone with his wife. "What else can we do? Maybe lunch every now and then? Scott, what keeps you so late at work? Is there anything that's not actually necessary? Or maybe something Genevieve could join in?"

"She's obviously welcome at any of the ballgames and school plays and stuff. She actually went with me over the weekend to the basketball tournament. But I doubt she'd want to go to all of them." Scott glanced up at the minister.

"Are you required to make an appearance at all of them, or is that something you've been doing extra just to make sure the students know you support them?" Marty's question caused Gen's head to jerk up. Had she thought he was required to go to all the games?

"There's no written rulebook for being a principal. At least not one that I've found." Scott shifted in his seat. "The school board obviously encourages me to attend various events, but it's probably not a requirement to be at every one. I can't remember Mr. Adams being at all the games when I was coaching."

"So, maybe Genevieve joins you at some and maybe you give up a few so you're home more?" Marty pointed between the two of them.

"That sounds like a fair compromise." Genevieve twisted and untwisted the end of her shirt. "I used to go to more of the games. I can't remember why I stopped. Maybe when he quit coaching."

"Which is funny, because you can actually spend more time with me now that I'm not coaching than you could when I was." Scott made sure his voice held more humor than irritation.

"True." She smirked.

"I assume there aren't ballgames every night of the week, though." Marty beat out a rhythm with his fingers on the edge of his desk.

"No." Scott shook his head. "Every now and then parents will come in right as school lets out and want to have long drawn-out conversations about their kid's grades or conduct. Sometimes I have to deal with school board meetings or fundraiser things. Occasionally they send me off to a training event. Even though school gets out at three, my hours are less concrete."

"Do you let Genevieve know when you have these things?"

Scott blinked. He was an idiot. Of course, she might want to know beforehand. Hadn't he been worried sick the evening her car died, and he couldn't find her? A text would've helped so much.

"From now on, I'll make sure you know if I'm going to be later than normal." Scott took her hand in his. "Would that help?"

She nodded.

"Okay. This all sounds like progress. You both have a better understanding of what the other is thinking, right?" Marty's gaze bounced between the two of them.

Genevieve and Scott nodded.

"Good. I want you to keep working on this, and I want to get together at least one more time. Is there a night next week that would work for you guys?" Marty went back around his desk and opened his calendar.

"As of right now, I can't think of anything I can't miss." Scott's answer brought a smile to his wife's face.

"Just dinner with my parents on Tuesday, like every week." She gave his hand a squeeze.

And there went the hope that had started to grow. Something between a groan and an exasperated huff escaped him before he could rein it in. She sent him a frown.

"Something wrong?" Marty glanced up.

"Tuesday nights are usually the nights when I'm least likely to have something going on. But that's the night she insists we go eat with her parents every week." Scott spread his hands in front of him. "I love my in-laws, but it doesn't make sense. Why does she complain about not spending time with me and then give up the one night I'm most likely to be home?"

<hr>

"We've always had dinner with my parents on that night." Genevieve stamped her foot. "You've never complained about it before. It's going to break their hearts if we don't go."

Marty knocked a paperweight against his desk as if it were a gavel. "Okay. New problem to work through. Calm down and think. Genevieve, what if the two of you do dinner with your parents once a month instead of once a week? Maybe another night, when Scott has something else going on, you could go over there again, just you?"

"But ..." Why was she fighting so hard against this? They'd

done it this way from the second week of their marriage, sure, but it wasn't like they didn't see her parents at other times. Would it really break her mama's heart, or was she simply looking for an excuse because it upset her to know he didn't want to do it that often?

"Take a minute and think, Genevieve. I know your parents, and I know what they'd want you to do in this situation, but you have to know it too." Marty squared her with a look that might as well have come straight from her father. "They raised you to believe when a woman gets married, she's to leave her mother and father and cling to her husband, like the Bible says. If holding on to this tradition pulls you away from Scott, is it worth it?"

"I'm not asking to give it up completely." Scott leaned forward. "I'm just so tired when I come home, it would be nice to stay in and relax."

She understood that. There were days when she had to drag herself out the door to go to her parents' house. She gave a little nod.

"Okay." She swallowed hard. "I'll talk to Mama and explain we need to switch it up."

"Atta, girl." Marty tapped his calendar. "Let's go ahead and pencil you guys in for Monday evening, then. If anything changes, feel free to let me know. In the meantime, I have some homework for you."

Both groaned in unison.

"You sound like a bunch of teenagers." Marty laughed. "Maybe because you're around them all the time?"

Scott chuckled. "Maybe."

"This homework is fun. I promise." Marty shot them a mischievous grin. "I saw an idea I want you two to try. It seems to me you've both become rather wrapped up in your own wants and desires, as well as in trying to make that 'perfect plan' you came up with for life come to be. We need to get you back to getting to know each other again and remembering why you fell in love in the first place."

Wasn't that sort of what Valerie had suggested?

"I want you to go on a first date."

Genevieve blinked. Hadn't that ship already sailed? They dated for over a year before they got married. This would be more like a ... fiftieth date or something.

"Hear me out." Marty twisted a pencil through his fingers. "Pretend like it's a first date. Sometime this week, set it up. Imagine you've only met once—or not at all. You know almost nothing about the other person. Then, Scott, you pick her up and take her somewhere you've never been. Ask the kind of questions you would ask someone you're just getting to know. Wear something to impress. Maybe end with coffee or something. And then, whether you guys are first-date kissers or not is up to you."

Butterflies stirred in Genevieve's tummy. She'd thought she was past the point where she'd have to go through a first date again. How could she pretend she didn't know the man she'd lived with almost five years? Or find something new and interesting to share with him?

"I'm thinking I may ask Samantha to try something similar." Marty winked. "Let me know how it goes."

She and Scott shared similar looks as they stood to leave. *A first date—again?*

19

"Try here." Valerie handed Scott a slip of paper with a restaurant name in a town about forty-five minutes away. "Parker and I stumbled across it coming back from seeing our daughter, and now we can't wait to go back."

"Thanks, Val." Scott tucked the info into his pocket. "What are you guys doing back already? I expected you'd stay longer. And even if you didn't, I didn't figure you'd be at school any this week, considering we're on break."

"Ansley had to work the rest of the week. And you know Parker. He doesn't mind going away for a night or two, but then he's ready to be back in his own bed."

Scott nodded. He'd like to have Genevieve back in his own bed and couldn't believe she was still sleeping on that lumpy mattress. No way was that egg thingy helping that much.

"And I'm here working on a fundraiser idea for the art department. All my supplies are here."

"I hate that you have to raise your own money." He leaned against his door frame. "If I could convince the school board to change the way they do funding, I would in a heartbeat."

"And this from a coach." She threw a wink his way. "No

worries. I've done this so long, I'll be able to keep us going a few more years, at least. You two have fun on your date."

Their date.

Scott moved back to his desk and picked up his phone. If Valerie hadn't happened to walk by a few minutes before, he'd still be trying to figure out where to take Genevieve. He'd never been good at planning things like that. It had almost been a relief to be married and not have to worry about it anymore.

Though now he wondered if he had stopped too completely.

Regardless, he needed to let her know how to dress Thursday evening. Two days away. And he was probably going to stew about it until it was over. He still didn't fully understand how they were supposed to pull off such a feat. How did a man have a first date with someone he was married to?

> Hi. This is Scott. I got us reservations for Thursday evening. Wear something nice.

Did that sound stupid? She knew who he was, but they were supposed to be pretending like they didn't know each other. He wasn't in the drama department for a reason.

> I'm looking forward to it. What time will you pick me up?

> 5:30 okay?

> I'll be ready.

Okay. That was done. Now, to focus on work enough to get through the next two days.

Except his mind kept wandering back to the date. Maybe it wasn't so hard to get into the spirit. Memories of their actual first date came to mind for the first time in years. He'd been so nervous, despite having talked to her multiple times a day for weeks, before he worked up the nerve to ask her out.

And he'd taken flowers. There was an idea. When was the last time he'd done that? Surely not all the way back to their first date?

Despite Marty saying gifts weren't her love language, Scott knew for a fact she liked flowers. Scribbling on a sticky pad, he made a note. "Buy flowers Thursday afternoon."

Then he added, "Bring nice clothes to work to change before heading to pick up date."

A grin took over his face, but he didn't care. This was sort of fun.

ANOTHER GLANCE in the mirror showed everything still in place. Genevieve smoothed down one of her long wavy brown tresses and repositioned her pearls. Was she too dressy? He'd said to wear something nice. Maybe the necklace was too much for a Thursday night date. She reached up to remove it, then changed her mind.

Marty's idea of pretending like this was their first date had sounded ridiculous at the time, but now that it was here, it was more real. She wiped her sweaty palms on the towel in the hall bathroom and left before she was tempted to peek once more at her reflection. She couldn't improve on anything else no matter how much longer she stood there. Might as well go wait in the living room.

The clock showed minimal movement of the long hand from when she'd looked only two minutes before. He'd said five-thirty, and it was only five-twenty-five. Not everyone arrived at least ten minutes early like her father. She perched on the edge of the sofa, where she had a clear view of the driveway through the window. Her knees bounced with unsuppressed energy. Would this work?

One minute 'til, a red pickup truck pulled in. She rose on

shaky legs and then sat back down. If she met him at the door, he'd know she'd been watching for him. Better to stand after he rang the bell and make him wait a moment.

Who was she kidding? She jumped up and grabbed the doorknob right as the chime sounded through the house. A quick twist, and there he was.

Or rather, he must be somewhere behind the bright bouquet filling her view. Slowly, the floral arrangement lowered and his eyes twinkled above it. Deep brown eyes, almost chocolate. They appeared sweeter because of the lightweight green sweater he wore over a pair of khakis.

"Hi." His voice came out husky.

She unfroze herself and accepted the flowers. "Hi. Let me just put these in some water. They're lovely."

"I hoped you would like them." He took a step inside and stopped as if he didn't live here. Like he was supposed to be pretending. "I wanted to get your favorite, but I wasn't sure what that was, so I asked the lady to include a bunch of different ones. Hopefully, at least one is the kind you like."

She smiled and breathed in the scent of the buds before placing the vase on the table. "That's so sweet. I love daisies. These right here."

"I'll remember for next time." Had he really not known she loved daisies, or was he still acting? She honestly couldn't remember if they'd had that conversation before. "Ready?"

"Sure." She grabbed her purse and stopped as she caught the look of approval in his eyes. She smoothed down the skirt of her floral dress and walked the few steps to him. "Is this okay? I wasn't sure where we were headed."

"You're perfect." He tucked a strand of her hair behind her ear and then offered his elbow. "A friend recommended a little Italian restaurant a few towns over. Normally, I wouldn't drive so far, but this one was featured on one of those shows on TV where they go to the neatest places. I thought it might be worth the extra time."

"Sounds fun."

He opened the truck door for her and then waited. Right. They were pretending they'd never done this before. Okay. She lifted a leg up to the running board and almost tripped over her skirt.

"Oh. Let me help." He caught her about the waist and lifted her easily up to the leather seat. It must have been the thrill of moving from one spot to another so quickly that took her breath away for a moment. Not the strength in his arms or the gentleness of his touch. Or the way his hands lingered for an extra second, their warmth permeating the thin fabric of her dress.

"Thanks."

"My pleasure."

The drive was lovely as he headed them into the foothills. She searched her brain for something to discuss. What did they talk about in situations like this? It hadn't been that long, had it?

"So, you've never been to this place?" Maybe conversation about the restaurant would spur on some more conversation.

"No. A coworker mentioned it when I let it slip I was looking for something different to take a special girl." He glanced at her out of the corner of his eye.

"Oh. Where do you work again?" She fought back the giggle trying to escape.

"I'm the principal at the upper school in town."

"Wow." She smirked. "I thought principals were old. Or do you just look young for your age?"

He gave her a disbelieving look before returning his eyes to the road. "Ouch. I happen to be the youngest principal in the state, thank you very much."

"I bet your parents are proud."

"My mama brags about me every chance she gets." He gave a nod. "I don't see my dad a lot."

"I'm sorry. I didn't realize they weren't together." She twisted her purse strap in her hands.

"Oh, they're still married. My dad is something of a workaholic. Even when I'm there for the weekends, he's not around much. Always something else to do at the office." His words had slowed down, and she wondered if he realized the similarities. "I guess that's why I've become a bit of a workaholic. It's something I'm working on."

She blinked back some tears. He was trying. She'd told her mom at dinner on Tuesday they were going to switch up the plan. The look of approval he shot her across the table had been worth it. And her parents had almost acted surprised their routine hadn't changed sooner. The rest of the week had gone as well, though his hours were shorter due to spring break. Next week would be the real test.

"Thanks for letting me know." She pulled her mind back to their current conversation. "Where does your family live?"

"My parents and sister are both just outside of Little Rock. Far enough away I don't feel stifled, but close enough I can still go back and see them when I want." He glanced her way. "My baby brother lives in Shreveport. The family sort of considers him a lost cause, moving out of the state the way he did."

"So, you're the oldest?"

"The middle." He pointed to some deer off the side of the road. "My sister is the oldest. What about you? Your family nearby?"

"My parents live in town. I see them quite a bit since we worship at the same congregation and get together for dinner several times a month. But I'm an only child."

"Here we are." He pulled into the parking lot of a place she never would've stopped at on her own. But judging from the number of cars there, the food must be good. He came around, opened her door, and helped her down. The thrills going through her belly at his touch were almost strong enough to distract her from the aroma of garlic permeating the air around them.

She breathed in deeply. "Smells great."

"Let's go find out."

Seated at a tiny table covered with red-checked cloth and enhanced by a short flickering candle, they glanced at their plastic menus and giggled at the cheesy Italian music playing through the speakers. Every dish carried by their table made her change her mind about what to order. It all smelled amazing.

Finally, they each agreed to order something that sounded good to both of them and share bites. A breadbasket was set in the middle of the table, the crusty exteriors dripping with garlic butter. She didn't bother to keep back a groan of pleasure as she bit into a chunk.

"That good, huh?" He reached for his own piece.

"We should definitely come here again." She glanced up, eyes wide. "Sorry. That was very assuming of me."

"I rather like the way you assumed." He gave her that crooked grin of his and made her heart flip over.

"So, you're a principal." She ran a finger over her glass to knock off some condensation. "Is that what you always wanted to be?"

"Pretty much. I was a coach for a while, and I really enjoyed it. Teaching algebra was fun too. But I guess I thought I could have a greater impact if I took the higher position." He twisted his silverware bundle around. "I want to be an influence in the students' lives, make sure their voices are heard, and try to make sure they're getting everything they need in education. It's challenging in ways that teaching and coaching weren't. But rewarding in other ways."

"That sounds commendable." Had they ever had this talk

before? She'd always known he wanted to be a principal, but she couldn't remember hearing the reasons before tonight.

"What about you?" He reached over and took her fingers. "You're a nurse, right?"

She nodded. "A school nurse."

"So, something we have in common." He grinned again.

"Yes. Although I probably don't have quite the impact you do. I'm much more behind the scenes. I send kids back to class when they fake a temperature, check for head lice, collect excuse forms from doctors' offices, keep immunization records up-to-date. Every now and then, I hand out a bandage." She shrugged. "It's a job someone else could probably do, but I'll keep it as long as they let me."

"You don't think you're needed?" A little furrow showed up between his eyebrows.

"I don't know. I guess maybe I take some of the pressure off the secretary and homeroom teachers, but I know a lot of schools have quit having nurses on campus." She twisted her face into a grimace. "Probably only a matter of time, with so many budget cuts going on."

"There's a sad thought. I can't imagine not having a nurse around in case I need a bandage." He winked. "Maybe your school will start a revolution and schools all over will follow their example of keeping one on staff."

Their food arrived, distracting her from any sarcastic remark she might have come up with. Who could be snarky when bombarded by the tomato and garlic steam assailing her senses? She took a deep whiff in appreciation.

"Want to say a prayer?" He grabbed her hands even before she nodded. "God, thank you so much for this evening together, a time to get to know each other better and enjoy good food. Bless us as we explore possibilities with this relationship. Amen."

"Amen."

Several moments passed while they both *oohed* and *aahed* over their choices. Her tortellini melted in her mouth, spreading its cheesy goodness to each corner. When he offered a bite of his lasagna, she agreed it was just as good. She nodded when he asked if she'd like some dessert too. They agreed to split a tiramisu, hopeful it would live up to the standard of the main courses. It did.

She licked her fork from the last bite and sipped the strong coffee. "Who would have expected a place like this in backwoods northeast Arkansas?"

"I'll have to thank my friend for her recommendation." He stood and offered his hand. "Ready to go?"

The ride back was quiet. It wasn't as hard to pretend this was a first date as she had thought. Sure, they knew each other. But they had learned more tonight. Before she was ready, he was in the driveway and opening her door.

His hands lingered at her hips after he helped her down out of the truck. "There's starlight in your eyes."

She blinked, afraid if she spoke, it might break the spell.

"Let me walk you to the door." His voice was low, husky. Full of promise.

She hadn't had a chance to tell him what happened the week before. Obviously, now was not the time. She couldn't ruin the evening. But she also couldn't let him kiss her until she knew how he'd react to what happened with Coach Drake. She mentally kicked herself for waiting so long.

He tugged her hand after she stepped onto the porch. She turned and faced him, her pulse pounding in her ears. He ran a finger over one of her cheeks, leaned in closer.

She flattened her hands against his chest and applied just enough pressure to make him pause. "I'm not so sure I'm a kiss-on-the-first-date kind of girl." She added a smile to lighten the mood.

"Really?" He lowered his voice to a whisper and put the words right in her ear. "I'm pretty sure I remember otherwise."

She closed her eyes as the memory of standing on her daddy's front porch with him all those years ago slammed into her. That date had been every bit as sweet. And his lips had been perfect against hers, gentle and full of ... not love yet, but something close to it. Oh, how she missed that!

She swallowed the yearning inside of her and took a step back. She pulled every ounce of willpower from her core—this had to be one of the hardest things she'd ever done. "Be that as it may, maybe we should wait just a bit longer."

He deflated a smidge. Then, a gleam came in his eye. Was he going to kiss her anyway? His fingers gently gripped her chin and turned her head to the side. He pressed his lips to her cheek, lingering a moment as if he wanted to trail along to something better. Then, he leaned back and gave her hand a squeeze.

"I really enjoyed tonight, Genevieve. I hope you let me date you again."

Could he hear her heart beating like crazy? "I would love that."

"Good night." He turned and walked back toward the driveway.

She waved and then let herself into the house. She sank down onto the guest bed and flopped backward. Maybe tomorrow she'd work up the courage to tell him why she couldn't kiss him yet. But tonight, she'd savor the memory of every moment of their perfect date. No need to ruin this night with something so sour.

HAD HE DONE SOMETHING WRONG? He'd felt certain she wanted to kiss as much as he did when they got back tonight. Had even entertained hopes of her returning to their shared bed.

Instead, she'd joked about not kissing on the first date.

"I'm reading too much into it."

He shook his head and tried to concentrate on the computer screen in front of him. It was the Friday of spring break and he didn't plan to work long. But a few emails had to be answered and voice mails returned.

Monday, he'd have to face the problem with Coach Drake.

Although Kimmy wasn't ready to give more information on who had made her uncomfortable, Drake's performance at the ballgames last week also had Scott on high alert. He needed to dig a little more and figure out what was going on.

But until then, he planned to wrap up his bit of work today and get home to spend some more time with his wife. Maybe, when they met with Marty on Monday, he'd give them a "clean bill of health" for their marriage.

And then maybe Scott could get that kiss he was craving like crazy.

20

Genevieve really meant to tell Scott about Coach Drake over the weekend, but every time an opportunity arose, they were getting along so well she didn't want to ruin the moment. Now, it was the Monday after spring break and work was busy with playing catchup after being gone for a week. No way she'd be able to sneak a coffee break with her husband. But maybe she could touch base with Marian about scheduling things like that for the future.

Her flats were quiet as she made her way down the hallway. Halfway through second period, the students were dutifully tucked into their various classrooms, and all was peaceful for another thirty minutes. Marian was hanging up the phone as Genevieve entered the office.

"Good morning, dear!" The older lady beamed a pleasant smile. "If you're looking for your husband, he's stepped out, I'm afraid. Had to run a couple of errands."

"Oh. Thanks." Genevieve leaned against the counter. "I hadn't really expected to find him. But I wanted to see if you could help me out with that."

"Oh?"

"Can you check his schedule for the rest of the year, find the few open spots he has in the mornings, and pencil me in for ten minutes a couple times a week? We'd like to steal a few minutes to be together during the day when we can. Nothing much. Just a coffee break."

"I love it." Marian clicked a few times with her mouse and nodded. "Yes. Would you like me to share his calendar with you? That way you could see when I've penciled you in and can add it to your own calendar."

"You can do that?" Genevieve peeked around the monitor.

"I can and will." Marian clicked a few more times. "I'll send it once I've got them all done. More couples need to think like the two of you. There aren't enough spouses who take a moment to just be together each day."

Genevieve ducked her head. "Well, we're working on it, anyway. Thanks again, Ms. Marian."

"Let me know if you need anything else, dear." Marian waved a hand at her and went back to clicking.

That had been much easier than Genevieve could've hoped. She had to force herself to not skip as she made her way back to her office. A tiny giggle bubbled up her throat and escaped. Here's hoping he was serious when he agreed to that idea last week. Otherwise, he'd be in for a shock.

Her heart stopped at the sight of the large man leaning against her doorframe, watching her walk his way. Not the guy she'd been wanting to see, that was certain. Coach Drake straightened as she got nearer.

"I thought you'd run away." One corner of his mouth lifted.

"Working on a project with Marian." She waved a hand toward her office. "Did you need something? I haven't seen any faxes come through for your players."

"I got a cut and was hoping for a bandage." He held up a finger wrapped in a paper towel.

She gave a nod and moved to open her door, but he didn't budge. "Excuse me."

He raised one eyebrow. Took one tiny step to the left. Waited as if to see what she'd do now.

Her heartbeat pounded in her throat. But not in the way Scott had set her pulse racing the other night. This time, it was more anger and … fear. She squeezed past him and pushed through her door.

"If you'll wait right there, I'll grab you one." She rushed into her backroom and flipped on the light. After a quick search through the supply cabinet, she located the requested item. She spun around to take it back out to him and crashed into his chest.

"Whoa, there." His hands grabbed either one of her arms as she wildly shoved away.

"I told you to wait out there."

"I figured the closer I was to you, the more quickly you could cover this up." He wiggled his injured finger.

"I can't do anything with you this close. Back up." She took a giant step the other way as soon as his hands released her. "How did you get a cut?"

"I was packing up the equipment and caught my finger on a screw that had poked loose in one of the crates." He shifted impatiently as she unwrapped the paper towels. "It's not terrible, but I figured Pete wouldn't want me to drip blood everywhere."

She quickly ran an alcohol wipe over the abrasion to clean it, dabbed some antibiotic ointment on the bandage, and handed it to him to wrap up.

"You're not going to do it for me?" His lower lip stuck out. "I can never get them on right. Either too loose or too tight or crooked. Please?"

She huffed. "Here." Pulling the bandage a bit tighter than she normally would, she figured it would serve him right if it cut the blood flow off from the end of his finger for a while. Maybe not the Christian way to act, but definitely the way she felt.

"What? No kiss to make it better?"

"No." She hissed through her teeth. "Maybe you should go home and let your wife do that."

"*Aw*, come on. Don't be mad." He took a step toward her again. "You don't need to be jealous of her."

She pointed at her own chest. "I be jealous of her? I'm not. Remember, I'm married."

"So, you know how this works." His smile was rather wicked as he took another step her way.

She had nowhere else to go. The wall was only a couple of inches behind her now. "No. Whatever you think is working, I don't want it. I already have the man I want. And I definitely don't want someone who belongs to someone else."

"Belongs?" He snorted. "Marriage is just for tax write-offs. No reason we can't be together when we're not with our spouses. Especially since they don't make us happy."

"Scott *does* make me happy." She pushed against his chest as he inched nearer still. "You don't. Please stop."

"You don't mean that."

"I do mean that." She pounded a fist against him to try and emphasize her point. "I never wanted your attention. And I definitely didn't ask for that kiss the other day."

"But you're not getting any attention from that husband of yours." His voice lowered to almost a growl. "Why not let me show you what you're missing?"

"No." She couldn't scream. The whole school would hear, and the students didn't need to see this. "Scott and I may have had some problems lately, but we're working on it. And you need to do the same with your wife. She adores you. Go back to her if you need to show someone attention."

"Gen?" Scott's voice sounded at her door with a sharp knock. "You in here?"

She froze.

The door clicked open in her outer office.

"Gen?"

Her heart rate reached speeds she hadn't realized possible.

She shoved against the solid wall of jerk who still leaned up against her, but he just smirked.

"So, no more kisses?" Drake's voice was just loud enough to be heard, and his expression said he was aware of exactly what he was doing.

No.

She contorted her arms to slip under Drake's, but in doing so, she knocked against the vase holding Scott's date-night flowers that sat on top of the cabinet. Almost in slow motion, it fell and shattered against the tile floor, water, glass, and petals going every which way.

Scott's face appeared in the doorway as she finally ducked out of Drake's grip. "What?"

"Scott!" She reached out and touched his arm, but he jerked away. "Scott, listen."

He slammed a paper cup on her desk, creamy liquid splashing out the small hole on top from the force of it. "I thought you might like a chai latte. But I can see you're already occupied."

"Scott, no. I just told him to leave." How she managed to get any words out around the lump in her throat, she had no idea. "Please believe me."

Scott's gaze moved past hers and zeroed in on what was behind her. A glance over her shoulder showed Coach Drake leaning against the doorframe with a self-satisfied smirk, his arms crossed over his chest. She wanted nothing more than to kick him in the ... well, where he'd remember it for a while.

When she turned back around to explain things to Scott, he

was gone. She grabbed a towel and pushed past Harmon Drake to throw it at the water on the floor. She'd clean it up better later. Right now, she was more worried about the relationship with her husband, which was more shattered than the vase. She set some paper towels over the splatters on her desk and then rushed out of the room. A second later, she spun back around and went back to evict the trouble-maker.

He remained in his cocky position, watching her, not moving. The bell would ring in a few minutes so whatever she was going to do, she had to do quickly. She marched up to him, reared her hand back, and swung as hard as she could.

"Don't touch me again." She barely refrained from rubbing her fingers where the sting of the slap throbbed. "Get out."

"Your loss, baby." He worked his jaw for a second, then straightened and sauntered out as if nothing had happened.

She wanted to jump up and down and throw a screaming fit, but there was no time.

The bell sounded as she stepped foot in the hallway. Not ideal timing. Not ideal anything. She pulled her door closed and wove her way down to the office. Marian cast her a concerned glance and shook her head.

"He came in all upset and went in—I guess his meeting went badly or something. But then immediately, a student was sent in who needed to see him, so he's facing that right now, and I don't know when he'll be done."

Genevieve stomped in frustration. Of all the times he wasn't available, this had to be the worst. How could she explain things if she couldn't get a moment to talk with him?

"Does he have anything scheduled for lunch?" She held onto the edge of the counter as Marian looked it up.

"Not on here."

"What time does he have open for that? Maybe I can bring him back something."

"Twelve-fifteen until one." Marian met her eyes. "Assuming

nothing comes up between now and then. Some days I don't think he eats lunch."

"Do everything you can to make sure he does today, please." Genevieve glanced at the clock. "I've got to talk to him."

———

AFTER FORTY-FIVE MINUTES of having Tyler Dikes in his office, Scott still wasn't sure he had punished him enough for cussing out his teacher. Scott sat back and rubbed his eyes with his palms.

This was all his fault.

Every warning sign had pointed at what was coming, but he'd ignored them all. Still, seeing his wife in the arms of Harmon Drake was the last thing he'd expected when he walked into her office. And he couldn't get the image out of his head.

"Your conference call starts in five minutes." Marian poked her head through the crack in his door. "Need anything before?"

"No. Thank you, Marian."

"Got a headache?" Her normally smiling face was frowning.

"You can call it that. I'll be okay."

Or at least, he'd give the appearance of being okay. What other choice did he have? His personal life might be falling all to tiny pieces around him, but his professional world went on.

Had this happened because he hadn't given Genevieve enough attention?

Was that why she wouldn't kiss him the other night? Because she'd rather have the kisses of ... that ... that cocky, self-righteous slimeball?

He couldn't let himself think about that. Especially knowing what a sleaze the guy was toward students and other teachers. If only he had more proof, he'd take it to the school board and get him out of their life.

But was it too late?

And even if he did get Drake fired, would it fix anything between him and Genevieve? Or had this been the final straw to break their marriage?

He swallowed a knot of emotion, took several deep breaths, and dialed in to the conference call. An hour of listening to other principals hash out the pros and cons of duel-credit courses verses AP held less appeal than normal. It probably wouldn't be stimulating enough to get his mind off what had happened earlier. And he desperately needed to stop thinking about that.

21

"Hey. I've been looking for you. Want to go—" Valerie froze when Genevieve got closer. "He found out?"

"Worse." Genevieve unlocked her office door and groaned at the mess remaining for her to clean up.

Her friend peeked over her shoulder. "Whoa. What happened here?"

"Coach Drake." Genevieve rubbed at a spot throbbing in her forehead. "He was aptly named. Harm. He definitely leaves it in his wake."

"He hurt you?"

Genevieve shook her head. "He came in with the excuse of needing a bandage for a cut. Then, he cornered me, evidently wanting to pick up where he left off before spring break. I was telling him to back off and leave me alone when Scott came in. Unfortunately, all he saw was Drake with his hands around me in the back room. By the time I got to Scott's office, he was already dealing with something else."

"Oh, Gen." Valerie flopped down in one of the plastic chairs against the wall.

"I'm hoping I can catch him for lunch. Maybe if I bring him

food, he'll agree to listen." She touched the still-warm cup of tea. "He was bringing me this. We had such a good week last week. I didn't want to ruin it by telling him what Coach Drake had done. I should have listened to you."

"What's his favorite food?" Valerie leaned forward and clapped her hands to get Genevieve's attention. "Go get it. I'll clean up the mess."

"I've got almost two hours until his break." Genevieve snapped. "We went to this amazing place the other night, but it was about a forty-five-minute drive. I wonder when they open."

Valerie held her phone out. "I happen to be the friend who recommended said place. Give them a call and see if you can have the order ready when you get there."

Ten minutes later, Genevieve grabbed her purse. "Okay. I'm leaving, so I'll have time to get lost and still find my way back. You sure you're okay cleaning up this mess?"

"Go. I've got this." Valerie dropped a piece of glass in the trash can. "I think I might know where I can find another vase too."

"You're the best." Genevieve hurried out the door. A peek in the office window showed his door still closed. If this food didn't catch his attention, she wasn't sure what would. Time to find their date spot.

<hr>

SHE WRAPPED an old blanket around the Styrofoam containers all the way back with the hope the food would still be toasty when she returned to school. The smell of garlic had her stomach growling with hunger on top of the butterflies that had taken up permanent residence. She wiped her sweaty palms on her pants legs and grabbed the sack of food. Time to face the dragon.

Marian nodded as Genevieve walked in. Scott's door stood

open just a crack. She swallowed and rapped on the frame before pushing it open a little more.

He didn't hide his posture fast enough. She caught the slumped shoulders and bent head before he put his perfect principal costume back on. When he caught her eye, a bit of the performance slipped once more.

"What now?" He turned his chair to face his computer instead of her.

"I come bearing sustenance." The word hardly described the amazingness of the dishes in her hands, but it was what she could come up with on short notice. She pulled the door closed behind her.

"Is that supposed to make everything better?"

"No." She set one container on his desk and opened it to show what was inside. "But I was hoping it would at least earn me the permission to tell my side of the story."

"Is that—" He leaned forward and lifted the lid higher, then examined the box. "Did you drive all the way out to that restaurant and back?"

"I know I was supposed to be at work, but honestly, our marriage is more important than my job." She lowered herself slowly onto the edge of a chair across from him.

He shook his head and ran a hand through his hair. "I don't know what to believe anymore. One minute you're asking for a divorce, the next you say you're more worried about staying married than staying employed. One minute, you're the woman I remember, holding my hand and giving me hope. The next I catch you doing the same with—" He waved his hand in the air toward the door.

She got the idea.

"I told you. It wasn't what you thought. I wasn't holding his hand or giving him any hope. Exactly the opposite." She leaned forward. "I was trying to get him to leave me alone."

"If he was making untoward advances, why didn't you

scream or yell or something?" Scott pushed out of his chair and paced to the window.

"Think about it. There are at least three classrooms within hearing distance of my office. If I screamed, how many students would've come running in to find who knows what?" She pounded the arm rest. "I didn't want students involved if it could be settled with adults only."

He turned to face her, took a step back.

"I promise, Scott." She stood. "I don't want anyone but you."

They both closed the distance, and she was never so glad to feel his arms wrap around her as at that moment. She breathed in his familiar citrusy scent, listened to his heart pound beneath her ear. He leaned back and cupped her cheek in his hand.

"I don't want to lose you." The tears in his voice choked her up.

"I don't want you to."

His lips lowered to hers, hovering a breath away. She choked back a sob. She still needed to tell him the rest. She pushed back just enough to make his eyes fly open.

"I have to tell you something else first." Her words were barely above a whisper.

HE LET GO AS if she were on fire.

"He didn't kiss me today." She hung her head.

"Today?" Scott's hands grabbed his head. "But he did kiss you?"

She nodded, tears slipped from her eyes. "That Wednesday my car died. He was the one who gave me a ride home. And he kissed me when I went to get out of his Jeep. But nothing else happened."

"Yet it took you this long to tell me?" It took every bit of effort he had to keep from yelling. How long had it been since her car died? At least ten days now.

"I didn't mean to. I never could find the right time."

He stood there, hands still gripping his hair, as if it could stop his brain from the imminent explosion. She couldn't find the time. They'd taken how many road trips together? Had eaten how many meals at the same table? How many times had he asked if something was wrong?

And she'd denied it every time. Had blown it off. Had said she wasn't a first-date kisser. Rage covered him like a bucket of water. But this wasn't the time or place to give in to it. More work faced him before he could leave and maneuver through any of this.

He straightened and put his principal face on again. "I can't deal with this right now."

She folded in on herself, as if he'd punched her. "So, when?"

"I don't know. I have to get through the rest of this day with this all hanging over me now, though. Thanks for making a Monday worse than normal."

"Are you still going to meet Marty with me?" She clutched her throat.

"I'm not sure, Genevieve. We'll see how the day goes." He picked up his lunch and handed it to her, untouched. "Why don't you put these in the fridge or something? I'm not hungry."

She took the container and clutched it to her chest. Hovered another moment and then walked back out of his office. Glancing around the space, he was almost surprised there was no evidence of the storm that had just rushed through. His insides still swirled in tumultuous waves.

That jerk had kissed his wife. The woman Scott hadn't been allowed to kiss the last few weeks. And she hadn't said a single word.

And Scott couldn't even fire him over it. Because who would

believe him to be unbiased when it was his spouse involved? His hands were tied.

***

GENEVIEVE SET the to-go containers in the fridge in the lounge, Scott's name in big bold letters. Maybe that would protect it from anyone foraging.

So much for keeping the food warm for him. Garlic and tomato sauce didn't have the healing power she'd hoped for. Somehow, she had to get through the rest of the day too.

Back in her office, a sticky note was on her screen. "Praying for you." Valerie's prayers better be fervent and strong. Nothing weak would fix this mess she had made.

Oh, God. What have I done? Help us, please. Don't let me lose him over this. I love him so much, and I'm sorry I ever forgot it.

The clock showed five seconds later than the last time she'd checked. She placed her hands on her knees, but it didn't keep them from bouncing. Marty acted as if nothing was wrong, but she hadn't yet told him about the fight she and Scott had earlier that day. If Scott didn't show up in five more minutes, she'd have to.

The door swung open.

"Sorry I'm late." He didn't glance at her. "I got wrapped up in a meeting right at the end with the parents of a new student. Couldn't get away any faster."

"You're only a few minutes late." Marty set aside what he had been working on and pulled out the familiar notes from their previous sessions. "I can tell something has happened, but I'm not sure I want to know yet, so let's go over what I had assigned you for homework. How was the date?"

Genevieve willed Scott to look her way, but he continued to study his cuticles. She'd have to be the one to answer. "It was perfect."

"Well, I love to hear that." Marty said at the same time that Scott snorted. "Scott? You didn't enjoy it?"

"I enjoyed the date." Scott raised his head and met the associate minister's eyes. "I didn't realize she was such a good actress."

Had she deserved that? It hurt, regardless. She pinched her lips together to keep from making a remark as cutting.

"I don't understand." Marty looked between the two of them. "Are you talking about her pretending it was a first date?"

"I'm talking about her pretending she was in love with me." Scott stood and shook his head. "I'm sorry. I shouldn't have come."

"Sit." Marty's voice brooked no argument.

The war going on inside Scott was obvious on his face. The principal in him, who didn't want to take orders from another, fought against the fact he was younger than Marty and should respect the older man. In addition, a battle waged about whether staying and fighting for Genevieve was worth it.

She couldn't tell. But she let loose a breath of relief when he sat again.

"Okay. Obviously, we can't do this without facing the elephant in the room." Marty rose and moved to lean on the front of his desk. "Spill it."

"She kissed another man!" Scott's shout reverberated in her ears, shattering pieces of her all the way down to her toes. The hurt and anger and jealousy and betrayal in his voice were sharper than any knife in her kitchen.

Marty turned his attention to her but didn't say anything.

"I-I didn't kiss him." It was hard to talk with so much emotion bottled up in her throat. "He kissed me."

"Someone just kissed you out of the blue?" Marty's frown showed he needed more details.

She shook her head. "He gave me a ride home when my car died. It sounded innocent enough when he offered, but he kissed me when he was helping me out of his Jeep. Nothing else happened."

"Until today." Scott's sharp voice made her sound like she hadn't explained all this before.

"I told you earlier. It wasn't what it appeared." Genevieve ducked her head and studied her hands. "He came in for a bandage. I asked him to stay near the door, but he followed me into my back room where I keep supplies. When I turned around, he was right there. He started trying to kiss me, and I pushed him back and asked him to leave me alone, to go get kisses from his wife. When Scott came in, all he saw was me surrounded by Coach Drake's arms."

"Why don't you believe her, Scott?" Marty's voice was calm, although she could see more worry in his expression than at any other time they'd been counseling.

"I wanted to believe her. Then, she told me about the kiss." He slashed his hand through the air. "If it was so innocent, why didn't she tell me sooner? Why keep it a secret for almost two weeks?"

"Because I knew you were going to react like this." She pounded the arm of her chair. "You're mad and not thinking reasonably. If I'd told you right after it happened, it would've been hard for either of us to come to Bible class that night. And then, every time I was going to, we were having such a good day together that I didn't want to ruin it. Plus, what would you have done to Coach Drake? I didn't want you to risk your job by hunting him down in retaliation."

"Wait." Scott looked at her for the first time since he had come in. "Bible class … it was that Wednesday night that Valerie pulled you out in the parking lot to talk, wasn't it? You told her and not me?"

"She didn't give me a chance not to. And in her defense, she warned me I should tell you that night."

The room fell silent for several ticks of the clock.

"This is not something you two can't come back from." Marty tapped the edge of his desk. "Genevieve, you're going to have to work on regaining Scott's trust. Even if you didn't want the kiss, it happened. You kept it from him. That's a big deal. Trust isn't something easy to earn back once you've broken it."

Moisture pooled in her eyes. How did she get here? She hadn't wanted to. It definitely wasn't in her plans when she gave Scott the ultimatum three weeks before. Could she find a way to earn his trust again? He'd been trying so hard lately to make their marriage better, and she might as well have thrown it in his face.

"Scott, you're going to have to do some soul-searching and think about forgiveness." Marty focused on her husband. "You told me several times that you meant it when you promised 'for better or for worse.' Well, this falls in the 'worse' category. You said those vows were sacred to you. Now's your chance to prove it. I'm not saying it's going to be easy. But I am saying it's doable."

Tick, tock.

Tick, tock.

How could Marty stand the sound of the seconds going by like that all day?

"Before this, your biggest problem was that you'd started to take each other for granted. You got comfortable in knowing the other would always be there and no longer tried to meet each other's needs. Now, you've added another layer of trouble to work through. But I have faith in you both. Don't avoid each other. Try not to yell. And if you need someone else to talk to, I'm here. Give me a call."

He made it sound so simple. It wouldn't be. The tension between them was tight enough to walk across. But neither of them were skilled in walking a tight rope. Were they willing to learn?

23

"You changed my schedule?" Scott stared at his wife through her open door.

"*Hmm*?" She glanced up from whatever she'd been studying with a perplexed frown on the computer screen.

"Did you add coffee breaks to my schedule?" He leaned over her lower door and unlocked it.

"You acted like you thought it would be a good idea last week. I did it before ..." She sighed.

His jaw worked back and forth, heat rising in his chest. "So, now Marian thinks I need to get up and come spend a few minutes with you three times a week. If I don't leave my office, she's going to know something's going on between us."

"Something *is* going on between us." She leaned back in her chair and crossed her arms. "Maybe if we hadn't been working so hard to cover it up, we wouldn't be in such a big mess now."

"Sure." He snorted. "Blame the mess *you* made on trying to maintain a good appearance."

"Well, we hadn't been doing that great of a job anyway."

"What's that supposed to mean?" He shut the upper part of her door to give them more privacy.

"That day Coach Drake ..." Her eyes darted to his and then down to the floor again. "Anyway, he said something about how people were talking about the fact we were having problems. But he wouldn't say who he'd heard it from."

"And you believe him?" Scott's voice held an edge.

"Honestly, I don't know what to believe anymore." She pushed up and paced to the far wall. "When he started coming around more, I thought it was a coincidence. That he just happened to show up at the exact moment I needed something. The first day it was right after my chair broke. He helped clean up the coffee I spilled and promised to have Pete fix the chair."

Scott barked a laugh.

"What?" She stopped her pacing.

"You thought he got Pete to fix your chair?"

"Well, I mean, he said he would." She pointed to the new seat. "And when I came in the next day, there it was."

"All he did was pass on to Pete that it was broken. After Pete told me, I went out and got you that one." He ran his fingers through his hair. "I can't believe all this time you thought it was him."

"Why didn't you say something when you came in that day?" Her voice sounded lost as if he'd told her the sky was green.

"I didn't see the need to. I promised you almost five years ago I'd take care of you, and I mean to keep that promise." He turned to go.

"Wait." Two quick strides had her next to him.

He glanced down at her hand on his arm but didn't say anything.

"Thank you." She ducked her head. "I'm sorry I let my loneliness distract me from seeing who was really rescuing me lately. Him mopping up a spill and killing a spider and giving me a ride were nothing. You took care of me so much better—

with the new chair, taking the punch, nursing me when I was sick, and, believe it or not, coming to my rescue yesterday. I'm not sure I could have convinced him to leave without someone else coming in to distract him."

He covered her hand with his for a second, closed his eyes, and swallowed. "I'd do it all again in a heartbeat. What do we need to do to help you stay safe from him now?"

"I have my phone set up to call you with one command if he comes in again. And I'm keeping that lower door locked to at least buy me a few seconds. He works here, too, so it's not like I can avoid him forever."

"He works here for now." He gently lifted her chin.

"Are you going to fire him?" She frowned.

"I want to. But I need to dig a little more." He shook his head. "I should have acted quicker on the rumors I'd been hearing, but I didn't take them seriously enough."

"You mean other people noticed him paying extra attention to me?"

"Not you. But I heard about a few others who have been uncomfortable with the attention he was giving them, including some students." Scott let his head fall back against the doorframe with a thump. "You're the only one I've actually caught him in the act of harassing, but I don't know if I can use a statement from you since you're my wife. It might look like we were setting him up, and I don't want to get caught in a 'he said, she said' battle before the school board. They're not going to like me firing him anyway, now that the team made it so close to state."

"You knew he'd been doing things like this and still didn't believe me when I told you I didn't want his advances yesterday?" She took a step back, her lips trembling.

"I was hurt because you waited so long to tell me. How did you think that would look, you waiting almost two weeks to say anything? It didn't look like the actions of someone who was getting unwanted attention. It looked like someone feeling guilty." He squeezed his eyes closed and then opened them again. "What would you have believed if the roles were reversed?"

Her eyes blinked a few times, a tear still escaping the corner. "We've really let our trust in each other fall lately, huh?"

"Yes. We really have." He glanced at the clock. "Marian only put ten minutes on the schedule for today, and I've already been here longer. I better get back."

She nodded.

"I'll be home in time to go to your parents' house with you." He paused in the open doorway. "Lock this door behind me."

She blinked again and then moved to do what he requested. He caught her hand as she finished moving the bolt back in place and gave it a squeeze. Then, he headed back down the hallway.

As promised, Scott walked through the door with fifteen minutes to spare. Genevieve would never admit she'd been uncertain. After all, he'd been the one who said he didn't like eating over at her parents' house every week. This would be the second week in a row, simply because her mom requested they come again this week before tapering off to once or twice a month. With so much up in the air between them, she also wasn't sure how they'd get through dinner without everything going crazy again, either.

He changed quickly and came back out, finger-combing his hair. She always wanted to smooth out the ridges he left when he did that. But whether or not he'd appreciate it, she had no idea. She controlled the urge in her fingers and forced her hands to stay in her lap.

"Ready?" He grabbed his keys off the table. "Your mom promised me meatloaf."

Her lips twitched. Meatloaf was one of the meals he refused to eat when they first married. Now, it was a favorite.

She followed him out to the garage and waited while he opened the passenger door of his truck. He easily lifted her up into the seat. When they were dating, this was always the moment he'd reach over and steal a kiss. She was exactly the perfect height to make it easy. When was the last time he'd done something like that?

She touched her lips with her fingers as he moved away without any sign of affection. Would they ever again be able to find that lighthearted sweetness, that romance? She missed it.

Her father gave Scott a hearty handshake. Her mother was the ever-gracious Southern hostess. Within ten minutes of arriving, they were seated at the table in their usual spots. Her parents held their hands out so that all could link together during the blessing.

"Father God, we come humbly before You this evening to thank You for this bounteous feast we are about to eat. While we're talking to You, we also want to hold up Genevieve and Scott for You to keep working on them and help them find their way back to a better relationship with each other and with You. In Jesus' name, Amen." Her father's prayer shook her to the core.

What did he mean a better relationship with God? God wasn't the one who was upset with her. God wasn't the one fighting jealousy or hurt. God hadn't neglected her for almost two years. That was all Scott.

"You okay, Gennie?" Her father's question broke into her mental stewing, and she realized he'd been holding out the bowl of mashed potatoes for who knew how long.

"No." She took the spuds and plopped a spoonful on her

plate. When she reached to take the next dish, all eyes were on her. "What?"

"You just said you weren't okay when your father asked if you were." Her mother took the bowl from her hand and passed it to Scott. "But you didn't say what was wrong."

Her eyes met Scott's worried expression and then returned to her own plate. "I don't know that this is a good place to talk about it. I didn't really understand or appreciate Daddy's prayer."

Clang!

Her father dropped his fork. Once again, no one moved, but everyone stared at her.

"You had a problem with my prayer?" Her father's voice held a note she hadn't heard in a while. It was the tightly controlled anger he used to keep right below the level when she'd done something really bad growing up. Like the time she'd dug up all her mama's tulips out of the front flowerbed to make a bouquet. Or the summer she'd cut her own hair when the babysitter wasn't looking.

"I had a problem with the fact you think my relationship with God is suffering." She cut off a bite of meatloaf with much more force than necessary, causing gravy to splatter over her peas. "Just because my husband and I can't get our act together doesn't mean I have a problem with God."

"Isn't He part of your relationship?" Her father's tone was like steel.

"We're both Christians, if that's what you're talking about." She took a sip of her tea. "You see us at worship services and Bible class every time. You know that."

Her father shook his head, a furrow of worry between his brows. "What has Marty been talking to you two about if it's not how to be Christian spouses?"

Genevieve set her fork down and leaned back. "I don't think what Marty's been talking about with us is any of your concern.

You're the one who told us to go talk to him. I thought you were glad we were getting counseling."

"Honey, that's not what he means." Her mother reached out a hand and touched Genevieve's sleeve. "He's simply reminding you it takes three to make a marriage work to its potential. If you don't have God involved in your relationship, you're like a stool with only two legs—you'll just keep falling over. With God as the third leg, you have stability."

"So, tell us how we need to incorporate God more than we already have," Scott spoke up for the first time since they sat at the table.

"You've gotta stick to His plan." Her father slapped one hand against the other. "God as the head of the family, then the husband, then the wife. She needs to respect and submit to you like God says, and you need to cherish her like Christ does the church. When you do it like that, it always works. Hands down."

Hadn't they been doing that? She was rather put out with the whole conversation. "Why do you think we aren't doing it that way?"

"You've been griping about him. He's been neglecting you. And have either of you stopped to study or pray about any of this?" Her father pointed back and forth between them. "Or are you relying on everyone else to do it for you?"

"If it's not important enough for you to pray about and study to see God's plan, then no matter how many others pray about it, it won't be fixed." Her mother's quiet voice carried a balm of peace. "Now, you both think about it, but we won't discuss it anymore. I want to hear about the spring festival plans for this year. That's only a few weeks away, right?"

Her mother had to be the only person in the world who could get away with such a drastic subject change. Her father picked up his fork as if there hadn't just been a near-miss of an argument. Scott answered her mom's questions. And Genevieve took a bite of her now-lukewarm meatloaf.

Had she been wrong about them doing things the right way? Had she and Scott been trying to build their relationship without God's help these last four years? How could that be?

24

"What's your pleasure?" Jimmy stood, pen poised over paper, as Genevieve sat across from Valerie for lunch on Wednesday.

"Surprise me." Genevieve set the menu aside. "I've never had anything bad here, and I don't expect to start now."

"Careful what you wish for." Valerie waggled her finger. "He does fry chicken livers, you know."

"Well, if I ever wanted to try chicken livers, this would be the place I would go. Jimmy knows how to cook." Genevieve flashed him a big smile.

"One order of chicken livers coming up." Jimmy winked her way before heading back to the kitchen.

"You're in for it now." Valerie took a sip of her soda. "What's gotten into you?"

"I don't know. I know I need to make some changes in my life." Genevieve played with her straw paper.

"Like what? Besides trying chicken livers."

"My dad pointed out during dinner last night that he doesn't think Scott and I have been following God's plan for marriage. He said we need to include God more in our relationship and study about what God means a marriage to be."

"I thought you guys went over all that with Marty when you did pre-marital counseling." Valerie leaned back against the booth.

Genevieve shrugged. "I thought so too. Maybe my dad doesn't think it sank in or something."

"So, when he said, 'what God means a marriage to be,' what's he talking about?" Valerie leaned forward and pulled a Bible app up on her phone. "To look up all the verses on marriage?"

"I guess. He mentioned God being the head, then the husband. And me submitting. And him cherishing." Genevieve rubbed at the headache that remained from the night before. "And he scolded us because, evidently, we haven't been praying enough about it, but we're expecting everyone else to pray about it for us. Which isn't true. We've prayed."

"I think he's just worried about you guys. I know the Coach Drake thing made you take a few steps back from where you'd worked your way to." Valerie made a face. "I wish I could have seen his face when you slapped him the other day. I wish Scott could've seen you do that."

Genevieve snickered. "Yeah. I don't know how big an impact it had on him, but I haven't seen him since."

"Good riddance."

They both sat back as their food was delivered. A plate of something similar to chicken nuggets sat in front of Genevieve, complete with fries and dipping sauce. She exchanged a glance with Valerie, shrugged, picked one up, and took a bite. Not bad.

"So, back to what your dad said. Something to think about." Valerie waved a fry in her direction. "When he talked about you submitting to Scott. You know that doesn't mean you're supposed to be like his slave, right? More like you respect him and are supportive and helpful. Not hard to do when the man is cherishing his wife like he's supposed to."

"That makes sense. Submit sounds so archaic." Genevieve took a sip of her tea.

"Remember a couple weeks ago when I got onto you for only talking about the bad stuff?"

"Yes." Genevieve paused with a bite halfway to her mouth. "I suppose that's not submitting?"

"Not really." Valerie wiped some sauce off her lips. "Think about it. If all you ever focus on is the bad, you're going to forget about the good. Not only that, but you make him look bad to others. A wife is supposed to support and build up her husband, to be his biggest cheerleader. Try to remember the good things. If you focus more on them, the bad things won't seem as bad."

"So, no more letting off steam when he does something really annoying?" Genevieve twisted her lips into a face that said '*oops!*'

"Only vent if you know you're going to explode much worse at him if you don't." Valerie reached over and squeezed her hand. "In that case, I'm here for you. You know I occasionally need to get things about Parker off my chest. But I try not to."

"Scott was furious that I told you about Coach Drake before I told him." Genevieve ran a fry through some ketchup, smearing it around her plate. "I really messed up."

"Has he quit talking to you completely?" Valerie's face showed she knew he hadn't.

"No. He actually went with me to dinner last night." Genevieve dropped her fry and leaned back again. "But it's going to take a lot of work to get his trust back."

"Don't give up. It's worth it."

"I know." Genevieve shook her head. "I was the one who

demanded a divorce a month ago. And now I'm the one fighting to stay married."

"Keep fighting."

GENEVIEVE WAS LATER GETTING a coffee break the next morning, but it was the time of year when she started inputting the inoculation records of the incoming freshmen for next August. It was time-consuming. Maybe someday, the middle school and high school would use the same system, and everything would simply flow over by itself—but this was not that year.

Her caffeine from early this morning had worn off, and she was more than ready for a second dose. She waved at several teachers on their planning period as she stepped into the lounge. She didn't get to associate with many of the faculty and staff here, but she at least recognized them. Someone had started a new pot brewing, and it was almost finished, so she leaned against the counter to wait for the gurgling to stop.

"*Ugh.* My in-laws are coming this weekend." An English teacher broke apart a granola bar at the table. "I told my husband he had to clean the bathroom. Half that mess is his anyway. I still don't understand how a man can miss such a large target."

"I know that's right." Another teacher sat to the right of the first, half-heartedly grading what appeared to be math papers. "And don't get me started on all the little black hairs he leaves in and around the sink."

"The worst." The third woman sat on the couch behind the other two but joined in their conversation. "And if your mother-in-law is like mine, she can find every little spec of dirt and grime you miss. The fact it was her precious baby who made the mess doesn't seem to matter."

"One time I found some of those black hairs in the cup I keep by the sink." English teacher shuddered. "It took me a while to get them all out of my mouth."

Genevieve opened her mouth to tell the story about the toenail clipping, then stopped. She was married to these ladies' principal, their higher-up. Would he appreciate her sharing a story that put him in that kind of light? Was that what a Christian wife should do?

She grabbed the pot despite the fact the machine still spat every few seconds. Drops of coffee hissed on the hot warming plate as she refilled her mug. A splash of creamer from the fridge, and she was ready to head back to her office, away from temptation.

Before yesterday, she wouldn't have thought a thing about joining in on that conversation. She would've taken much pleasure in "venting" about the various ways her husband drove her crazy. Thoughts of what Valerie had cautioned her at lunch the day before ran through her mind.

Valerie mentioned she'd only been talking about the bad things her husband did and never the good. The women in the lounge sounded bitter and unhappy as if they were better than their husbands. Is that what Genevieve sounded like?

No wonder Coach Drake had heard rumors. Although she didn't talk to many other people in the school, if he'd heard her at all lately, it would've been only complaining. That definitely didn't lead people to believe her marriage was great.

Gossip.

That's all it was. It wasn't venting. It was trying to one-up each other over who had the best husband horror story.

Valerie's words came back to her. *If all you ever focus on is the bad, you're going to forget about the good. Not only that, but you make him look bad to others. A wife is supposed to support and build up her husband. Try to remember the good things.*

Maybe next time Genevieve came across a situation like the one she'd left in the lounge, she'd mention something good about her husband. Those women seemed to love trying to one-up each other. Wouldn't it be funny to change their stories from who had the worst husband to who had the best?

"I'm sorry, God." She prayed aloud once she was back at her desk. "Help me to do better."

A glance at the school calendar showed a softball game that afternoon. She'd bet almost anything Scott would attend. Maybe she should join him. Might earn her a smile—or what qualified as one the last few days.

She had to find a way to get the sadness out of his smile and work it back up to the one she fell in love with. The one laced with fun, attraction, trust, and appreciation. The one that still stole her breath when it came her way. When she got that smile back, she'd know they were truly mending.

Lord, please. Please help me find that smile again.

"THIS SEAT TAKEN?"

Scott's eyes left the ballfield to meet hers. "I didn't know you wanted to come."

"You didn't ask." She climbed up the two bleachers and sat on the cool metal beside him. "How late am I?"

"They're just starting the second inning." He pointed to the scoreboard. "The first went pretty fast. No runs yet. Three up, three down for both sides."

"Sounds like we're pretty evenly matched today."

"Fairly. The other school has an amazing pitcher, and this is our pitcher's first year, so we'll see how she does. She's got a good arm, but I'm not sure about her stamina. After a few innings, it's harder to get the ball where you want it to go."

The girl wound up and windmilled her arm, quickly letting the ball go at the bottom, so it zipped through the air and past the batter.

"I never made it past slow-pitch. Seeing a softball flying at that speed toward me was too intimidating."

"It's sometimes intimidating to just watch." Several pitches later, Scott glanced over at her. "I'm sorry I didn't ask you to come with me. We could have walked up together."

"We can walk back together when it's over." She slipped her hand under his arm and snuggled in a little closer.

The sunshine was warm, but the wind still had a bit of a bite to it. He shifted to put his arm around her instead and tucked her into his side.

"I might even treat you to dinner."

"A girl could get spoiled hanging out with you." She smiled.

The naturality of their teasing lightened his heart, despite knowing they had much more to work on and learn.

"That's how every girl should be, right?"

"I used to know a guy who thought so." She playfully bumped into his side.

"Whatever happened to him?" He raised an eyebrow. "Anyone I know?"

"I see him around occasionally. I hear he likes ballgames and Italian food."

"Sounds like my kind of guy." He whispered it in her ear.

A shiver wound through her back. "Mine too."

"That's good to know." He cleared his throat and turned back to the ballgame. "We're starting to make a spectacle of ourselves."

"People keep telling me more couples need to be like us." Genevieve shrugged. "We must be doing at least something right."

"Probably more than we think we are." He nodded.

"And maybe more with each day."

He met her gaze and grinned. Sadness tinged the edges of the moment, but it was also laced with hope ... and love. Cheering erupted around them, and they pulled their attention away from each other and back to the game. Dating at school events wasn't the easiest, but it was worth it.

25

On Saturday, Scott read his mom's text again.

Think I'll come see you two this weekend.

Nothing like giving a head's up. He glanced at his watch. If she was driving up right now, she'd be here in less than two hours. Not good.

A cheer went up as the baseball team scored two more runs. He'd meant to stay at least through the rest of this game, but he had some damage control to do at home. The team would have to win without him.

Can I get an ETA?

I haven't left yet. I'll be there by dinner.

So much for getting a straight answer. What did he need to do before Mom got here?

The bed.

He jumped up and headed toward his truck. There was a

furniture store on the way home. Time to finally replace that mattress. Something he should've done before now.

Especially after Genevieve had started sleeping in there. Despite being livid about her insistence on separate rooms, that didn't mean he shouldn't still take care of her. Well, she still wasn't going to sleep on a new mattress because Mom would be in there tonight. And she needed to move back to their room whether she was ready or not.

———

GENEVIEVE LOOKED up from the flowerbed she was weeding in front of their house. Scott's truck had just pulled back into the driveway, and a new mattress filled the back. She stood and stretched the kinks out of her spine.

"I thought you were at the baseball tournament today."

He lifted a hand. "I went for a while, but they don't need me there all day. Besides, Mom texted and said she wants to come spend a few days with us."

"So, that's why you finally replaced the old mattress?" She brushed the dirt off her fingers as she walked over to the truck's tailgate.

"There was a good sale." He slid the bulky purchase his way. "And I promised I would. Can you handle catching the end as it comes off the truck?"

"Got it." She bent her knees as the weight pushed against her arms. It was more awkward than heavy, but it still required more effort than she usually expended. She walked as quickly as she could to keep up with his long stride toward the front of the house.

"If we can get it up on the porch, I should be able to slide it down the hallway."

"You sure? Because I don't mind doing this." Her foot hit the trowel she had left lying on the sidewalk and her leg twisted beneath her. "*Oof!*"

"You okay?" The mattress hit the ground but didn't fall flat as it was at least partway up onto the porch already. Scott knelt beside her and gently felt along her ankle. It was one of the first times he'd touched her more than holding hands or lifting her up into the vehicle in weeks. She was tempted to twist her leg every day.

"I'm fine. Just a klutz." She pointed to the offending shovel. "What I get for leaving out my weeding tools."

He stood and pulled her up with him. "How's that feel? No pain?"

"Nope." She rotated her foot all the way around to show that she could. "Honestly, it appeared worse than it was."

"Okay. Let me scoot this through the house, and then we'll try the box springs."

She reached down and pulled another long grass runner from between her azalea bushes. The timing of this visit from his mom was a bit strange. In a few weeks, they'd be headed down to see her for Easter, to see Scott's three-year-old nephew hunt eggs, and enjoy his mom's ham. What triggered this?

Scott came back out, and she followed him to help move the box springs. They were a bit lighter but comparably as bulky. She glanced down as they neared the porch to make sure she didn't step on anything else, although she wouldn't have turned down another opportunity for his hands on her.

"Okay. I've got it from here." He set his end down and maneuvered it through the living room and down the hallway.

She followed along behind, grabbing fresh sheets from the hall closet and carrying them into the room. "Does your mom know I've been sleeping in here?"

"No." He huffed as he lifted the box springs into place. "And if it's all the same to you, I'd rather she didn't."

She didn't have a response to that. What could she say? It

was her own fault she'd been sleeping in a different room from her husband. She'd considered moving back for weeks now but hadn't found a way to do it graciously. Not to mention the tension that remained between them over the stupid Coach Drake incidents. At least her mother-in-law's surprise visit afforded her an easy way back into her own bed.

His biceps bulged as he manhandled the mattress to move it into place. Was he still lifting weights with the boys a few times a week like he'd done when coaching? He definitely hadn't lost any of his muscle definition. He lifted his head and caught her gaze. She blinked and ducked her head. As attracted as she found him right now, he obviously didn't feel the same toward her.

"I'll get this old mattress set out of here, if you'll let me by." He touched her shoulder.

"Oh." She jumped a bit. "Of course. I'll put clean sheets on the bed. I can move my stuff in a bit."

He nodded.

She took several deep breaths once he was out the door with the mattress. *Get it together, girl. I'm not a teenager crushing on a boy. It's okay to be attracted to my own husband.* She mentally gave herself a shake. *Yeah, but what if he never feels that way about me again?*

She couldn't go there right now. Marty said there was still hope. Maybe her moving back to their shared bed was exactly what they needed to take the next step to getting their relationship where it ought to be. She stretched the edge of the mattress pad into place and snapped the fitted sheet open to spread over the new bed. It did look much more comfortable.

Scott came back in and grabbed the far corner she hadn't gotten to yet and slid it down. In the past, when he'd stepped in to help make the bed, it often led to them *in* the bed. She was afraid to look at his face for fear of seeing a lack of desire there.

It'd only happened a few times, but it was a sweet memory, and she didn't want it tarnished.

"Got the top sheet?" His voice held a bit of huskiness, and he cleared his throat.

She grabbed the edge of the cloth and lifted it in the air to help spread out the folds and wrinkles. He caught the other side and brought it down, his gaze holding hers above the crisp linens. She needn't have worried. His eyes said he remembered exactly what she remembered, and the thought was just as sweet to him.

He was the first to look away, but not before her pulse quickened to a sprint, and the ever-present butterflies started a square dance around her tummy. He turned and hefted the box springs leaning against the far wall to maneuver it back out of the house. He paused right beside her and cupped her cheek.

"I need to get these over to the dump before it closes, but I'll be back after that to help clean up and straighten things. Mom isn't going to be here until around dinner. Maybe I can grill."

She closed her eyes and leaned into his hand for a moment. "Okay."

He dropped a quick kiss on her forehead and then was gone.

She'd never wished for a time machine more than lately. But if she could go back to before she gave the ultimatum—or even back to before they started taking each other for granted —she would in a heartbeat. She gathered up her hairbrush and a few other items that had lived on the dresser in this room for a month now and carried them back to the bedroom that was supposed to be shared. Ready or not, it was again. She dropped her items on top of her dresser and went back for the curling iron and socks that remained down the hall. Most of her clothes had stayed where they were because she hadn't wanted the hassle of moving everything.

She spread a hand over the bedspread and did another

quick glance around the guest room before deciding it appeared its normal self and wouldn't give away the secrets of its recent occupancy. The rest was up to how she and Scott behaved. But knowing his mom, Genevieve wondered how they'd pull that off. That woman was amazing at sniffing out secrets. The fact she hadn't noticed when they were up there to meet his niece astounded Genevieve. Unless that's why her mother-in-law was coming now.

"EVERYTHING OKAY WITH YOU TWO?" Mama Stewart washed a bunch of spinach in the sink for their salad that evening.

"Why do you ask?" Genevieve glanced through the screen door to where Scott manned the grill. What she wouldn't give for the excuse to be out there instead of here, where she was the one being grilled.

"Something seemed off the last time I saw you. It's been eating at me since you came to see Beth." She wielded a knife and started slicing up a cucumber and tomato.

"Off?" Genevieve could only answer a question with a question so many times. Exactly how long did it take to get steaks done to medium? "Like what?"

"I'm not sure." Her mother-in-law put a hand to her hip. "But the fact that you're not trying to reassure me right now is only making it worse."

Genevieve focused on checking the potatoes in the oven. She squeezed the foil-wrapped spuds with her mitted hand, but they still needed a bit longer. Hopefully, her mother-in-law would think the heat from the oven caused all the heat in her cheeks.

"I'm going to go ask Scott how much longer on the meat. The potatoes aren't completely done yet." She dashed through the door before his mom could protest and almost collided with the man himself.

"What's wrong?" He caught her by her elbows and glanced around her to where his mom remained in her hand-on-hip position.

"She's asking me if things are okay with us—said something felt off the last time we were around her, and she wants to know what." Genevieve hurried the whispered words to him, hoping he understood. "You said you didn't want her to know about our sleeping arrangements, but I honestly don't know what else you want me to not say."

"The meat's almost done." He squeezed her arms. "Get me a platter, and I'll come help field questions. I should've known she had an agenda for coming so suddenly."

Genevieve breezed back inside, grabbing a platter out of the cabinet. "He says it's almost ready. How's the salad coming?"

"Fine." Her mother-in-law's short answer stung her with guilt, but she really wanted to handle this the way Scott wanted her to. No need to upset him any more than she already had.

She handed over the platter outside and waited while he pulled the steaks off the grill. He shot her a glance. "She's not going to bite, you know."

"I don't want to say something you don't want me to say." She gripped the back of the Adirondack chair as if it were a lifeline to help her navigate this crazy path.

"You won't." The trust in his voice caused her heart to skip a beat. "But it's okay. I'm coming."

Scott put a hand to the small of his wife's back and steered her toward the kitchen. His mom shot him a knowing look. He set the meat in front of her and kissed her cheek.

Genevieve busied herself with pulling potatoes from the

oven and setting the table. Mom clanked the wooden salad bowl in the middle of the table. Scott raised an eyebrow as he laid out forks and steak knives but said nothing. After the short prayer, silence reined again as they served their plates.

Three bites into her steak, Mom slammed her knife down on the table. "I failed you, didn't I?"

Scott choked on the drink of water he had just taken. "What?"

"You two. You're having problems, aren't you?" She pointed between Genevieve and Scott. "I could sense something off when you were down the other day, but I couldn't put my finger on what. You both said the right things and smiled enough, but you never touched each other."

They hadn't touched that whole day? Scott thought back but couldn't remember all the details. Mostly how sweet the baby had been and how happy Lacy was, despite her exhaustion after giving birth.

"Mom." Scott placed his hand on the table. "We hit a rough patch, but we're working through it. I didn't want to worry you."

"You didn't think I'd want to pray for you?" She shook her head. "Or might have some advice to share on things that help when one person in the relationship is a workaholic."

Scott's mouth opened and closed again. The comparison had been niggling around in his conscience for a while now, but he hated admitting it. Evidently, his mom recognized the same thing.

"I've seen the signs over the last year or so." His mom picked at a spot on the tablecloth, and Genevieve cringed. Obviously, they hadn't gotten it clean last from the last time it was used. "Your father always working when I needed him was something that caused problems in our marriage."

"You and Dad had problems?" Scott leaned back in his chair.

"We obviously worked through them. We had three kids

afterward." She gave a cocky grin.

"Mom! I don't want to think about that." Scott waved his hands in the air as if he could eradicate the thoughts from reaching his head.

She laughed and swished her napkin toward him. "Seriously, is that what's causing the problems between you two?"

He exchanged a glance with Genevieve. He hesitated, because it wasn't the only problem, but it would be the one easiest to admit. They both had issues to work through, but some didn't need to be discussed with anyone else. Gen pressed her lips together and squared her shoulders.

"It's one of the problems, but not the only one." Genevieve speared a bite of tomato on her fork. "Although we had several marriage counseling sessions before, they must not have sunk in enough. We're getting back to some of the basics and remembering what God desires from us as husband and wife."

Scott shot her a glance partly grateful and partly awe. "And once it was brought to my attention that I was putting more into my job than my marriage, I've been trying to find a better way to do things."

"And I have found ways to be with him even when he's doing school things." Genevieve pushed a cucumber to the side of her plate.

"That's sort of what your dad and I used to do. Sometimes, still do." Her mother-in-law got a dreamy expression on her face. "Meeting up with him somewhere for lunch, just the two of us, always helps us both have a good day."

Her insinuation that it might be more than lunch had Scott cringing again.

"But I don't want you two to end up like us." She brushed a wayward hair off her cheek. "I did a lot of the parenting by myself. And it wasn't easy. I never considered how it would impact your future relationships to see ours working that way.

Always having your dad away must have taught you that it was the way things were supposed to be."

Scott leaned forward and took his mom's hand. "Mom, I never thought that. I was always jealous of my friends whose dads were able to come to all their ballgames. Or were home in the evenings to hang out instead of working late. Now that I know I was headed in the same direction, I promise Genevieve won't have to raise our children by herself like you did. But for the record, you did a great job."

"Are there children coming?" His mom perked up at that thought. "I mean, you're not getting any younger. And neither am I."

"Thank you for that reminder." He sat back again. "No children yet, but it's something we plan to address someday." He shot Genevieve a wink, and her cheeks turned rosy. Hope of getting back to that level of relationship exhilarated him.

"Well, I'm glad to hear you're working on it." His mom picked her fork back up. "I'm sure making you move back into the same bed should help."

Genevieve and Scott locked gazes, eyes wide. How had she known?

"You left a sock under the bed, dear." Mom popped a bite of meat in her mouth with a smirk. "And a bobby pin on the dresser."

Genevieve's lips twitched with amusement. As much as Gen had complained about his messy habits, she had a few of her own, and seeing his mom call her out on it had them both starting to giggle. Sure, the dinner conversation hadn't been all pleasant, but maybe this was a sign they were heading the right direction.

Though he might need to do a bit more work on spending so much time at the office. And a niggle of an idea started to form that shook him to the core and stole his breath. Could he make such a sacrifice?

26

The weekend was long, but good, in spite of the lunch on Sunday where Scott's mom ganged up with both of Genevieve's parents to give them more advice on how to make their marriage stronger—not to mention not letting it get to the point of needing extra help in the first place. After about ten minutes of that conversation, Scott rose from the table, pulled Genevieve up beside him, told all the parents they loved them, and led her out of the restaurant. She stared at him in astonishment in the car, but he just shrugged.

"We've already been over that. They know we're working on it." He grabbed her hand and held it on the console. "I didn't feel the need to be subjected to more of the same, nor to let you sit there being picked apart."

"Thank you." She pointed back inside. "Won't your mom still need a ride back to our house?"

"I haven't left yet. We can wait out here until she's ready."

She shot him a grin. "*Ooh*, she's going to let you have it when she gets out here."

"Maybe. But it's our marriage. And it's time for them to butt out a little and trust us to keep working on it."

239

THE SINCERITY of his words from Sunday grew stronger the more they replayed through her head over Monday and into Tuesday morning. A glance at the clock showed five minutes until Marian had scheduled their coffee break. Genevieve was at a stopping point, so she decided to meet him at his office instead of making him come to her. She stood, stretched, and grabbed her mug to head down the hallway.

Marian waved at her as she entered the office. But before she could say anything, a surly teenage girl stomped through the doorway and thrust a note into Marian's face. Her expression said she was anything but pleased at having to come to the office. Although it was obvious why she'd been sent. Her skirt was short enough that Genevieve was amazed she couldn't see the bottoms of the girl's undies. And the cut of the top wasn't much better. The girl popped her gum while she waited for the secretary to read the missive.

"Wait just a moment, Tansy." Marian waved the paper in the air and then headed off to knock sharply on Scott's door. She stuck her head through the opening but pitched her voice where the words weren't clear out here next to her desk. Scott's voice rumbled in response and then Marian turned and waved the girl to come her way.

The girl tromped over and huffed as she passed Marian to enter the office. Marian cast a glance of exasperation over her shoulder before following the teenager through the doorway and pulling the door closed behind her. Genevieve leaned against the counter, perplexed. If it was a matter of breaking dress code, a single glance would tell him the girl was in violation. Why had Marian gone in too?

A few moments later, Marian led the girl back out, and gently steered her into a plastic chair against the wall. "We'll just call your parents, shall we?"

Marian drummed her fingers while she waited for someone to answer the phone. She glanced up at Genevieve and must have noticed the confused expression because after leaving a message, she leaned forward where her whisper could be heard by Genevieve, but not Tansy. "Coach Stewart always has me come in when it's a girl violating dress code so he won't have to look at her and see something he might possibly not want to see. He said he respects the girls and his wife too much for that."

Genevieve glanced at his closed door and wished it were open so she could run and throw herself into his arms. A prick of guilt stabbed her for worrying about him looking at cheerleaders the other day. Such worries seemed ridiculous in light of what the secretary said.

"I'll be back in a few moments, Genevieve. We're going to rummage through the pile of lost-and-found clothes to see if we can find something more suitable until Tansy's parents can get here. Scott's wrapping up one thing and then said he'd join you."

"Thanks, Marian." Genevieve hoped her voice conveyed the whole depth of her gratitude. She was grateful not only for the help at getting coffee breaks set up, and the friendship, but also for helping her husband maintain his promise to stay pure for her.

She sat in the molded chair Tansy had vacated and closed her eyes for a moment. *Lord, please forgive me for not trusting him. Please help me to be a better wife, to live up to the respect he gives me. Help me overcome the stupid lapse in judgment I made several weeks ago when I started listening to and leaning on the wrong man instead of my husband.*

As if thinking of him had conjured him up, Coach Drake's cologne assaulted her nose and brought her eyes wide open.

"Back in the principal's office again?" He leaned against the counter directly across from her, his ankles crossed and a smirk on his face. "You must be a naughty nurse, indeed."

How had she ever thought his interests were sincere? Now, all she could see was the slime ball he truly was. She glanced again at the closed door and wished her husband would open it right now.

"What? No retort?" Coach Drake leaned forward again, his face only about a foot from hers. "After that slap the other day, I expected a much feistier come-back."

"I'm not playing your games. Please leave me alone." She crossed her arms over her chest and leaned as far away from him as possible, considering the window behind her head. "Like I said the other day, you need to go pay attention to your wife and daughter."

"They're not as much fun." He poked his lower lip out in what she assumed was a pout. On him, it looked more like a fish face.

"Maybe you should try playing a different game, then." She somehow kept from laughing at the mental image in her head. "I don't find the one you're playing now to be fun, either."

"You did for a little while." His voice dropped lower as he closed in a bit more.

"No." She hissed the reply through her teeth and contemplated which way would be the best exit from this. How long did it take to find something to cover that girl more than what she had on? Why wasn't Scott coming out of his office already? Surely, the reminder had popped up on his screen. She shifted to her left a tiny fraction, planning to make a break for it if Coach Drake got any nearer.

"You said I was a hero." Some saliva erupted from his mouth as he practically spat the words at her.

"No. I said you'd been acting like a hero." She wiped the wet from her cheek. "Being a hero and acting like one are two totally different things. You want to see a hero? There's one right behind that door."

Timing was everything. Scott opened his door as she said that. There wasn't any "hallelujah" music in reality, but Genevieve could hear the choir in her head. She watched his face as he took in the situation and was relieved no hurt flitted across those brown eyes of his.

"Get away from my wife." His tone wasn't loud, but it carried authority.

Coach Drake straightened, one eyebrow raised. "Going to live up to her hero worship again, are you?"

Scott's gaze flitted to her and then back to the man between them. "I don't know what you're talking about, but I do know if I see you lay a hand on my wife or any other woman in this school again, you're going to be fired immediately."

"And how do you plan to do that?" Drake's cocky attitude emanated from every inch of his stance and posture. "I took the boys almost all the way to state. The board isn't going to want a coach as good as I am let go."

"They will if they know you've been sexually harassing your coworkers." Scott's reply froze time for a moment. The clock ticked over another second, and another, and another. Had he procured proof that some of the other rumors were true?

"It's your word against mine." Coach Drake's shoulders suddenly didn't seem as broad or straight. "No one's going to believe the man who couldn't get the basketball team to regionals the three years he was coaching. They'll say it's jealousy. That you made it up. Got your wife to agree to lie for you."

"What about the other women you've been giving inappropriate attention to?" Scott leaned against his doorway as if he had all the time in the world. "They'd have no reason to lie for me."

"You have no proof."

"Sure about that?"

Was he bluffing? The other day, he said he didn't have the evidence he needed to validify the rumors. But surely if he had enough proof now, he'd just fire the dirt bag. She glanced from her husband to the man who'd wreaked such havoc with their fragile marriage lately and back again.

Apparently, Coach Drake couldn't decide if Scott was bluffing or not, either. He straightened and thrust his chin out. "This isn't over, Stewart."

"It is over." Scott's jaw tightened. "One way or another, it's over."

"I'll come back when Vice-Principal Anne is in. She's easier to deal with than you are." Coach Drake stalked out of the office.

"I bet she won't be." Scott's mutter carried across the room.

Genevieve sprang from her chair and ran the short distance to her husband. Without waiting to see what kind of reception she'd receive, she threw herself at him, wrapping her arms around his waist. After a split second, his arms enfolded her and pulled her in tight.

"You okay?" He stepped them both back into his office and shut the door without letting her go.

She nodded her head, her hair catching in his short beard hairs. "I was so glad you came out when you did. I'd been trying to figure out how to get away from him if you didn't open the door soon."

"What was he saying to you?" His hand ran circles on her back.

"That I was feisty, and he'd rather play games with me than his wife. And that I called him a hero—which I didn't. I said something about him playing the hero, but I know better now. He was only acting like what he thought I wanted." She shook her head. "Stupid me. I had a hero all along."

"Is that why he said that about the hero worship?" His finger ran down her cheek.

She nodded, her eyes closed to try and keep the tears at bay.

"I'm not a hero. Just a man, trying to do the best to take care of his wife." His words mumbled into her hair, but she could still hear them.

"It seems to be working." She giggled. "I'm still alive almost five years into the marriage."

He chuckled. "Not exactly what I meant."

"I know." She snuggled closer. "We probably wasted all our coffee break time, didn't we? Do you have something else you're supposed to be doing right now?"

"Nothing more important than this." His whisper set those blasted wings beating like crazy around her tummy. Could they stay like this all day? She wouldn't complain despite the extra work it would leave for tomorrow. Although Marian might not appreciate having to deal with having both Principal and Vice-Principal out at the same time.

"Do you really have enough proof to fire him?" She pushed back a hair's width—just enough to be able to look into his face.

"Almost." His lips tightened in a line, and she could read the frustration in his eyes. "No one wants to admit it outright. I guess they're all afraid of what he'll do in response, or afraid others will think less of them. But if I could get only one or two of them to write a statement, he'd be gone before the end of the day."

"Where did you hear the rumors?"

"Marian overheard students talking about it in the bathroom one day, but she doesn't know which students." He inched them backward until he could lean against the edge of his desk, her body tucked between his legs. "I know I can't always rely on student rumors, but in this case, having seen the way he's treated you, I know it's a probability.

"And at least one other teacher has mentioned feeling uncomfortable, but she didn't give a name. I'm hoping Anne can convince her to give it up as well as maybe lead us to another person who feels the same way. Not that I want anyone else to have suffered like that. I simply have a bad feeling there are more."

"Don't give up yet." She put her hand against his cheek. "If he keeps it up, he'll get found out."

"I don't want to risk someone else going through what you've gone through before he gets too sloppy to keep it a secret." He banged one of his hands against the edge of the desk.

"Let's pray about it." As the words left her mouth, she wondered at the oddity. When they first married, they'd prayed about everything that bothered them, but lately, they'd fallen out of the habit.

"Great idea." He pressed his forehead to hers and closed his eyes.

"God, thank You for this woman You have given me. Help me as I continue to try and be a better husband. Help us both as we try to repair the damage we've done to our relationship. And God, please, help us with this situation with Coach Drake. I know he has a soul, too, and he isn't acting like one of your children. Help us find the proof we need so we can stop his actions before someone else gets hurt. And please heal those who have suffered from his choices. In Jesus' name, Amen."

"Amen." Her reply came out on a breath, and her eyes fluttered open.

With their heads pressed together like this, it was the closest they'd been in a long while. His eyes searched hers for a moment, as if uncertain what he would find. She tried to put all the love and faith running through her at that moment into the look she gave in return. It must have worked, because he tilted his head the slightest bit, started to move closer, his lips only millimeters away.

A sharp rap at the door pulled them apart with a groan. So close. He straightened and stepped an inch away, but not far enough that she couldn't still feel the warmth from his body.

"Come." His voice was mostly the normal self-assured bass she was used to. She was probably the only one who would notice the little break near the end.

Riley poked her head through the entryway. "Hey Coach Stewart, I ... Oh, sorry!"

"It's okay. Is it time for our meeting?" He gave her a grin that didn't show any of their frustration. "You're here about the booth for the seniors at the spring festival, right?"

"Right, but we can wait."

"It's okay." The moment was shot anyway. Genevieve gave his arm a squeeze and shot him a look of regret. "I was about to head back to my office."

Scott caught her fingers and gave them one final tug before letting her go. Riley's face blushed as Genevieve passed her, and Genevieve wondered if her own matched. Getting caught about to kiss her husband. That hadn't happened in a while. She might as well be a teenager again for the emotions dashing this way and that inside her.

If only Riley had waited two more minutes.

If only his schedule weren't so full for the next few weeks as he planned the spring festival.

"Coach Stewart."

Scott grinned at Marian as she hovered in the door Tuesday afternoon. "What's going on, Marian?"

She twisted her hands together in an atypical show of

worry. "Remember when I told you about that conversation I overheard a while back?"

"How could I forget?" He motioned to the chair in front of his desk.

"I might know who one of the girls is now."

His heart skipped a beat. Could this be it? What they'd been waiting for? Enough proof to get rid of the problem of Coach Drake?

It might be better if it were another teacher, but if he'd been harassing a student, there'd be no question of firing him. The school board didn't tolerate child abuse. Or anything that hinted at it.

"The last time Tansy was in here, we agreed something else was going on to make her show out so much." Marian leaned forward. "When I was helping her find ... more appropriate clothing this morning, I happened to look down at her shoes. And I noticed they looked exactly like the ones that day under the stall."

"You're sure?"

"They're canvas ones she's drawn on with markers. No other pair in school looks like them."

He leaned back and sighed. "And you're certain she's one of the girls who received Drake's attention?"

"Her voice." Marian brushed a tear from her cheek as she nodded. "I probably overstepped my bounds, but I asked her if anything had been happening lately to make her feel uncomfortable. And she hesitated before denying it. There was something in her eyes ... as if she wanted to confide in me but couldn't."

"Anne comes back tomorrow, right?"

"Unfortunately, no. She got confirmation today that it's the flu."

"*Ugh!* Assuming she's back early next week, let's have Tansy meet with Anne then and see if she'll talk to her. Maybe bring in the counselor. Sometimes Ginger knows how to put things in such a way where students will open up more readily. And maybe make an appointment to get Kimmy back in here too. With Anne or me. We can let her know our suspicions and that we're trying to put an end to all this."

"I'll work on that right now."

"I'm ready for this to be over."

He folded his hands and rested his forehead against them as Marian pulled his door mostly closed behind her. "God, please let this be what we've been waiting for. Help us be able to get Tansy the help she needs. Give these women the bravery to help put an end to this mess. And God, while we're talking, can You help me find a way to get a kiss from my wife again? I miss her."

Maybe a selfish prayer there at the end. But it had taken all his self-control to not kick Riley out earlier so he could have ten more minutes with Genevieve. They'd been so close!

27

"Mr. Stewart?"

"Hi, Kimmy." Scott motioned her into his office Thursday after school. "What can I do for you?"

"Actually, it's not only me." She opened the door farther, and a couple of other teachers stood there with her. "Mind if we all come in?"

"Of course." It wasn't about math, because at least three different departments were represented in the teachers who sat across from him.

Kimmy glanced between her coworkers and then straightened her shoulders, obviously the designated spokesperson. "Remember the other day when you told me you'd support me if I wanted to file a sexual harassment complaint?"

His heart leapt and he took a deep breath to calm his pulse. "Yes."

"I'm ready. And Cynthia and Diane are too."

"All the same person?" He willed his hands to remain calm as he waited to hear their answer.

"Yes, sir." Kimmy leaned forward and changed to a whisper. "Drake. Coach Drake."

Inside his head, fireworks exploded in a celebration that he finally had what he needed. But at the same time, his heart broke for these women who had suffered such a situation under his watch. Had there been anything else he could've done to prevent this? How many more were out there and simply too afraid to admit it?

"Let's get this squared away. I'll call the head of the board tonight, and we'll get the ball rolling." He opened the folder on his computer he'd hoped to never need and printed off the forms for their statements. "I had heard several rumors about Drake but hadn't received enough proof to do anything about it yet. Now, we can."

The women all relaxed in their chairs.

Kimmy eagerly accepted a pen from him. "Thank you so much."

"Thank you for being willing to come forward."

And thank You, God! Thank You for finally ending this nightmare.

GENEVIEVE HADN'T BEEN able to catch a coffee break with her husband in several days. It was Friday afternoon. One week until the spring festival the school held each year. Every class sponsored a booth with a game of some sort. There would be bounce houses, food trucks from a couple of towns over, a bake sale, and a faculty versus students softball game. The event was always fun, but it held her husband captive until it was over.

She glanced at the clock. If she tried to enter one more spring physical without some extra caffeine, she'd be sure to get something wrong. Especially considering the morning she'd already been through—two cases of head lice in the sophomore class. Both girls had been practically inconsolable at being sent home for such a condition, even though it wasn't their fault. The nasty creatures preferred clean hair. She ran the end of her pencil absent-mindedly across her own scalp, scratching at phantom itches.

Pushing back from her desk, she made her way down the hallway and peeked into the office to see if Scott was free. His door was closed. She let out a small sigh and focused on Marian's stress-filled voice. One look at the secretary's face told her something was serious. Marian scribbled furiously on a small notepad beside her, then turned and clicked faster than Genevieve knew was possible, moving her mouse across her screen and clicking again.

"Thanks for the heads up. We'll make sure he stays safe until you can get here." Marian set the phone down and closed her eyes for a second.

"What's going on?" Genevieve moved to right in front of the desk.

"Silas Bates. His mom and dad just finalized their divorce. His dad had all his parental rights taken away. That was his mom on the phone. The dad's not taking it well. We're going into a soft lockdown right now." She turned and clicked a few more times on her computer. "Oh, no. He's one of our baseball players, and they were going to practice during the last two periods today. He's probably on the field now, and I'll never get Coach Pryor to answer his phone."

"I could run out there."

"No." Marian clicked a few more times. "I already sent the message about the lockdown to everyone, so you wouldn't be able to get back in without the proper code or key. No one should be out of the classrooms right now. I'm going out there and get those boys into the building again. I need you to stay here and see if you can get the police on the phone. The mom said Mr. Bates was probably on his way now, and she wasn't sure how he might act when he got here. She's coming, too, but wanted to give us a heads-up. Evidently, the dad got a head start."

"Are you sure? It's no problem for me to run out there. I can call to have you let me back in." Genevieve thumbed over her shoulder.

"I'm not allowed to let anyone in unless it's a student or the police right now." Marian patted her hand. "Here's the information. Coach Stewart is probably on his way back from where he was observing a class. Of course, Vice-Principal Anne is still out for the rest of the week. That flu she caught was a doozy."

Marian's voice faded as she scooted out the door. The woman couldn't be a day less than sixty-five, but she moved quickly.

Genevieve blinked and sat down on the vacated stool. Her fingers ran down the list of phone numbers next to the computer until she located the police department. She dialed the number and tapped her fingers while listening to it ring on the other end. In a small town like this, there shouldn't be that much to keep them busy. Why had they still not answered after four rings?

"Police department." A tired-sounding voice finally answered. "How can I help you?"

"Hi. This is Genevieve Stewart at the high school. We're on a soft lockdown right now. A parent is headed this way and is very upset about losing his rights to his son, who is a student here. We were hoping you could send a few officers this way, to be on the safe side."

Scott walked in, and she waved a hand to get him to stop.

"Do you know if he has a gun?" The officer still sounded like this was a boring conversation. Didn't she hear what Genevieve had just said?

Genevieve scanned the sheet Marian had scribbled but

didn't notice any words like gun or weapon. "Not that I know of."

Scott leaned over and read through Marian's notes while Genevieve waited for more information on the phone.

"Okay. Let me see where my closest officers are, and I'll get them headed your direction." Without waiting for a confirmation from Genevieve, the officer hung up.

Genevieve stared at the handset in shock. "*Um*, okay?"

"What's wrong?"

"I called the police department to get some backup. That lady acted like it was no big deal, said she'd see if she could find some officers to send our way, and then hung up." She set the phone down a bit harder than necessary.

"From these notes, we don't know that it will be a big deal." Scott ran his finger down Marian's scribbles again. "Just that he's upset and might be on the way. Soft lockdown is simply SOP. Where's Marian? Why are you here?"

"I happened to walk in at the wrong moment." Genevieve pressed her fingers to her forehead. "Marian ran out to the baseball field to get those players into the building since that's where Silas is right now."

Scott shook his head. "Why didn't she just call Coach Pryor?"

"She said he never answers his phone." Genevieve spun in the stool to face her husband. "You have a bit of paint or something ... right there."

Scott swiped at his cheek.

"No. Here." She wet her finger, reached up and scrubbed at a spot above his right eyebrow. "What have you been doing?"

"I helped the juniors with part of their booth earlier." He waved her away when she licked her finger to try again. "I'll wash it off later."

"Suit yourself."

Movement caught her eye across the vestibule. Someone

approached the front doors. Marian said they were locked, right? Was it the dad? He didn't look violent from here, but the front walk had him in shadows this time of day.

Scott started to move that way, and she shot an arm out to catch him. "What are you doing?"

"I thought I'd go see what he wanted."

"Marian said we can't let anyone in." She tightened her grip on his bicep.

"She can't." He pulled her fingers loose. "I can."

"Scott, no. At least wait for the police to get here." Her heart pounded in her ears. Anything worthy of locking down the school was worth taking more seriously than he was.

"There's no need to get the police involved if I can talk him into leaving calmly." Scott took another step toward the door.

"But what if you can't?" Her words came out more like a cry.

He slowly rotated back to face her. His eyes revealed hurt, and she realized her words showed no trust in him. It wasn't that she didn't believe in her husband. She just didn't have faith in Silas's dad.

"Scott. We don't even know if he's armed." She tried to swallow past the lump in her throat. Or was that her heart?

He reached out and squeezed her hands as the pounding began on the front doors. "It'll be okay. I won't let him hurt you. Feel free to go back to your office and lock the door, if you want."

"I'm not worried about me." She clung to his fingers for seconds longer. "I don't want to lose you."

Time paused for one short eternal moment before the banging grew louder and more insistent.

"I'd better at least stick my head out and talk to him there. Otherwise, he's liable to break a hole through the glass." Scott pulled his hands away and walked out of the office.

Genevieve blinked back tears of frustration and nerves. The man didn't need to know she was scared of him. That would only make it worse for Scott. She busied herself looking at Marian's computer screen.

Several instant messages had popped up from teachers wanting more information about the lockdown. She replied that they needed to keep the students in the rooms, no matter what, but didn't tell anything else. No need for the students to find out. That would only make the situation worse for Silas.

Had Marian reached him by now? Had she convinced Coach Pryor to move the boys inside? Not knowing was worse than murder. Or maybe not. She reprimanded her thoughts as they strayed to darker images than she wanted to imagine.

Scott led the man through the foyer and into the office. "Let's step in here and see what we can figure out, okay?"

"You always keep the doors locked like that?" The man glanced over his shoulder.

"State policy. People have to be buzzed in. That makes sure the kids are safe and no unwanted visitors can get in. Things are different from when we were in school." Scott's voice stayed pleasant enough, but Genevieve was sure a band of tension thick enough to cut had entered the room with the two men.

"But you said I can pick Si up early?" Mr. Bates's voice was off a tinge. Alcohol? That could only make matters worse.

"Let's come in here and pull up his file to see who all is on the authorized list of people to pick him up, okay? If your driver's license matches up, there shouldn't be a problem. The state requires all these little precautions, of course." Scott left the door open a crack, far enough she could still hear. "You got big weekend plans for your boy?"

"Yeah. Camping. Haven't been able to take him out in a while, you know. With it being so cold and then baseball stuff. Thought this would be a good weekend to get away."

The sadness in his voice brought to mind Parker's lesson on marriage from weeks before in their Wednesday night Bible class. Were Mr. and Mrs. Bates looking more like the torn pieces of construction paper now? She obviously didn't know all the details, but they'd been married long enough to have a fifteen-year-old son. If she and Scott had gone through with her ultimatum, would her voice sound so forlorn? Would she always be looking for ways to hold on to what she'd lost?

Granted, they didn't have children yet. But what could come between two people who had been together so long? What drove them apart?

"Did you look him up yet?" Mr. Bates's voice sounded a bit impatient. "Can I get my son now?"

"I'm sorry, Mr. Bates. The system is giving me fits right now." Scott's voice remained calm, probably to try to keep the father in front of him from getting more riled up. "You know how computers are. They're great when they work, but when they don't, life is even harder. Let me see if I can pull his paper file instead, okay?"

"Okay."

Scott's time-buying tactics had worked so far, but Genevieve wasn't sure how much longer that would last. Where were those officers? Where was Marian?

THE BELL RANG for the classes to switch, but the school remained eerily silent. No voices, no locker slams, no squeaky sneakers. Only the overly loud tick of the clock in the office.

"What did that bell mean?" Mr. Bates's voice was pitched a little higher.

"We're on a special schedule today but didn't get the bells changed. Normally, that would mean the end of sixth period. In a few minutes, it will ring again to signal seventh." Scott shut a file cabinet drawer with a bang. "Isn't Silas a junior this year?"

"Sophomore."

"Right. No wonder I couldn't find him. Hang on just another minute. We'll get this figured out."

From the corner of his eye, Scott caught a glimpse of Genevieve peeking through the crack in his door. If only she'd gone to her office like he'd suggested. The thought of her getting involved in whatever might happen in the next little bit had him on edge more than normal.

"You're not really going to let me take my son, are you?" Mr. Bates's tone had drastically changed. There was an edge to his voice now, a steel pain hardening the words.

"What are you talking about?" Scott tried to keep his tone normal, but a note of caution crept into his voice. Where were those officers? In a town this size, they couldn't have been more than ten minutes away, even on the outskirts of the city limits.

"Look, Mr. ... Stewart. I'm leaving here with my son. Now." Bates's chair scraped back, the noise loud against the quiet of the building.

THE BELL RANG AGAIN, each reverberation echoing the waves of fear rolling through Genevieve's chest. She leaned forward enough to peek through the crack in the doorway, but still couldn't see anything. She couldn't do anything if she were in that room with them, but she longed to at least know exactly what the situation was.

Footsteps echoed down the hallway. Marian hurried into view right as pounding sounded on the front doors. Finally!

"What's that? Some other parent you're keeping kids away from?" Mr. Bates was shouting now. "This isn't a school. It's a prison. Just because my lousy ex-wife doesn't think I can be a good dad doesn't mean I can't. I have rights, too, ya know. Now, get my son in here, or you're really going to regret it."

Genevieve hopped down off the stool as Marian scurried to open the doors for the officers.

"I wouldn't do that, if I were you." Scott's voice was a different kind of steel. The kind that said he was going to protect everyone in this building if his life depended on it.

Oh, please, God, don't let his life depend on it! Keep him safe!

"Or what?" Something crashed. "Huh? Was that important to you? Not any more important than my child! How about this?" Another thump. Each noise sped Genevieve's heartrate further.

The officers rushed through the office, not waiting for any more information. "Get down on the ground!"

More skirmish sounds came from inside. Marian's hand pulled Genevieve down and restrained her from running to check on Scott. Had any of those crashes hurt him? Was he okay? Why hadn't he said anything in the last few minutes?

A policeman led Mr. Bates back out, hands in cuffs. "Officer Rimmel will take down all the statements. But you should be good to release the students from lockdown now. I'm going to walk Mr. Bates out to my vehicle."

Marian could hold her back no longer. Genevieve rushed through the office door. A small shriek escaped her lips. Her husband slumped on the far side of the room, one of the chairs from in front of his desk broken beside him. She placed her fingers to his throat and her breath whooshed from her lungs as she felt the flutter in his veins.

"Scott." She patted his cheek. "Scott, honey."

"I'll have an ambulance here in a jiffy, ma'am." The police officer tipped his hat and spoke into his radio.

Scott's eyes blinked. Her heart rate slowed down another fraction. He blinked again, and she could tell the moment those brown irises focused on her.

"Do you realize how scared I was?" She might have swatted him if he weren't already hurt.

"I'm getting the idea." He pushed with his arms, a small groan escaping him as he sat a bit straighter against the bookshelves. "I don't think the chair actually hit me. I lost my balance trying to dodge it and hit my head on these blasted things."

She felt along the back of his hair and confirmed a lump creeping up on the back of his head. "Does it hurt anywhere else?"

"You mean besides the bump you keep pushing against?" He tilted his head to move it away from her probing.

"Good to see your sarcasm wasn't damaged." Another piece of the fear that had reigned for the last half hour slid off her shoulders.

The corner of his mouth turned up. "Yeah, well. My mama always told me I have a hard head."

Before she could respond, more commotion broke out in the outer part of the office. A woman's hysterical voice was pitched so high Genevieve almost wanted to cover her ears.

"Silas! Where's my boy?"

"Mrs. Bates, we're having him brought right now. Please calm down. Everything is under control." Marian's soft ways made Genevieve smile. Even when the older lady was so frazzled earlier, she still knew exactly what needed to be done and accomplished it.

"Mom? Seriously!" Silas entered. "I told you Dad would do something crazy if you pushed him. Why didn't you back off?"

"I couldn't risk it. I couldn't risk him being able to harm you."

"Harm *you*, you mean." The teenager sounded older than his fifteen years.

"There, but for the grace of God." Scott's quiet voice brought her attention back to him. Tears held at bay until now escaped down her cheeks. He lifted a hand and wiped one away.

She couldn't speak past the lump in her throat. He pulled her head down to his shoulder and rubbed circles on her back. She was supposed to be taking care of him, and yet here he was comforting her instead.

"Mr. Stewart?" An EMS worker came through the door, already opening the black bag in his hands. "Let's get you checked out, shall we?"

Genevieve pulled herself away, though it took every ounce of self-control to do so. He gave her hand one more squeeze and then nodded for her to go give her statement. She would go through the motions of getting through the rest of the day, but the words he'd spoken a moment before would haunt her. They needed to sit and really talk soon, but when would they find time?

28

Scott's wiffly snore next to her ought to be comforting. The EMTs had checked him out and declared him concussion-free. Still, she lay awake, listening to the steady in-and-out of the breaths coming from his side of the mattress.

Her eyes closed again, but every time she allowed that to happen, scenes from the afternoon ran across them like a movie on a screen. The slightly lost and bitter look on Mr. Bates, the hysteria and panic and anger on Mrs. Bates, and the hurt and disappointment Silas Bates wore like a second set of clothes.

There but for the grace of God. Scott's words from earlier echoed through her mind.

What-ifs and might-have-beens bombarded her brain, no matter what she did. She rolled to her other side, facing away from her husband. If he'd taken her seriously, he might not be her spouse now. If she hadn't agreed to give things a second chance, she might wear some of those same emotions the Bates radiated. Would she have become bitter and ugly and angry with life?

She flopped onto her back once more and let out a sigh.

When she was a little girl, her father taught her a trick to relax. She imagined an elevator at the top of her head, going down toward her toes. As it passed each part of her body, all those lights were to go out and sleep. But tonight, such a simple method wasn't cutting it.

Genevieve threw back the covers and padded down the hallway. Maybe some tea. Water in the electric kettle. Chamomile in the mug. Now, to wait for a boil. She leaned against the counter and watched the moon as it guarded her yard and all around.

She could've lost Scott today. And she admitted now she didn't want to. Sure, she could do without some of his habits. She scrunched her nose and rubbed at a sticky spot on her arm from where a spill had been left on the countertop. His clothes were probably in the floor in front of the hamper. There would inevitably be more toenails on the counter—though hopefully not in her mouth again—and there were sure to be more nights when they didn't have time together except for a goodnight kiss. But she'd rather have all that than to be alone always.

His arms wrapped around her from the back, and she startled.

"Didn't mean to scare you." His beard caught pieces of her hair as he snuggled her up against him. "You okay?"

"Just restless. Thought maybe some tea might help." She leaned into his strength.

"Crazy day, huh?"

"The worst." She closed her eyes. "Let's not have one like that again, okay?"

"Sounds like a good plan to me."

Their bodies swayed to a rhythm no one could hear but them. The kettle clicked off, steam escaping through its mouth. The clock in the living room ticked over another hour. The air conditioner kicked on down the hallway.

"I don't think your tea is going to get made if you don't add the water." His voice pulled her eyes open again.

"This is more comforting than herbs anyway." She hugged his arms closer around her.

"Why didn't you say something?" He tugged a strand of her hair. "I would have held you like this back in the bed instead of out here in this cold kitchen."

"I didn't want to wake you. You needed sleep after the day we had."

"And you didn't?" He grabbed her hand and tugged. "Come on."

She followed him back to their room. He tucked her in and then climbed into his side of the bed before pulling her over to the middle. She curled in his arms, breathed in his familiar scent, felt more of that leftover tension ease from her body.

"So, what am I comforting you about?" His voice was husky, whether from drowsiness or something else, she wasn't about to ask.

"I can't stop thinking about today. Those people. Seeing you slumped there on the floor." She half-buried her face in the pillow.

"Hey." He tugged her around. "I'm fine. Not even a concussion, remember? A few bumps and bruises."

She shook her head and nestled it in his shoulder. "The way they were yelling, all the bitterness and anger. That could have been us. I don't want to be like that, Scott."

"I don't, either." His whisper in her ear sent a shiver down her back. "But we won't be. We're not going down that road. We've seen where it can lead. And, though things aren't back to honeymoon-perfect, I'd like to think we've at least come a little closer again, haven't we?"

The nod of her head bumped his chin and cheek.

"Want to hear something else good?" He nuzzled his nose into her cheek.

"*Hmm?*"

"A few teachers came forward and agreed to sign statements against Coach Drake. The president of the board is meeting with me Monday to go over it all. Drake's not going to get the chance to hurt anyone else at the school."

She raised up on an elbow and tried to make out the expression on his face. "Really?"

"Really." He pulled her back down. "So, I'm safe. You're safe. Our marriage is safe. You feeling better? Think you can sleep now?"

"Thank you." She kissed his cheek.

"For what?"

"For everything. For being you. For getting up in the middle of the night just to make sure I come back to bed."

His arms squeezed around her in a hug. "Any time."

She snuggled into the place she'd missed these many months, the little hollow between his bicep and heart, the perfect size and shape for her head to rest. His arm stayed around her waist. His breathing evened out once more, a slight whiffle emitting from his nostrils as he took up his snore again. She let her heavy eyelids drop and wondered only for a second if that elevator had made it to the bottom floor yet.

"WELL, I HATE THIS." Tim Miles ran a hand over his bald head. "And to think he got our boys almost all the way to state."

"Yes, sir." Scott handed over the forms the teachers had filled out last Thursday. "But as you can see, we've had several teachers with the same complaint toward him."

A couple of the other men tutted as they read over the statements.

"And, unfortunately, we've had a student come forward, as

well." Scott passed over the page Anne and Ginger had helped Tansy fill out that very afternoon.

The room was silent.

There was no way Drake was getting out of this mess now. Not when a teenage girl had admitted to him kissing her. It was a good thing the school board would handle it from here, because Scott wanted nothing more than to beat the man black and blue.

Tim cleared his throat. "A student?"

"Yes, sir. We'd noticed she'd been acting out and getting into trouble more lately. Marian overheard some of the girls talking about Coach Drake one day. We had her meet with Anne and Ginger this morning to see if we could confirm what Marian had overheard. Ginger is going to do some extra counseling sessions with her, and her parents have been brought in. Otherwise, we're not telling anyone else."

A man across the table muttered a foul name under his breath. Several others nodded. The papers were passed around, but no one offered any objections or arguments in Drake's favor. Not that Scott had expected they would.

"Do you know if Drake is still here this afternoon?" Milton Smith stacked the papers with a whack.

"I'm not sure. I can call his cell phone."

"I have his number. I'll do it and see if I can get him to meet us in here now. No need to let this go on any longer than it already has. You can find a sub for his classes for the rest of the year?"

"Even if I have to take them myself." Scott nodded.

"I guess this means we need to start looking for another basketball coach." Tim sighed.

"I might actually have an idea about that." Scott swallowed a lump of nervousness. "Though, I'm not sure how much you'll like it."

Several of the men exchanged glances and then returned their attention to him. "Well?"

Straightening his shoulders, Scott took a deep breath and put his plan into action.

THUNK. *Thunk. Thunk, thunk, thunk, swoosh!*

Genevieve dried her hands and went to peek out the living room window. Scott still wore his slacks and button-down, though the sleeves were rolled up. And somewhere along the way, he'd changed to tennis shoes. He dribbled a basketball rhythmically between his legs and then up the length of the driveway before releasing it to a perfect swish through the middle of the hoop mounted above their garage door. He hadn't done that in a long time. It used to be where he went when he needed to think something through.

She stepped through the door and leaned against a porch rail, watching him. His meeting with the school board had been this afternoon, and he'd stayed late for that and final preparations for the festival this Friday. She hadn't seen him since their quick coffee break that morning. They'd agreed Genevieve would stay out of the Coach Drake situation unless the board required another witness, though they couldn't fathom them needing more proof on such a serious charge.

He looked over after making another goal and waved. The ball rolled back in his direction, and he caught it and started dribbling again. Toward the road the streetlights were on, giving him the light to make a three-pointer. He raised his hands in the air as he ran up the walk toward her.

"Show off." She grinned at him to show she was teasing. "You haven't shot hoops in a while, though no one could tell by watching you."

"I'm a little rusty, but not too bad." He propped the ball on his hip and studied his feet. "Which is good ... because I'm going back to coaching."

"You mean until they find a replacement for Harmon Drake?" She frowned. That was a bit much to put on someone whose plate was already as full as Scott's.

"No. I mean, I'm going to take back my teaching and coaching position." Without raising his head, his eyes glanced up as if to gauge her reaction.

"What? But, Scott, you love being—"

"Hear me out." He dropped the ball and held out his hand. "Here. Let's sit and talk." He pulled her inside and sat on the sofa.

"Scott, you can't give up your job. You worked so hard for this." She grabbed both his hands in hers and squeezed his fingers.

"I love teaching and coaching too. And I love you." He tilted his head and gave her a sad smile. "I'm not saying I won't ever want to be principal again. But for this point in our life, I really think God's leading me to go this direction. I'll still be here, still doing something I love, but I'll have a bit more freedom—as long as it's not basketball season—and more time for you. You're more important."

She blinked back moisture pooling in her eyes. "You'd give up your dream job for me?"

"That first meeting with Marty ... he told me if I didn't change some things, I was going to lose you. I don't think I realized how serious everything had gotten. I realized we were having more fights than usual, but I let myself get so distracted and involved elsewhere, I didn't see what was happening right in front of my eyes. I hurt you. And I never wanted to do that. And I never want to do it again."

She swiped at her cheeks. "I wasn't exactly being a model wife. I mean, it takes two to have a fight. I let everything stew inside me and focused only on the bad things instead of trying to find the good or talking to you about it. And then I blamed you for all our problems instead of taking responsibility for any of it myself."

"I found something." He squeezed her shoulders and got up to grab a remote from beside the television. "Watch this."

The screen came to life with a view of her and him standing on the stage at the church building. The bride handed her bouquet to Valerie and then sent a thousand-watt smile in the direction of the groom taking her hand. Genevieve snuggled against her husband of almost five years to watch their younger selves get married again.

"Repeat after me." Marty shot a wink at Scott and then coached him through his vows.

"Genevieve, I give you this ring as a token of my love for you. God has built into you the qualities essential to become my wife. You've added joy, love, and beauty to my life. I promise to love you, constantly giving up my rights for you even as Christ did for His bride, the Church. I promise to lead you as God directs in our lives and to be responsible for your well-being and the well-being of our children. I always want you to be my best friend. Regardless of what happens in our lives, we can rejoice and enjoy life because God has enclosed us in His hand. We love, Genevieve, because God first loved us."

Scott paused the video. "Somewhere along the way, I forgot some of that. But I want to try again, if you'll give me a chance."

She nodded. "I need to remember mine too. Will you play the next part?"

After a few awkward moments while she slid the ring on his finger on screen, Marty prompted her in her vows.

"Scott, I give you this ring as a token of my love for you. Because I have seen God lead us together in such a special way, I give myself to making our marriage and our life such that the world looking on us will know that He is real. I promise that I will love you in the midst of the everydayness of life. I promise that I will live openly and honestly before you so that we would not live out our lives in separation and isolation. Because I trust you with my life, I promise that I will defer to your leadership. Before God and before men, you will be the head of our home. And so do not urge me to leave you or to turn back from following you, for where you go, I will go; where you lodge, I will lodge. Your people will be my people, and your God, my God. And may the Lord do to me and worse, if anything but death should part you and me."

"Maybe I need to post a copy of that on my mirror to remember every morning all I promised. I think I've broken quite a few of those." Genevieve picked at a dry spot on her finger.

"We can ask Marty to print them out for us again. I'm sure he has them saved somewhere." Scott ran a finger down her cheek.

"I'm so sorry I didn't go to you first—so many times, not only the one about Coach Drake. You're supposed to be the one I run to, the one I confide in, the one I trust most. Instead, I let myself get caught in a bad situation and then made it worse. Do you think you'll ever forgive me?"

"I think I already have."

She looked up into eyes filled with so much emotion she almost couldn't take it all in.

Marty on the screen said, "You may now kiss the bride."

And Scott, in real life, took him at his word, leaning down and pressing his lips to hers, ever so softly at first, and then more. While the wedding played in the background, with their friends and family cheering them on, Genevieve found the sound appropriate. After all, back then, they'd had no idea what all they might face in this adventure called marriage. That applause meant more today now that they'd made it to the top of a mountain and were headed back down again.

"I'll still be principal for the rest of the year, and probably part of the summer." Scott pressed his forehead against hers. "Can you put up with me? Keep living with my crazy hours and emergency meetings and exhaustion?"

"As long as you keep trying." She scrunched her nose. "And can put up with my relearning how to be a good wife."

"I'm sorry I took you for granted the last few years. I promised for better or worse. And I meant it. But hear me today when I promise I will try my hardest to not take you for granted ever again."

"I promise too. I don't want to take you for granted ever again, either." She sealed it with a quick peck to his lips.

He pulled her into a hug. "Now, to get through the rest of the school year. Spring festival later this week, baseball and softball season, prom, awards ceremonies, graduation. It's a lot. I'm tired just thinking about it."

"And don't forget we need to squelch the rumors going around school that we're having issues." She raised her eyebrows.

"Ever find out who's spreading those?" He pushed back just enough to look at her.

"Not sure they actually exist, but Coach Drake swore that's why he started hanging around my office." She shuddered.

"More coffee breaks and lunch breaks will help." He chuckled. "And you could be my date to prom."

"Do I have to wear one of those dresses?"

"*Mm.*" The sound coming from his throat was rather appreciative. "That might be fun."

The video caught their attention again as laughter broke out. On the screen, Scott pushed cake into Genevieve's face as she shrieked and batted him away. She wiped chocolate crumbs from the front of her dress and accepted the kiss he offered as apology, giggling as frosting transferred from her face to his upper lip.

"Let's be that couple again." She smiled at the memory.

Friday dawned a beautiful day. Genevieve and Scott walked hand-in-hand toward the cafeteria where part of the spring festival was set up. With elementary, middle and high schools all participating, it took up not only the cafeteria, but also the football field and several things between. The aromas of cotton candy, deep-fried everything, and smoking pork filled the air from various nearby food trucks.

"Need any tickets today?" Marian and the other secretaries manned a table right inside the doors, rolls of paper tickets stacked almost to their chins.

"Are there some good games and activities this year?" Genevieve handed over a five-dollar bill.

Marian passed back twenty tickets and winked. "Something tells me you'll want to spend at least a few of these."

"Thanks so much, ladies." Genevieve saluted them and then turned to take in the growing chaos. Most of the games geared toward younger children were in here, as well as the bake sale run by the junior class. "I heard there are some chocolate chip cookies that can't be beat."

"That way." Scott pointed to the other side of the room. "I

might have purchased a bag when they were setting up last night. Had to make sure the rumors were true, ya know."

"Of course." She grinned.

Their week had been chaotic, with this festival taking up much of his extra time, but they had managed to steal a few breaks during the days as well as enjoy some snuggles each evening. He had even started kissing her goodbye in the mornings and hello in the evenings again, a habit she didn't want them to break. Wednesday night, she'd asked Marty for copies of their wedding vows, and she'd laminated them in the workroom yesterday, so they could be displayed on their bathroom mirror. Neither of them wished to risk forgetting their promises to one another again.

Scott glanced at his watch. "I'm supposed to help the seniors with their booth in half an hour. I better start that way considering how many people will probably stop me between here and there."

"Okay. I'll catch up in a bit. I think Mom and Dad are supposed to be around here somewhere." She pointed the other way. "Besides, I want some of those cookies before they sell out."

"Have fun." He pecked her cheek and headed back out the door.

The crowd grew by the minute. In a town this size, most employers understood that the students would be out of classes, and they set special hours or closed completely to accommodate the parents. She wandered past fishing games, ring toss and duck pond games, a face-painting booth, and a table full of arts and crafts made by some of the older elementary kids.

The bake sale table had a crowd around it, but she wiggled her way through to the front and surveyed the various bags of sweets. "Okay, which cookies are the best?"

"These over here, Ms. Stewart."

"Give me three, please." She handed over the cash and accepted the plastic bags. Cookies for her now, and then some to share with Scott later. If he was lucky. She tucked those into her tote.

Valerie waved from behind a table full of art. Her students sold some of their best paintings, drawings, and sculptures every year to help keep the room stocked with supplies. Genevieve stepped up and examined an acrylic painting of a sunflower field.

"I love this." She flipped it over to see the tag.

"I loved it too. I almost didn't want to put it out here, but we need the money."

"Did you paint it, Val?" Genevieve studied her friend.

"Yes. I always do a few extras." Valerie shrugged a shoulder. "Might as well use the pieces I make to show off different techniques during the year."

"Is the budget tighter this year than before?"

"Always." Valerie accepted the payment and wrapped the painting in brown paper. "But we'll make it through. I'll work for free if I have to."

"You almost are anyway." Genevieve added her artwork to the cookies.

"Scott won't let the art department die completely." Valerie winked. "He knows how important it is."

"Oh." Genevieve wondered how much she should say. Scott wasn't announcing his job change until the beginning of summer. But not many people were around.

"What's wrong?" Valerie tilted her head, setting her dangly earrings swaying.

"Scott isn't going to be the principal next year." Genevieve kept her voice low.

"What?" Valerie leaned forward. "What happened? They didn't fire him for letting go of Coach Drake, did they?"

Genevieve shook her head. "No. Nothing like that. He's ...

well, he's going back to coaching and teaching for a while. Said it gives him more time for family. Less stress. And he loves it, too, so he acted like it wasn't that big of a deal."

"He's doing it for you." Valerie squeezed her shoulder. "And I'm glad for both of you. Speaking of Scott, I think you might want to wander over to the senior booth in a few minutes. You're going to want to see what he's volunteered for."

Genevieve shot her friend a look, but Valerie shooed her on her way and went to help another customer. Slightly confused and more than a little intrigued, Genevieve stepped out into the sunshine and wandered past the tantalizing aromas down to the football field. More people meandered around other activities. The sophomores had set up a maze made out of cardboard boxes. The basketball team had various heights of hoops, and people tried different shots to win prizes. Balloons, music, and laughter filled the air.

She walked to her left, knowing the seniors usually set up their area toward the far goal posts. Sure enough, after passing several other games, she came to a group of kids she recognized as twelfth-graders. Riley waved her over, giggling. She stood behind a table where they took the tickets. Pie pans full of whipped cream filled the space before her.

"Hey, Nurse Stewart. Want to try your hand?" Riley pointed to the pies.

"At making pie?" Genevieve frowned.

"At throwing pies." A tall, gangly boy laughed. He pointed to the big temporary wall beside him with a hole right in the middle. "The more tickets you give, the closer you get to stand to throw the pie. When you're ready, Coach Stewart will stick his head out, and you cream him."

Laughter bubbled up in Genevieve. "Coach Stewart, huh?"

Scott's face poked through the hole, and he wiggled his eyebrows.

"There a reason you didn't want me to know about this?" Genevieve waved her hand toward the booth.

"Nope." He shook his head as much as he could in the tight space. "I didn't figure you'd be interested. I mean, a good wife wouldn't want to smear whipped cream all over her husband. Or laugh at him while someone else did it."

She propped a hand on her hip. "Seems like a good husband wouldn't smear cake all over his wife's face, either, but we have video evidence of you doing just that."

"*Hmm.*" He made his face look as innocent as he could. "Oh, well. Go ahead and try if you want. I've seen you throw. I'm not worried."

"That so?" She pulled out the length of tickets and handed them to Riley. "How close do I get to stand for twenty tickets?"

All the seniors burst into laughter as the tall boy led her about a foot from the wall.

"How's this, Coach Stewart?" Genevieve hefted the pie, as if to test its weight. "Think I can hit you from this close?"

"You might regret this." He squeezed his eyes closed.

She took the aluminum pan and gently pressed it into his face. Then, she smeared it back and forth a few times, for good measure. When she pulled back, whipped cream covered every inch of his head, clinging to his beard hairs and poking out of his nose. She wiped some off around his eyes and he blinked a few times. Even through the cream, she could see the wicked expression.

His head disappeared from behind the wall. Where was he going? As he rounded the corner, her heartbeat picked up speed. He was going to smear it on her!

She backed away, but he walked faster. She dropped the pan and broke into a sprint—too late to escape his long legs. He caught her hand and pulled her around, locking her into an embrace. He shook his head.

"I warned you." His voice was husky.

"What are you going to do?" The bravado faded from her voice. Giggles came from all around, as more people came over to watch.

"Yeah, Scott. What are you going to do?" Her dad's voice teased from a few feet away.

"Daddy!" Genevieve squirmed.

"You said you wanted to be more like that couple." Scott drew his face nearer to hers.

"All these people are watching!" She hissed the words, sure he'd lost his mind.

"Good." His whisper was filled with laughter. "They can put a stop to all those rumors you mentioned."

He closed the last half-inch of distance and placed a smacking kiss right on her lips. A cheer erupted from the gathered crowd. She couldn't help but start laughing, and felt his grin against her lips. This was utterly ridiculous, and yet perfect. His eyes sparkled as he let her go.

"You've got a little something." He motioned to the area around her mouth.

"*Um-hmm.*" She accepted a towel from Riley and wiped her face before passing it on to her husband. "How much longer are you working this booth?"

"Until ten." He pulled the cloth away, revealing cream still lodged in his hair and beard.

She giggled and turned to the crowd. "Everyone hear that? Who's next? We've got almost forty minutes left to pie Coach Stewart!"

"You're going to have a lot of making up to do later." His whisper tickled her ear and most likely left more whipped cream in her hair, but she didn't mind.

"I'll look forward to it." She winked at him.

"I love you." He kissed her nose and then turned to go back to his booth.

"I love you too." She made sure her words were loud enough for all to hear, but especially her parents.

If they hadn't stepped in and cautioned her from continuing down the road of leaving Scott, she wouldn't be this happy today. But here she was, looking forward to celebrating five years of marriage this summer, and maybe even growing their family in the next year. Blessed in her imperfectly perfect marriage, for better or for worse, but never for granted.

A NOTE FROM THE AUTHOR

Dear Reader,

This is not a typical romance novel. But my heart refused to let me not write it. Why? Well, multiple reasons.

For one, after being married almost twenty years myself, I'm well aware of how hard it is to keep love alive after the honeymoon. When the regular day-to-day-ness of life sets in, it is so easy to forget to make each other a priority. Don't get me wrong. I have a great marriage. But that doesn't mean we don't have moments where we take each other for granted and have to step back and remember to keep our priorities straight.

For another, we have so many friends and family members whose marriages have fallen apart. Some didn't even last a full year. You guys! A year! I feel like my husband and I didn't even fully know each other after one year of marriage … and we'd dated for three before that. Needless to say, it broke my heart to see all these marriages falling apart.

This story is not based on any real-life couple in particular. More, it's a combination of a lot of little ideas and situations. Mostly, I wanted to explore the idea of a couple on the verge of divorce whose family and friends were against it. Would they have enough influence to help the couple change their minds?

I hope you've enjoyed this different kind of romance novel. Maybe even gained a few ideas to apply to your own marriage. Mostly, I pray all your marriages are strong and that you don't take each other for granted.

As always, reviews are greatly appreciated, if you feel the urge to leave a few words. Pass this story on to anyone you think it might bless. And until next time, thank you so much for reading my book.

God bless you!

Amy

DISCUSSION QUESTIONS

1. Genevieve starts the story with an ultimatum. Do you think things would have changed for her and Scott if she hadn't made such a drastic demand?
2. Scott thought everything in their lives was going great. How easy is it for people to be so caught up in living their dreams that other parts of their life fall by the wayside?
3. Do you think Scott and Genevieve would have been able to work things out if not for their family and friends encouraging them to try?
4. Along the same lines, often a couple will look like they're doing great on the outside, when behind closed doors they're falling apart. What can we do as Christians and friends to help others make sure their relationships don't fall apart? What can we do ourselves to make sure our friends know when we need help and support?
5. As Genevieve and Scott start their counseling, one of the things they have to do is make each other a priority. How hard was it for her to find ten minutes

of the day to spend with him? Do you often have the same problem? What can you do about it?

6. Can you imagine going on a second first date? How hard would it be to pretend to not know the person you're sitting across from when you've been married to him for years? Do you think you would learn anything important?

7. As if their situation wasn't in a bad enough place, when Genevieve keeps getting hit on, it adds fuel to the fire. Is it often easy to let something worse into your relationship when things are already bad?

8. Date nights don't always have to be a meal. Genevieve and Scott ended up going to a play and a basketball game at school. What other "normal" things might a couple do that could be considered a date? Do you try to work in everyday dates in your life?

9. Scott made a very hard decision at the end of the book. Do you think it was the right choice for him? For their relationship?

10. This is a romance about people already married. Sometimes, when you're in a secure relationship for a long period of time, you forget why you fell in love in the first place. Do you think more couples need to take time to go back and remember how they got there? Do you think more couples need to stir up the embers of romance even after marriage?

ABOUT THE AUTHOR

Amy R Anguish grew up a preacher's kid, and in spite of having lived in seven different states that are all south of the Mason-Dixon line, she is not a football fan. Currently, she resides in Tennessee with her husband, daughter, and son, and usually a bossy cat or two. Amy has an English degree from Freed-Hardeman University that she intends to use to glorify God, and she wants her stories to show that while Christians face real struggles, it can still work out for good.

Follow her at https://amyranguish.com or http://www.facebook.com/amyanguishauthor

Or https://twitter.com/amy_r_anguish

Learn more about her books at https://www.pinterest.com/msguish/my-books/

And check out the YouTube channel she does with two other authors, Once Upon a Page (https://www.youtube.com/@onceuponapage3326)

ALSO BY AMY R. ANGUISH

Window of the Heart by Amy Anguish

The Stained-glass Legacy Series—Book Three

Lennox Malone may not believe in love, but she's determined to do the best job she can as her friend Sara Beth's maid of honor. Problem is, the man in charge of fixing up the chapel doesn't match her determination. Fighting against preconceived notions, a past that catches up to her, and an attraction she wants nothing to do with, this wedding is turning into more than she can handle.

Ty Dunne might be laid back and easy-going, but he's determined to make sure the chapel is ready for his cousin's wedding. Not only is it his duty as best man, but he wants to preserve the family's history in the building. If only he could live up to his family's other expectations —or those of Lennox Malone, the fiery redhead he can't stop thinking about. Before he can go any further with her, though, he has to convince her that love is real and worth the risk.

Lennox has built her walls high and sturdy, but Ty is determined to find a way in—even if it's a window. Maybe the history of the chapel itself along with the romance of a wedding will help.

Get your copy here:

https://scrivenings.link/windowoftheheart

Destination: ~~Fun~~ Romance

Roadtrip Romance—Book One

It's not every day you bring a boyfriend back as a souvenir.

Katie Wilhite is ready to settle into her new job as a librarian now that college is through, but friends Bree and Skye want one more girls' trip, and when Bree insists this is her bachelorette fling, Katie agrees. What she didn't agree to was allowing fun and flighty Skye to dictate the itinerary or for her anxiety to kick in harder than ever ... right in front of a cute guy.

Camden Malone had no idea when he agreed to be the voice of reason on his cousin Ryan's vacation that the trip wouldn't stay in New

Orleans as planned. But when Ryan plots with Skye so that the guys can tag along with the girls all week, he isn't nearly as upset as he should be. Not with Katie's fiery temper and flashing eyes intriguing him more by the minute.

Can Katie relax enough to trust Camden and a possible future, or will she continue to push him away as only a vacation fling? And can Camden move past a rocky history of his own to be able to jump into a better future? For a trip that was supposed to be all about fun, there's a lot of romance going around.

Get your copy here:

https://scrivenings.link/destinationromance

Roadtrip for ~~One~~ Two

Roadtrip Romance—Book Two

Recovering from heartbreak is hard when

the ex-fiancé tags along ...

Dallas wasn't in the plans when Bree Henley set out to use the nonrefundable honeymoon tickets from her canceled wedding. Nor was running into ex-fiancé Nathan Hart. But their mutual friends and the weather have other ideas. A hurricane cancels their cruise and Bree decides to turn the disaster into a roadtrip for one, never imagining Nathan would object.

Nathan is furious when he uncovers the plot to get him back with Bree. But he can't just let her go roaming around the big city of Dallas alone. Though he knows calling off their wedding was the right thing to do, he still cares for Bree. And before he knows what hits him, he's volunteered to tag along. Suddenly, it's a trip for two.

Spending the week together might remind them of why they fell in love. But is it enough to overcome the obstacles standing in the way of "til death do us part"?

Get your copy here:

https://scrivenings.link/roadtripfortwo

Operation Find a ~~Job~~ Guy

Roadtrip Romance—Book Three

by Amy R. Anguish

She's set on saving her car ... and her heart.

Skye Jones has one goal for the summer—keep her father from taking away her convertible. That's the *only* reason she agrees to work at her sister's bridal shop in Boulder, Colorado, while she searches for a non-boring job. Why else would she have anything to do with weddings when she has no interest in marriage?

Benjamin Smith somehow ended up as a groomsman in two weddings over the summer, so he's spending a lot of time at Happily Ever After events. Falling for a blonde with no dreams of settling down wasn't in his five-year plan, yet the more he sees Skye, the more he wants to figure her out.

But all she sees him as is a boring attorney–her complete opposite.

Besides, romance is supposed to be for Skye's friends, not her. And she's in Colorado to get a job, not a guy. Right?

Get your copy here:

https://scrivenings.link/operationfindaguy

Love Delivered

A novella collection, including "Romance at Register Five"

by Amy R. Anguish

Mack McDonald isn't happy about the Grocerease app coming to his grocery store. But he's committed to the sixty-day trial period, and braces himself to lose money. Kaitlyn Daniels loves how the Grocerease app helps her make ends meet so she can assist her mom, the reason she moved to small Sassafras, AR. Mack and Kaitlyn struggle to overcome differing opinions on the perks of the app. But if they don't, it could keep them from something even better.

Get your copy here:

https://scrivenings.link/lovedelivered

No Place Like Home

Can love secure Adrian's wandering heart?

Roots are overrated, at least to someone like Adrian Stewart, preacher's kid, who has never lived anywhere longer than six years. That's why her job with MidUSLogIn Inc., is so perfect for her—lots of travel, and staying nowhere long enough to have it feel like home. But when work takes her to Memphis, closer to her family for the first time in years and in the same small office as Grayson Roberts, she starts to question her job, her lack of home, and even her memories of her rocky past with the church.

Gray is intrigued by Adrian from the moment he sees her, and he's determined to get to the bottom of why this girl, who loves old movies and hums when she works, won't go to church with him. As they grow closer, he wants more too, but how can he convince her to stay in Memphis when she doesn't believe in home—or God? Can he use his own broken past to break through hers?

Get your copy here:

https://scrivenings.link/noplacelikehome

Saving Grace

Michelle Wilson's one goal in life was to become a top journalist at the local paper back in her hometown of Cedar Springs, AR. But on the way to bringing that dream to reality, a life-changing wreck interrupts Michelle's plans and adds an orphaned baby into the mix. Now, she has tough decisions ahead—did God put her in that accident to save baby Grace? And if so, why is it so hard to convince everyone else she should be the baby's new mommy?

Greg Marshall has been Michelle's best friend his whole life. He's thrilled she's moving back home, but not so sure about her sudden desire to be a single mom. His feelings for her have grown through the years, but she's never seemed to notice. Can he help Michelle with the adoption and grow their relationship at the same time?

Get your copy here:

https://scrivenings.link/savinggrace

Faith and Hope

Get your copy here:

https://scrivenings.link/faithandhope

An Unexpected Legacy

Get your copy here: